EMMA CANE

A Promise at
BLUEBELL HILL
A VALENTINE VALLEY NOVEL

AVON

An Imprint of HarperCollinsPublishers

*To my husband, Jim, who brainstorms the best widow
plots. Though I'm a writer, words cannot express my
love for you.*

AVON BOOKS
An Imprint of HarperCollins*Publishers*
10 East 53rd Street
New York, New York 10022-5299

Acknowledgments

My thanks to all the people who helped me research this book: Ginny Aubertine, Binnie Syril Braunstein, John Desantis, Gregory Roepke, Rudy Suarez, and Christine Wenger. Any mistakes are certainly mine.

Chapter One

In the workroom of Monica's Flowers and Gifts, Monica Shaw stood at a large table, critically studying the flower arrangement for a wedding the next day. It was May in Valentine Valley, Colorado, the start of wedding season, one of her busiest times of the year. She loved every moment of it, from helping a nervous man find the perfect flowers to ask his girl to marry him, to making the bride feel like she was the centerpiece of the altar, framed in beautiful flowers: roses, tulips, and dahlias, with a spray of white delphiniums. And she was good at what she did, as more and more of her customers confided that they'd been referred by their satisfied friends. The walls of the workroom were covered in photos from her successful events and reminded her of happy occasions and a job well done.

The bell at the front door jingled, and she glanced through the window that separated the workroom from the showroom. The door swung closed behind a tall man dressed in khakis, a dark blue polo shirt, and a windbreaker. He looked good—broad, muscled shoulders tapering to narrow hips. He had a square-jawed Captain America face, beneath a military cut of deep auburn hair, and carried himself with a regality that seemed out of place in a flower shop—heck, in the whole town.

Dark sunglasses still hid his eyes as his head briefly turned from side to side. She knew the girly stuff he saw in her showroom: flowers, terrariums, plants in baskets along one side, and on the other, homemade crafts she took in on consignment, like quilted baby blankets, knitted layettes, ceramic vases, and leather frames. Behind the front counter were coolers full of flower arrangements anyone off the street could buy. Surely, he was there for roses—he looked like a rose sort of ladies' man, no spontaneously picked wildflowers for him.

He finally took off the sunglasses, revealing the deepest blue eyes she had ever seen, piercing and intelligent, cool and impassive, above a nose with a slight crook in it, as if he'd broken it once and hadn't bothered having it fixed. With those eyes, he took in her work, her life, and didn't even twitch a lip in a smile. She immediately didn't want to like him, just from that lack of expression—but she was far too fascinated already.

Through the window, Monica watched Karista, her freckle-faced teenage sales associate, drop the tissue she'd shredded just looking at the stranger to approach the counter and speak to him. The words were too muffled for Monica to hear, but when the man turned away, it was obvious he meant to browse. He glanced at Sugar and Spice's daily pastry laid out on the little wrought-iron table, today a raspberry torte, but moved on. How could he resist that? Not many people did.

Perhaps he was a Josh Thalberg groupie, trying to score leather-carved goods before they were all gone. Josh's fame had started in her store, but now he was creating expensive shoulder bags for an Aspen boutique and exclusive necklaces for his wife's lingerie store, Leather and Lace. He didn't have as much time for the checkbook covers, key chains, and frames he'd done for Monica in the past. People were starting to express their disappointment that she didn't have a larger selection, and she was surprised how much his popularity was playing with her head—as if her flower arrangements weren't enough to lure customers anymore.

The stranger did pause to look at Josh's work, intricate and unusual, standing out next to the crocheted baby bonnets. Then he gave Karista a nod, slid his sunglasses back on his face, and headed outside.

Monica hurried through the swinging door, and asked, "Who was that?" just as Karista exclaimed, "Did you see him?"

They laughed together.

"He can't be from around here," Karista said, light brown ponytail bobbing as she shook her head. "But he doesn't exactly look like a tourist, either."

"And he was just browsing?"

"That's all he said. Real deep voice, too. Called me 'miss,' all formal."

Monica came around the counter and moved through her shop until she reached the big plate-glass windows that bracketed the front door. She leaned across her flower displays and could just see the stranger studying the sign above the shop next to her own, SUGAR AND SPICE, before going inside the bakery.

"Do you see him?" Karista asked as she reached her side.

"He just went into Em's place."

Emily Thalberg was one of Monica's best friends. She'd arrived in Valentine Valley a couple years before to sell a building she'd inherited but ended up finding a passion for pastry and marrying a local cowboy, instead.

"And now he's left Em's empty-handed—guess he was browsing there, too—and is heading into Wine Country. Weird."

"He could just be sightseeing. You never know what tourists want to see," Karista added with a teenager's faint disdain.

Monica grinned. "He doesn't look like a tourist." Then her stomach growled. "Hey, Karista, I'm going to take my lunch outside and sit in the sun."

"You just want to spy on him," the girl teased.

"And maybe I do. I'll let you know while you slave over those bows that need to be made."

Karista gave a cute, fake pout and followed her behind the counter. Monica took her salad from the flower cooler, grabbed a fork, napkin, and her water bottle, and headed outside to sit on the bench in front of one of her big windows. It was a crisp mountain day, brilliant blue sky encompassing the nearby Elk Mountains like an umbrella. Some of the hardier summer perennials were already filling planters along Main

Street. Freestanding display signs stood on the sidewalk outside several businesses, advertising the day's
specials. Her block was filled with two-story clap-
board buildings painted blue and yellow and red like
a field of flowers. At the end of the street, closest to
the mountains, rose the stone tower of town hall, the
highest point in Valentine. The Hotel Colorado took up
the whole block directly opposite her, three stories of
stone, with arched columns along the first floor like the
vaulted ceilings she'd seen in photos of castles.

Was the stranger noticing the prettiness of this little
town? Or did he have something else in mind? He
didn't seem like a browsing tourist. Sure enough, as she
worked her way through the salad, she saw him appear
out of another couple stores along the north side, then
cross the street and go from store to store along the
south, too, making his way slowly back toward her.
Occasionally, he answered a phone call or text. She
didn't hide her curiosity, and she noticed him look at
her. When he came out of another store, he glanced
again, and this time she gave a little wave. What the
hell. Maybe he'd come talk to her, and she'd figure out
what was going on without having to chase him down.
He didn't wave back.

She noticed the oddest thing about him, how he
looked at every person he passed, even glancing down
at their hands, both men and women. He seemed so . . .
alert, not caught up in his "browsing," not like a tourist
out for a sightseeing stroll. And if he was killing time
before some kind of event, well, he'd chosen an odd
way. Most guys would find a bar and watch a game. In

fact, he'd already gone into the Halftime Sports Bar
and come back out again.

He reached the hotel and put a hand on the big glass
door to go inside—and then turned and looked at her
again. She stiffened, waiting, then felt a sharp sizzle as
he headed back across the street and straight toward
her. Why was she letting this guy get to her? He was
staying at the hotel, obviously just passing through, and
man, did he look full of himself. And they hadn't even
exchanged a word!

That was about to change.

He stepped onto the sidewalk and stopped in front
of her. A couple strolling hand in hand shot him a look
as they had to veer around him. They went inside her
shop.

"Excuse me," he said, in the deepest, most delicious
voice she'd heard in a long time, "but is there a reason
you're watching me?"

Shielding her eyes with one hand, Monica gave him
a sunny smile. "Is there a reason you're going from
shop to shop, staying nowhere long, like someone
casing each place?"

From behind the sunglasses, he lifted an eyebrow.
"I'm new to town—you're bothered that I'm checking
out places I might like to shop or eat?"

She thought she detected the faintest trace of amusement in his voice, as if he was trying to suppress it.

"Or you might want to buy flowers? Or jewelry?"
she asked sweetly.

"I'm here a few weeks for business. Have to fill my
time somehow," he added lightly. He glanced from her

lunch spread to the flower-shop sign. "So you work here?"

"I'm the owner."

He nodded as if in understanding. "No wonder you feel like you can interrogate customers."

She laughed. "Only ones who are trying to appear mysterious." She put out a hand. "I'm Monica Shaw. I don't suppose you want to sit down on this bench so I don't pull something in my neck trying to get a good look at you."

"Travis Beaumont."

His handshake was firm and warm. He sat down beside her, his back as straight as a character from one of her favorite historical romances—the duke who deigned to visit a commoner. But he didn't seem to be arrogant, just . . . alert, as his gaze scanned the street before resting with interest on her face again.

"Nice name, Travis Beaumont."

"Thank you. Not that I had anything to do with it."

"Your parents gave it to you, and you didn't make it up here on the spot?"

He cocked his head, his voice pleasant as he said, "If I didn't want you to know my name, I wouldn't have told you."

"Right, like the mysterious business trip." She held up a bag of almonds. "Want some?"

"No, thank you."

She got the feeling that he was waiting to see what she'd come up with next. Maybe he was flattered by her curiosity. "Have you ever been to Valentine Valley before?"

"No. I've been to Denver, but that was it. Have you lived here your whole life?"

"Yep. A small-town girl, that's me. Except for college, of course."

"Where did you attend?"

"Think you know me from somewhere?"

"No, because I'm pretty sure I'd remember you."

"Flatterer." She took another bite of her salad, chewed, and swallowed before answering. "I have a business degree from Colorado State, and took courses in floral design. So I've answered your question, and now maybe you'll answer another of mine. Where are you from?"

"Right now, Washington, D.C."

"But that's not where you're originally from, of course."

He linked his hands together, forearms resting on his thighs. "I'm from a small town in Montana that you would never have heard of. My turn to ask. Do you own the shop with anyone else?"

Now *that* was a curious question. "Nope, I'm the sole owner."

He shrugged his shoulders. "Sorry if I'm out of line. You just seem young."

For some reason, she got the feeling that wasn't the whole explanation.

"I was going to ask the concierge a question," he continued, "but maybe you can help me. Do you know a place off the beaten path where my men can relax this evening?"

His men. Spoken like a soldier. Travis Beaumont

seemed nothing like the laid-back guys she knew. But that was most of his appeal. And his handsome face, of course.

"Tony's Tavern. It's on Nellie Street, by Highway 82. Dark bar, pool table, darts. Maybe I'll see you there."

He stood up. "Thanks for the information. Nice meeting you." After nodding, he headed back across the street and disappeared inside the hotel.

Monica slowly gathered her lunch and took it inside. The strolling couple was just taking a bag from Karista, and they smiled as they passed Monica and went outside.

The door had barely closed when Karista said, "I could hardly concentrate on them—what was that hot guy saying to you?"

"Not much, but it was fun anyway."

Now she'd have to decide if she actually meant to search out Travis Beaumont at Tony's. There was something far too intriguing about him.

Secret Service Special Agent Travis Beaumont stood at the window of the third-floor hotel room that he'd begun to transform into a command center. He stared thoughtfully at Monica's Flowers and Gifts down below, with its backdrop of mountains, some still dusted with snow at the peaks. Behind him, a number of agents were setting up conference tables, radios, printers, and computers, which would eventually connect all the agents on the ground with headquarters and the White House. President Alanna Torres would be visiting Valentine Valley within two weeks, attending her son's wedding—not that more than a handful of people in town knew those details yet. Travis had been entrusted with his first assignment as lead agent with the advance team. And he wasn't about to blow it because of a cute, flirtatious woman with the most incredible deep brown eyes.

He told himself to stop, that he was sounding hung up on her. But there was no denying she was gorgeous, with a headful of black curls like a starburst, flawless light brown skin, and high cheekbones that gave her an exotic look. Her slim, cropped pants had hugged her hips, while her short-sleeve top had shown off toned arms. It had taken everything in him not to stare at her, to pretend indifference. It had been a while since he had felt this attracted to someone. After his divorce two years ago, he'd shied away from dating altogether, then occasionally had a meal out, mostly with women his buddies had set him up with. Nothing had clicked.

But all he'd had to do was look at Monica Shaw's wry grin to feel his pulse rev up. And that was bad news.

Walking the streets of Valentine Valley had almost reminded him of his own hometown, where, as a boy, he could race the streets, playing cop or soldier, and someone would always be looking out for him, prepared to tell his mom if he was up to no good—or prepared to keep him safe. But this small town was now part of his job, and he would have to know it inside out, meeting with the police and fire chiefs, even the medical personnel at the closest hospital. And if he didn't have an exact presidential itinerary yet? Well, that was nothing new. Sometimes, the president's junior staffers were clueless.

But at least there were parts of his job that were easy. His site agent had already scheduled a meeting at the Sweetheart Inn, where the wedding would take place. His transportation agent would be meeting with the local cops to get a feel for every street in town. He'd soon have 3-D models of Main Street from the Forensic Services Division, so they could find every vulnerability to guard the presidential motorcade. To that end, he'd spent his first afternoon looking at the street from on the ground, checking out the stores, the number of customers, the sightseers. He also needed a place for an observation post, with a great sight line to the front entrance of the hotel since the president would be staying there.

His team would be doing background checks on all the owners, of course, but the flower shop had an ideal location, right across the street, and a second floor. He saw the curtains of an apartment, not a business. The countersniper team would have a tactical advantage from such a location.

It didn't hurt that the owner was easy on the eyes and that she'd sort of flirted with him. That usually didn't happen. He knew he gave off a serious, no-nonsense vibe, and most women were looking for fun. Not that he'd ever get involved with someone while on the job— it was difficult enough to deal with an ex-wife who was also an agent and the constant travel. He didn't have time for anything else. It was serious, crucial work, protecting the president, especially the first female president. The usual average of ten threats a day against a president were 50 percent higher for President Torres. All of them were taken seriously. He was focused on his job, and nothing would stand in his way.

But part of his job was making sure his team relaxed when they needed to, letting off steam during their brief hours away so they could be more alert on the job. Even though he didn't take advantage of the fun— besides a good beer and maybe a game of pool—he was one of them. He wanted to lead by example, and he wanted their respect.

And if they saw Monica flirting with him—well, it couldn't hurt him, as far as his men were concerned. And meanwhile, he'd be sizing her up, deciding if she'd be the perfect host for a countersniper team. He found himself hoping she'd show up at Tony's Tavern.

Chapter Two

Monica met up for dinner after work with all the girls at Rancheros, the Mexican restaurant farther down Main Street. The décor was old-world, with wrought-iron lampshades over each booth and an actual fountain in the center of the restaurant.

Emily Thalberg, pastry chef extraordinaire, arrived next, perky as the girl next door—even though she'd been raised by a bohemian single mom in San Francisco.

Sliding in beside Monica, she pushed her strawberry blond hair behind her ears as she grinned. "Let's pull the table closer to us, or Whitney will never fit into the booth."

"I heard that." Whitney Winslow-Thalberg appeared, her voice faintly sarcastic, waddling like the eight-month pregnant woman that she was. She sank onto the opposite bench very slowly.

"How you feeling?" Monica asked, smiling at her.

"If one more person asks me that . . . But at least I can tell the truth to you guys. Grouchy. That's how I feel. Grouchy and uncomfortable. And I have a whole month to go of this. But I'm glowing," she added with cheery sarcasm, "let's not forget I'm glowing!"

Whitney's black hair was cut stylishly, expensively, in layers to her shoulders, and she had a dimple to the right of her mouth that winked whenever she smiled— and she smiled a lot now that she'd married Josh. She wore the most elegant maternity clothes that Monica had ever seen, but that happened when you traveled the world with your supremely wealthy family. Not that you'd ever know Whitney's family was in the same league as the Hiltons. Whitney was the most unassuming, sweet woman—and owner of a slightly naughty lingerie chain, Leather and Lace, with underwear named just for her. Monica had a hard time staying out of her store, and it wasn't just because the owner was one of her best friends.

"There's my favorite sister-in-law!" Brooke Thalberg cried out as she approached. She bent over the bench and almost put her face into Whitney's stomach. "And my soon-to-be favorite niece!"

Whitney rolled her eyes, but the fondness in her gaze spoke for her. During the Christmas season, Whitney had married into a great family, the Thalbergs, who owned the Silver Creek Ranch south of town. Brooke, long brown hair in waves about her face, worked alongside her brothers and her fiancé. She also had a side business, a riding school, housed in a newly built indoor riding arena.

Brooke and Monica had grown up together, best friends all through school even though Monica had been a cheerleader and run track, while Brooke had been into barrel racing like every good cowgirl. They'd spent more time at Monica's house than on the ranch, mainly because Monica's grandpa had lived with them, and he was always too sick to do much. Monica had hated to leave him alone. He was a fascinating guy who'd marched for civil rights and taught her much of what she knew about gardening. He'd affected the course of her life, and she'd tried to follow in his footsteps, definitely where activism was concerned. She'd gone door-to-door to save Bluebell Hill, a gorgeous meadow in the foothills of the mountain that overlooked the whole valley, even led a boycott of the produce of an "organic" farmer she'd filmed using pesticides. Not that she'd made much time for environmentalism lately except for the occasional letter to the editor, she thought, wincing.

While they were waiting for their drinks and still browsing the menus, Emily said, "Monica, did you see that hot guy going from store to store this afternoon?"

"You sound like Karista," Monica said, shaking her head, "all excited about someone who happens to be handsome, as clean-cut as a soldier, and in a suit tailored to perfection."

Brooke whistled her enthusiasm. "Tell us more."

"How do you know he went from store to store, Em?" Monica asked. "Considering you're a married woman, I didn't think you'd spy on a guy."

"Mrs. Ludlow literally marched her walker up to the front window to see what he did when he left."

They all grinned at the image.

"You seem to know a lot about what he did, too," Emily said, narrowing her blue eyes with friendly suspicion.

"That's because I actually talked to him."

"So who is he?" Brooke demanded.

Before she could answer, their waitress, Lisa, daughter of another local rancher, Deke Hutcheson, came to take their order. She asked when the baby was due, talked about her son's riding lessons with Brooke, but Monica could see the impatience building around the table. All the girls wanted to know about Travis, and she didn't know what she wanted to tell them. For the first time, she wondered if she should keep something to herself. And just the fact that she had that thought made Travis far more important than he needed to be. So after they'd placed their orders, she told them everything.

Emily clapped her hands together. "He sounds like he'd be fascinating to get to know."

"Even though he's only in town briefly," Whitney said, helping herself to salsa and chips.

"Minor details," Emily insisted. "He'll be blown away by our Monica."

Monica smiled. "That's not necessary. I'm just really curious why he'd hide what he does, why he seems so formal."

"Maybe he works for the Mafia," Brooke offered.

They all laughed.

"He could be a criminal, but I don't think so." Monica crunched a chip and swallowed. "In my mind, I thought of him as Captain America, all patriotism, like if he was wearing a suit, he'd have a flag pin on his lapel. He did pause and look with a lot of interest at Josh's leatherwork, Whitney."

Whitney beamed with pride. "How could he not? My husband is so talented. Oh, not that he wouldn't love your flowers, too!" she insisted.

Monica grinned. "I pegged Travis as the macho type, so I'm thinking flowers aren't his thing."

"But maybe florists are . . ." Brooke mused.

"Are the shoulder bags selling well in Aspen?" Monica continued.

Whitney's eyes widened. "It's just . . . amazing. He can't make them fast enough, and, of course, they take a lot of time because his carving is so intricate." She looked earnestly at Monica. "I know he also has some frames in various stages for you."

"That's nice of him, but I understand that he'll make the most money on those bags and the necklaces he's doing for you." For a while there, it seemed every customer wanted only Josh's work, not her own. But she'd come to terms with it, taking some online classes to improve her design creativity, which was all she could control.

"We have more important things to discuss," Emily said. "We're having a baby shower tomorrow!"

Whitney blushed and rested her hand on her stomach, that maternal glow she'd mentioned very evident. Monica felt a twinge of happy envy for her. She looked around at all her friends as they discussed the shower—and it hit her for the first time that she was the last single girl. Emily and Whitney were both married, and Brooke was engaged. Monica was thirty years old now—thirty! How had that happened? She'd enjoyed her twenties like every other girl, but lately, as she watched her friends fall in love, she'd begun to feel that her life was . . . lacking.

Maybe that was why she found herself intrigued by Travis and his unusual demeanor. Would he show up tonight at Tony's Tavern? Would she?

She would. Not that Monica confirmed that for any of her friends. She decided to go to Tony's alone, hoping that any embarrassment she might end up suffering would have limited exposure. Unless, of course, the Thalberg brothers and their sidekicks were there. She wouldn't think about that now.

In her little apartment above the flower shop, she dressed carefully, a white, sleeveless, drape-necked top that showed off her lean arms and hugged in all the right places, above deep pink jeans and high heels. She wore dangly earrings and dangly bracelets, making her feel feminine and sultry, ready to flirt and dance and have a good time.

She tried to be very quiet going down the back steps and getting in her car. Brooke and Adam lived above Sugar and Spice next door, and she didn't want any questions. She drove to Tony's even though she could have walked the seven blocks—but in heels? She thought not.

The tavern looked like a dive bar from the outside, but the regulars liked that because it kept most of the tourists away. Inside, there were flat screen TVs on the wall between mounted animal heads and neon beer signs. She walked through the front of the tavern, down the long bar, where customer after customer turned his head to look at her as she passed. She knew or recognized most of them. Even Tony De Luca did a double take as he poured a drink behind the bar, eyebrows raised. A single dad, Tony had been a few years ahead of her in school. He hung out with the Thalberg men and still played hockey and baseball on their rec teams, so she knew him pretty well. She gave him a broad smile, lifting her chin and shaking her curls, feeling sassy. It had been too long since she'd put her sexy on.

She didn't see any strangers, so she kept going into the back room, where a pool table was spotlighted in the center, tables and chairs scattered along the walls, a jukebox shining from one corner.

She saw Travis Beaumont almost at once, standing with a group of men near the pool table. He was wearing the same navy blue polo shirt but had changed into jeans. No sunglasses, either. She could look at those handsome high cheekbones, as sharp as if someone had sculpted them, all night long. She felt a little shiver of desire. It had been a while since a man made her feel that way. He spotted her, and an even more aggressive awareness shot through her, and she felt trapped in his gaze, impassive though it was. What did he keep hidden beneath all that control? She shivered, realizing that she wanted to find out.

Though he didn't smile, he raised his beer to her in a little salute. She smiled back, then noticed his friends—or should she say "his men"? There were four guys and a woman, all dressed casually, but they, too, wore the same watchful expressions, even when they were smiling at something one of them said. They all eyed her, and it wasn't sexual in any way. It was like they took her apart with their gazes, then looked away after determining that she was harmless. Maybe they were bodyguards; she'd seen a few of those during her days skiing the hills of Aspen.

Or soldiers—that seemed more precise. They had the same vibe as Adam Desantis, Brooke's fiancé, who'd just gotten out of the Marines a couple years ago. They appeared like people who'd seen more of the world, dealt with its ugliness, and had it change them. She couldn't even take offense at the way they studied her because when the next guy came through the door, they did the same thing to him.

One of Travis's colleagues gave her a closer look, a black guy with a shaved head and biceps that bulged beneath a tight Henley. He smiled at her, and she smiled back, even as he said something to Travis. She didn't know what Travis said, but the man gave a slightly disappointed nod and turned back to watch the pool match.

Had Travis dissuaded his interest? That was unexpected.

As the man himself came toward her, she settled her hip on a stool next to a long shelf built into the wall at bar height. Bowls of popcorn were scattered down the length, along with empty glasses and bottles of beer.

Raising her voice to be heard over the country music, she said, "Nice seeing you again, Travis."

"Same to you, Miss Shaw."

"You can call me Monica, you know. I won't bite."

He didn't crack a smile although she thought the corner of his mouth might have twitched. Ah, there was someone human under there.

"Monica, may I order you a drink?"

"That's better. I'll take whatever beer you're having."

He arched a brow, then caught the eye of Nicole, the waitress in tight jean shorts and a low-cut top, passing through with a newly empty tray. After he raised his bottle of beer, she gave him a big smile, nodded, and moved back into the main barroom.

"Those must be your 'men,' " she said, gesturing with her chin toward the pool table. "And your woman, too?"

"Not my woman, but yes, she works with me. She's one of the guys."

"She looks pretty cute for 'one of the guys.' "

"She's married."

Smiling, Monica said, "It's very obvious they all work with you—for you?"

He nodded.

"Ah, so you're the boss. Actually, you feel like the captain. I think you were in the military. You all act like a platoon or something."

He nodded again. "I was a Marine."

She felt like she'd scored a point in an imaginary game. "One of my best friends is engaged to a former Marine. You don't exactly remind me of him because he's always been a lot more easygoing, but there's . . . something about the two of you."

He didn't say anything, so she chattered on.

"Are all the rest ex-military?"

"Not all."

As Nicole brought her a beer, she gave Monica a smile and an arched eyebrow that was the same as a thumbs-up.

Hiding her grin, Monica took a sip and studied Travis. "You're making me treat you like a surprise gift, one I have to unwrap to see what the truth is."

He arched a brow, then she felt herself blushing.

"Damn, that came out wrong," she admitted. "You're a mystery, Travis Beaumont, and that's hard to resist in this small town."

"Can I ask you a question?"

"Sure. I'd appreciate being distracted from my embarrassment."

He didn't smile, but she thought those incredible eyes might actually have twinkled.

"I saw signs in various windows today. There's an archaeological dig nearby? One they're threatening to close down and build over?"

"Yeah. Did you hear about the big archaeological find outside Snowmass Village a couple years ago? Dozens of mastodons? They're calling it Snowmastodon." She quirked a brow. "Get it?"

He nodded, and, again, she was hoping for a smile, but she was disappointed. Maybe his smile would be too powerfully handsome for her, a mere mortal, to bear. But all kidding aside, everyone should smile more, even if only to make themselves feel better. She smiled a lot while she worked, but then again, she was dealing with beautiful flowers and customers who were happy to give them as gifts or decorate their homes. She wondered what Travis really dealt with on the job. Maybe he didn't have much of a reason to smile, and that was sad.

"Anyway," she continued, "they were bulldozing an expansion of the reservoir in Snowmass Village and unearthed thousands of mammoth bones: mastodons, an Ice Age bison, and lots of others. Over thirty mastodons, the biggest mastodon find in the world. The museum in Denver will be doing years of preservation and research. But they had to close the site up after seven weeks of searching, and it's all capped with clay and back underwater. Well, a few months ago, we found our own little archaeological site when the Renaissance Spa, south of the Silver Creek Ranch, started working on its expansion. The spa is saying they have to start building again, so their indoor pool can be done before winter. The scientists are claiming they're not being given enough time to investigate. The public is on mammoth overload—some people are even asking why they should bother digging here for one little mammoth after the huge find in Snowmass? But it's our history, you know?"

"Sounds like you're on the side of science," he said, reaching past her to grab some popcorn.

She could smell his citrusy aftershave, and it made her a little dizzy. She briefly closed her eyes, both amused and exasperated with herself. "Yeah, these mountains have always needed protection. They're dotted with old silver-mining holes. Think of all the forests that have been cut down, and now the government is leasing way too much protected wilderness for natural-gas exploration." She leaned closer. "Shh, you didn't hear me say that. My dad is an engineer for a natural-gas company."

"My lips are sealed."

And that, of course, made her look at his lips, and she had the strangest momentary sensation that he was looking at hers. Then he glanced back at his friends—to get himself under control? Remind himself of his position? She didn't think he needed to be reminded of that too often. He seemed to take whatever he did very seriously. She was dying to ask about his job again, but he'd already rebuffed her today. She'd play it cool.

Clearing her throat, she said, "So there's a local group of environmentalists trying to keep people interested in the dig, and if enough are interested, maybe the spa will delay its new pool a couple more weeks."

"I hope it turns out for the best."

She sighed, already knowing that her dear friends, the widows, were involved. Three old ladies, activists all, lived at the Widows' Boardinghouse. They worked part-time for Emily while actively directing the Valentine Valley Preservation Fund, which offered grants for new and renovating businesses. They used their committee to make sure they were in on all the happenings in Valentine—and they created their own "happenings," too. They'd already started work on their plans to highlight the plight of Valentine's mammoth.

He sipped his beer and looked around the growing

crowd in the poolroom. His friend, he of the bulging muscles, seemed to take that as permission to approach.

"Travis, we're goin' to play some darts," the man said, a Southern drawl making his deep voice musical. "You and your friend up for it?" He turned and flashed her a gleaming white grin.

She held out her hand. "Hi, I'm Monica Shaw."

His hand encompassed hers in a warm grip. "Royce Ames. Good to meet you."

"I'm up for darts," she said. "I've never played a real game, just shot at the board. You guys can show me, right?"

Nodding, Royce pulled her toward the dartboard in the corner. She glanced over her shoulder at Travis and tossed her head toward the corner, welcoming him to join them. He shook his head, and she gave a little shrug as she turned back to Royce. That was too bad because she thought Travis needed to find something fun to focus on instead of examining the room as if for enemy combatants. It seemed he wanted his "team" to relax but not so much himself.

Royce and two of his friends taught her a game, and they were much more easygoing than their "leader." Royce had a naughty sense of humor, and it was obvious he was interested in her. But there was something about Travis, the way he stood alone, shoulders back, in command, that captured her attention and concern. The Royces of the world didn't need help to let off steam, but the Travises sure did.

"Would you like to dance?" Royce asked after a second game of darts was over.

He'd put aside his beer unfinished, as if he weren't allowed to touch it anymore. Stranger and stranger.

But it was an up-tempo song that she was already tapping her toes to. "Sure."

She moved her hips to the music, and though she made a show of having a good time with Royce, she could feel Travis watching her. It made her feel over-heated, sexily self-conscious, and even more curious about her mysterious ex-Marine.

After a second dance, Royce looked over her head, then grimaced. "Time to go. Have to work in the mornin'."

He must have gotten some kind of signal from Travis. "What do you do?" she asked innocently, as the song ended.

He grinned. "Can't say right now. I'm under orders."

"You're all making me too curious."

Royce shrugged good-naturedly. Why couldn't she like someone this easygoing? But no, she had to be drawn to the mysterious, intense loner whose idea of fun seemed to be watching others having it. But she knew herself well—his behavior was the very reason she was interested and curious. It was obvious he needed to let loose once in a while.

Travis approached. "Are you staying, Monica?"

Royce waved good-bye to her and returned to his coworkers.

She smiled up at Travis. "I have to work in the morning, too, so I'll head home."

"Let me walk you to your car."

"Because Valentine Valley is such a scary place after dark?"

"Because I'm a polite kind of guy."

She could feel her smile fade as she briefly studied him. Usually, this was when even a polite guy tried to kiss her, but she didn't worry that was going to happen with Travis. She nodded, grabbed the sweater she'd left on her stool, and preceded him through the bar, leaving his friends behind to put on their jackets and settle up their bills.

Outside, the May evening was already brisk, into the fifties and dropping steadily, so she slid her arms into her sweater.

"I parked around back—even more reason for a big man to escort me," she teased.

Again, he gave her that faint lip quirk that might have been the very beginnings of a smile. Why did he hide himself behind impassivity?

Overhead, the sky was pitch-black, and brilliant stars were scattered like glitter tossed by schoolkids. Beyond the parking lot, she could see the lights of the only apartment complex in Valentine. But she didn't see any people, and besides the muted sound of music from inside Tony's, she and Travis seemed totally alone.

And then she heard the faint sound of off-key whistling. Travis was already alert, his head moving side to side as if he thought everything that crossed his path could mean life or death. It would have been amusing, except at that moment, a shadow seemed to extend from a Dumpster behind the bar, just to her right. Everything proceeded to happen both in an instant and in slow motion.

"Hey, baby," said a man with a slurred voice. He reached forward as if to grab her arm, beer breath leading the way. Startled, she dropped her purse.

And then, suddenly, Travis had the man against the Dumpster, a hand at his throat. The shadowy stranger made a single strangled sound that was abruptly cut off, and he grabbed Travis's hand in both of his, as if to pry him away. His feet kicked feebly.

Monica stumbled sideways in shock, barely having felt Travis move past her. By the light on the back wall of the tavern, she could see the impassive planes of his face, the deadly cold expression, his eyes shadowed and dark.

"Bad idea to approach the lady," Travis said in a low voice.

Before she could protest that the guy couldn't breathe, Travis let him go, and he collapsed to his knees, coughing and wheezing. Travis stepped away and watched, fists on his hips as if holding himself back.

"Just—just takin' a piss, man," the stranger gasped, hands at his throat, his eyes a little wild in the meager light.

"Didn't anyone ever tell you you don't scare women by approaching them out of the dark?" Travis demanded, hauling the man up by his jacket collar and sending him reeling toward the front of the tavern. "And you *never* touch them without permission."

"Right—sorry," he said hoarsely, then gasped another, "Sorry!" at her. He turned and tried to run although he veered sideways before righting himself and staggering out of the parking lot.

Monica simply gaped at Travis, who still stood stiff and defensive, as if expecting an army to attack.

"Uh . . . thanks," she said, gathering her wits. "You move fast."

He shrugged, and some of the tension left his shoulders. "Training. Hope I didn't scare you."

"No, a drunk trying to grab me did, though."

"Did he touch you? I wasn't quite sure if your purse fell, or he tried to grab it."

"It was all clumsy me, I'm afraid. Not sure what that guy was trying to do."

They both dropped to their knees by her purse, and she couldn't be surprised when Travis produced a flashlight from his pocket like a magician.

"He was pretty drunk," Travis said, and now his voice sounded a little regretful. "He probably didn't intend much except to hit on you, but I couldn't take that chance. I couldn't see if he had a weapon."

"That's okay. Not sure anyone's protected me like that before. If he'd have had a knife . . ." She shuddered, and suddenly her hands were shaking in the tiny beam of the flashlight.

To her surprise, Travis put a gentle hand on her shoulder. "You going to be okay?"

"Yeah, yeah, of course," she said, giving a shaky laugh. "Not used to surprises—or unpleasant ones, anyway. Thanks for your help."

They silently gathered up her wallet, cell phone, and everything else. He slid a tube of lip gloss into her purse, then took her hand to help her to her feet. She stared up at him for a lingering moment. They both seemed to realize they were still holding hands and let go at the same time.

"Thanks," Monica said, repeating herself. She turned and led the way through the parked cars. She noticed that he remained behind her, as if that guy would be stupid enough to come after her. Of course, he could have gone to friends for backup . . .

No, she wasn't thinking that way. He'd seemed a harmless drunk in the end, and Travis had certainly scared him off.

And impressed the hell out of her.

"This is mine," she said, leaning against the mini-van and looking up at him. She gave him a bright smile and tried to be normal again. "Bet you think it's a sexy ride for a single girl."

"It's a curious choice," he said.

"I have a larger van for flower deliveries, but during all the major seasons, I sometimes need more vehicles. It just made sense. Fits my ski equipment, too. Do you ski?"

"Not regularly, but I used to back in Montana growing up."

"Black diamond runs?"

"Of course."

"So you can be competitive—just not at darts."

"I can be competitive at anything, but I know when to stand down."

"More military talk. What do you mean?"

She leaned against her van while he stood with his hands behind his back, as if he was used to remaining at attention all the time.

"I've told you those people in there work for me—we're stuck together twenty-four hours a day when we travel, but that doesn't mean I need to subject them to my presence every moment of the day. You forget, they probably need some time away from the boss."

"Royce doesn't seem like the kind of guy who'd let your presence inhibit him."

Travis released his breath in almost a little snort. Of laughter? Disbelief?

"Royce isn't bothered by much of anything, and since we room together when quarters are tight, he's pretty tolerant of me. But the others don't seem as free to be themselves around me."

"Then you're being a nice boss."

He cocked a brow. "Nice? I think I'm being practical."

"Oh, sorry, practical."

She gave him her best smile, and although he studied her, he didn't smile back. She couldn't think of another thing to say, only found herself noticing the way the shadows molded the strong bones of his face. He was a man who protected people, a thoughtful boss who put his employees first—she liked that. But if he was always so concerned for his people, when did he let loose himself?

"You have your keys?" he asked quietly.

She gave a little jerk, coming out of her trance. "Sure. Right here. Good night. And thank you again for your help."

"You're welcome."

She dug them out of her purse and got into the van. The engine turned over immediately, and when she glanced out of her window, he was already striding back toward the front of the tavern.

Who *was* this guy, and why did he bring out her curiosity and fascination?

Chapter Three

Back at the Hotel Colorado, Travis changed into sweats and tried to relax even though his adrenaline was still high from the encounter with that drunk—or maybe from the evening spent watching Monica light up Tony's Tavern with her smile and bubbling personality.

He had to share a room with his good friend, lead advance agent for the countersniper team, Royce Ames. Rooms were at a premium since the hotel would soon have to vacate the entire second and third floors for the presidential visit. President Torres had given permission to release dates in advance, and the hotel had been glad to accommodate them since they were in on the secret of the president's eventual arrival.

Now Royce was stretched out on his bed, remote in hand, flicking through channel after channel. Travis sat at the desk, reading a civil-war book, but he wasn't seeing the pages.

He was remembering the way Monica Shaw danced, arms upraised above her head, hips bumping to each beat of the music. Her face had been full of sensual pleasure at the movement of her body, and it made him think of—

No, he wasn't going there. And she hadn't been dancing with *him*—but she'd wanted him to ask, he damn well knew it.

He couldn't afford to be distracted. His job was to keep the president safe, not to party with the locals. A couple years back, the agency had implemented new rules, one of which was no drinking less than ten hours before shift. It made it easier to keep his detail under control, but it also left an occasional hour for TV, books, and thinking about a beautiful woman whom he'd be running into far too much—running into temptation. And dwelling on it wasn't like him.

The next day, on a misty Thursday afternoon, Monica went to the Widows' Boardinghouse early to help set up for Whitney's baby shower. The widows, with their energy and enthusiasm never flagging, had already done much of the decorating in their big old Victorian. Emily's husband, Nate, had renovated the house for his grandma a few years back, and now they had a comfy kitchen with a breakfast nook and gleaming oak cabinets, all decorated in a cow theme—fitting, since the boardinghouse was part of the Silver Creek Ranch, and Mrs. Thalberg, a rancher's widow, lived there.

Monica had slept surprisingly well after the incident in Tony's parking lot. She'd felt protected and safe, and now that time had passed, told herself the guy was only drunk anyway and probably wouldn't have hurt her. But in the dark night, she couldn't have known that, and neither could Travis. He hadn't hesitated to put himself between her and danger. She shivered, and it wasn't from fear. Damn.

She was chopping vegetables and laying them out on a cow-spotted tray while Heather Armstrong set up food warmers in the dining room. Heather, short red hair still windblown, was Emily's best friend from San Francisco, who'd recently moved to Valentine Valley to start anew with her business, As You Like It Catering. Last year, she'd met and fallen in love with Emily's brother, Chris Sweet, in what was a whirlwind affair, even for Valentine Valley.

Emily and Brooke were admiring the cake from Sugar and Spice, formed to look like a baby carriage.

"Didn't Steph do a great job with the decorating?" Emily gushed. "Those roses along the bottom are all hers!"

Steph, Emily's teenage sister, was a high-school senior, blonder than her older sister, who'd taken Emily's surprise appearance into their family pretty badly a couple years ago. Since then, she and her sister had grown so close that she now worked part-time at the bakery, with plans to become a full partner someday.

Steph walked in from the parlor, pink and blue crepe dangling around her neck. "If I'm so good, guess I can skip college. I did manage the bakery just fine when you were on your honeymoon."

"You will not skip college!" Emily said with mock sternness before morphing into pride. "Did you guys hear she's going to Johnson and Wales University in Denver? Culinary arts *and* business. My sister is so smart!"

Steph made a big production of rolling her eyes as she looked for the best place to hang more decorations, but Monica could see the pleased pink in her cheeks.

"Are you going to barrel race there?" Brooke asked.

Brooke had been training the teenager for years. It was amazing how fast the two of them could make their horses circle the barrels.

"It's not one of their sports," Steph said, "but I'll pick up a few tournaments here and there."

"But your studies come first," Emily reminded her.

"Yes, *Mom*," Steph said heavily, even as she elbowed her sister.

Monica looked around the kitchen, her smile broadening as the widows bustled in from various parts of the house. She loved all these women, old and young, whom she'd spent her life with, who'd taken care of her. The widows had been the grandmothers she'd been denied—her mom's mom had lived on the East Coast, and while she'd been alive, they'd only been able to see her once or twice a year. Her dad's mom had died when Monica was a toddler. Mrs. Thalberg, Brooke's grandma, with her brilliantly dyed red hair and artful makeup, had been a rancher's wife, and she'd adopted jeans and vests, when most other women of her generation still preferred tailored pants. She'd treated Monica and her twin sister Missy like the sisters Brooke had never had. When Mrs. Thalberg came for Grandparents' Day back in elementary school, she'd acted as

Monica and Missy's grandma, too, since their own grandpa was always too sick to attend—though he did remember to send wonderful notes that they'd find in their desks on that special day.

Mrs. Palmer, Brooke's future grandma-in-law, was the odd one of the three, with her big blond wig and boldly patterned dresses she must have made herself, because Monica had never seen dress fabric with giant stars (like she sometimes wore when she read tarot cards). Only one of the widows, Mrs. Ludlow, seemed like your typical grandma, with her blouses and slacks, cloud of white hair, and a walker. None of them were strangers to activism, due to their various causes around Valentine, but Mrs. Ludlow had a secret—she'd actually been arrested. Not that Monica brought it up because she herself was a little notorious in environmentalists' circles. She didn't dwell on it.

More of the guests began to arrive, including some of Monica's family, too. Her sister Missy could never come to these kinds of things. Monica knew that her mom was always disappointed though she never showed it. Missy was a reporter for CNN in Washington, D.C., and didn't get all that much time off.

The guest of honor arrived last, and although the shower was hardly a surprise, when Whitney saw all the women gathered—including her jet-setting mom— the pink decorations for her baby girl, and the beautiful cake, she burst into happy tears.

All through lunch, the house was full of the cheerful sounds of women talking. Heather was teased because she should be the next one engaged, and Brooke, too, who hadn't set a wedding date yet. Since Whitney already knew that she was having a girl, the adorable baby clothes she received were in a rainbow of pastels, pink and purple and yellow, sized from birth up to a year. She even received some bigger items, a stroller, two car seats, and a portable play yard.

"Didn't those used to be called playpens?" Monica's mom said, shaking her head as everyone smiled.

Janet Shaw had close-cropped hair and darker skin than Monica. Her dad always used to call her his princess, but come to think of it, lately Monica hadn't heard that. She frowned at her mom. Did she look a little . . . tired? Maybe preoccupied? When she saw Monica watching, she smiled the same old smile, but Monica wasn't convinced that all was right in the world.

"Missy wishes she could have been here," Janet said to Whitney, as everyone began to go through the gifts piled on a side table. "She went in on the stroller with us."

"And I've only met her once, last Christmas," Whitney said, surprised. "That was very nice of her."

Monica tried to hide her frown as she studied her mom. She hadn't heard about Missy's involvement. Why couldn't she get away from this feeling that something seemed off with her mom?

Later, as everyone was having cake, Mrs. Ludlow called for attention from her rocker near the fireplace. "I have a wonderful announcement to make," she said. "You all know that my granddaughter, Ashley, is a lawyer in Washington, D.C."

Monica knew a lot about Ashley. After being involved in student government together in high school, they'd gone on to the same college and dove into environmental activism. Together, they'd tied themselves to ancient trees about to be cut down and spent a month one summer living in a tree house in a forest scheduled to make way for more coal mining. Monica became well-known for writing grant proposals to further the interests of their various groups. Ashley took that to the next level, becoming an environmental lawyer, working from the inside to help important causes. But not before Ashley had chickened out on the biggest protest Monica had ever been involved in—the one that gained her the most notoriety.

There'd been another rumor she'd heard about Ashley, but Mrs. Ludlow had never confirmed it, saying it was Ashley's private business.

"I haven't talked about it much, because my granddaughter asked me to keep quiet," Mrs. Ludlow continued, "but for over two years, she's been dating the son of President Torres."

Though she said it matter-of-factly, her cheeks blushed with pride, even as gasps and murmurs circulated through the parlor. *That* was the rumor, Monica mused, glancing at Brooke, who nodded back at her in confirmation.

"And now they're getting married," Mrs. Ludlow added.

The "mom" corner of middle-aged women called out their congratulations, and the younger crowd looked at each other in wonder. What would it be like to plan a presidential wedding?

"Are they getting married in the White House?" Monica asked.

"What if we're invited!" Brooke said excitedly.

Mrs. Ludlow shook her head, then took a sip of iced tea. As she patted her lips with her napkin, Monica could barely restrain her curiosity. *Come on, Mrs. L., spill!*

"No, Ashley wants a more traditional wedding in her hometown, so she'd like it to be at St. John's Church and the Sweetheart Inn. But we cannot breathe a word beyond this room, not yet."

More excited gasps. Monica glanced in surprise at the elder Mrs. Sweet, Emily's grandma and the owner of the Sweetheart Inn, dressed far more elegantly than anyone else—except maybe Whitney's mother. Surely, the inn needed at least a year's notice to hold such a wedding. But Mrs. Sweet, cool and serene, her white hair drawn back beneath a broad-brimmed straw hat, just gave the smallest, knowing smile. So she'd been asked in advance. Mrs. Palmer and Mrs. Thalberg, not close friends of the other woman, exchanged a re-signed look. They'd been on the receiving end of Mrs. Sweet's "airs," as they liked to call it, their whole lives. Emily said she sometimes felt trapped between her real grandmother and her other newly acquired ones.

Mrs. Ludlow raised a hand as the questions began. "I can't tell you more details right now. You all surely understand that a presidential wedding has far more complications than any of us can imagine."

Emily's jaw dropped. "The president . . . she's coming here?"

For a moment, you could have heard the proverbial pin drop.

At last, Mrs. Ludlow beamed. "Of course she is. Isn't it wonderful? Now, of course, I'll want to host a bridal shower. Monica, I shall need to talk to you about flowers, and perhaps some kind of little craft item for favors, and—"

"But when is the wedding?" Vanessa Winslow asked impatiently.

Whitney frowned at her mom, but everyone knew that Vanessa moved in wealthy circles, and she probably wanted to make sure she was in town for such an event. She'd recently bought a condo in Aspen to be near her daughter part of each year.

"Soon, is all I'm allowed to say." Mrs. Ludlow used her walker to rise to her feet, like a queen finished with her audience. "Ashley would like me to tell Monica and Emily that she'll be contacting you both about wedding details. We all understand it's terribly last-minute, but she'd love to use your services during the wedding weekend—you, too, Heather, my dear."

The three young women stared wide-eyed at each other, and Monica knew just what the other two were thinking—being part of a presidential wedding could put their businesses on the map. Even Aspen residents and tourists would have to take notice after that. She felt a thrill of awareness, various flowers cascading through her mind like a rain shower, demanding to be chosen for the rare honor of a presidential wedding. They might need flowers for the hotel, too, where the president would be—

And then she stiffened, realization dawning. Travis! *That* was why he was in town, looking all mysterious and military-ish—he had something to do with the president and the wedding. And who else dealt with a president? The Secret Service. If it was true, he was taking the "secret" part very seriously, but now all the protectiveness he'd displayed on her behalf made sense.

Monica now understood that Mrs. Ludlow had been ordered to keep things under wraps, just like Travis had been. No wonder he'd been walking the streets of Valentine, looking things over. He had a very important job to do.

Or was she jumping to conclusions?

"Ladies, you know what we have to do," Mrs. Palmer suddenly said in a loud voice, her Western drawl cutting across all the other conversations. "We have to speed up our 'Men of Valentine Valley' calendar photo shoot." She rushed on, acting as if she hadn't heard the groans. "Think of all the people who'll be in town to purchase our calendar, raisin' money for a good cause."

The widows were always looking for ways to raise money for the Valentine Valley Preservation Fund, Monica knew. Last year, they'd gotten in some pretty hot—and illegal—water using Josh's newfound leatherworking fame. Okay, not so much because of his craftsmanship, but the sexy "cowboy artist" photo that had gone viral. Josh had at last agreed, along with his friends, to do a G-rated calendar showing off Valentine Valley's . . . assets.

"Oh, that's a good idea, Renee!" Mrs. Thalberg said enthusiastically.

Sandy Thalberg, Whitney's mother-in-law, winced. "You know I've never been thrilled with the idea, Mom. The boys all might have felt . . . forced."

"Forced to show off their muscles?" Brooke scoffed. "They were all for it. Except my Adam, of course, who's pretty humble."

Monica rolled her eyes, and Emily gave a delicate cough.

"Chris kind of enjoyed it," Heather admitted. "Then again, I received a grant from the preservation fund for my building renovation—thank you again, ladies," she said to the widows. "I hope he didn't feel he had to participate on my account."

"Oh, please, he's Mr. January, 'caught' reading in front of a fire," Emily said about her brother. "How difficult is that?"

"Well, he loves to read," Heather said, both hands raised in a shrug.

"Bare-chested in winter?" Monica's aunt, Gloria Valik, plump and good-natured, elbowed her sister. She was Nate's secretary at the Silver Creek Ranch.

Janet snorted. "We only have their word they're bare-chested. Have any of you seen the photos?"

Monica looked around as the widows projected serenity, and everyone else shook their heads. "What did Dom say, Mom?"

Her brother, Dominic, a food broker who often traveled internationally for his clients, would never be shy about doing a macho calendar. But, then, she wouldn't exactly know his deep feelings—they'd spent a lot of the last decade treating each other like friendly strangers. She sighed.

"Oh, you know Dom," Janet said. "I'm almost embarrassed to say what his response was about the calendar."

"Come on, tell us!" Brooke urged, grinning.

Janet sighed. "I know he enjoyed his photo shoot, because he got February, and women—oh I can't believe I'm saying this—women love chocolate for Valentine's Day."

Brooke roared the loudest with laughter.

"I got it," Emily said ruefully, but she burst out laughing, too, joined by the others.

Monica wiped her damp eyes, surprised that her mom wasn't enjoying the joke as much as the rest.

"They've already completed the photos for the fall, winter, and spring months," Mrs. Thalberg pointed out. "We only need Will Sweet playing baseball—"

"Without his shirt?" Steph asked innocently, then giggled.

Her grandmother, Mrs. Sweet, sniffed as if she smelled rotten eggs even though they were discussing her grandson.

"—and Scott Huang playing pool," Mrs. Thalberg continued as if she hadn't been interrupted.

Monica had to admit that a photo of Scott, an army veteran, using his prosthetic arm to play pool, would be pretty inspiring.

"And, of course, we want that group shot at the hot springs," Mrs. Palmer said. "We'll take care of the calendar, don't you worry." She looked right at Monica. "And anythin' else that needs to be prepared before the president visits."

Monica hoped no one noticed the pointed stare. She still received the widows' monthly e-newsletter about important Valentine Valley causes, but it had been a long time since she'd marched at their sides. With the president coming because of Mrs. Ludlow's own granddaughter, she couldn't believe they'd try anything crazy.

"Monica," Mrs. Thalberg said, "could you give me a hand in the library?"

Oh no. Everyone was chatting about the wedding or Whitney's baby gifts, and Monica was forced to slink away through the French doors into the library, following the widows. She kept hoping someone would notice and call her back, but she wasn't so lucky. The library had once been a man's office, but they'd added lots of bookshelves and comfortable chairs to go with the desk. A bag of knitting was propped beside one chair, and, for a moment, Monica tried to pretend they were only grandmas.

But they weren't that innocent. They now looked at her with focused determination. Before they could speak, the door opened, and Monica's mother slipped in and closed it behind her.

"Mom—" Monica began.

"Count me in," Janet said firmly.

"Count you in on what?" Monica asked, glancing at the widows, hoping they'd go along with her supposed confusion.

And, to a degree, they did. Mrs. Ludlow slowly bent over for her knitting, and Mrs. Thalberg sprang to help her. Mrs. Palmer went to the desk and pulled open a drawer as if looking for something.

"Don't act all innocent," Janet said, her voice full of enthusiasm. "My daughters were often involved in your protests and your sit-ins and did a lot of organizational computer work for you. Do you know how many letters to the editor I helped edit? It's obvious, with the president coming, that you all think this is the perfect way to spotlight your latest cause."

"What cause?" Monica asked with exasperation. "Mom, it's been a long time since I did any actual protesting." And she wasn't quite sure how she'd let her old concern about the environment get put on the back burner. Of course, she'd been focused on growing her business the last few years, but still . . .

"I've seen the posters you've put up around town," Janet said to the widows, "calling on the citizens of Valentine Valley to demand the mammoth dig be allowed to finish at their own pace."

Monica remembered the discussion with Travis. Posters had been harmless enough, but anything more . . .

"But the posters aren't working," Janet continued. "People don't even notice them."

Mrs. Ludlow sat down heavily. "You're right. We've known it for a while now. You wish to help?"

"I think we need to think bigger," Janet urged, her smile a little . . . forced.

Monica gaped at her mom, having no clue what was

going on with her lately. Janet had never been fond of her daughters' activism, worried they'd either get hurt or develop some sort of reputation, but she'd understood and never got in their way. She'd cooked hot dinners for them when they'd lived in the tree house, proofread Monica's grant proposals. When the whole country seemed to know who Monica was, Janet had stood beside her even though Monica could see the disappointment in her eyes.

"Mom, the widows do have another event planned. You know there's a Mammoth Party next week, right? They've put ads in the paper and in all the church bulletins."

"Signs will be going up soon," Mrs. Palmer said absently.

But the widows were all focused on Janet, each sporting a special gleam in her eye.

"Janet's right," Mrs. Thalberg said, her voice cool and firm. "The science party isn't enough."

"But the scientists will be displaying information about the dig," Monica insisted. "Kids will be able to hunt for their own dinosaur bones. People will really have to think about the importance of science."

No one was listening to her. She could feel the fervor of "the cause" rising in the air, a tension and excitement. Why wasn't she as excited? Probably because her own protesting had distorted her relationship with her brother. He'd meant to go into the navy until asthma had stood in his way, and maybe that fueled his patriotism. He considered Missy and Monica *un*patriotic for that last, infamous protest.

"We'll call an official meeting of the protest group," Mrs. Ludlow was saying. "Janet, we're so glad you'd like to join us."

"Wait, wait," Monica said, raising both hands. "You all need to think before this goes further. Yes, the president will be here, but not in an official capacity, but for her son's wedding—your *granddaughter's* wedding, Mrs. L. Do you want Ashley's wedding disrupted? I don't remember your son's being all that thrilled with your activism."

"I would never do anything to embarrass Ashley," Mrs. Ludlow insisted, undaunted. "And we will certainly not disrupt the wedding."

"Or even hold our protest on the wedding day itself," Mrs. Thalberg added. "Don't worry, Monica. We can call attention to an injustice without overdoing it."

Monica blinked at them all in disbelief—they "overdid" things all the time!

"Let's get back to the shower before people start to talk," Mrs. Palmer urged, standing at the French doors and looking through the sheer curtain like a spy. "Look for our e-mail, where we'll throw out dates for a meetin'."

Monica sighed, eyeing her mother, who gave her a "jaunty" grin and walked back into the parlor. Monica followed, and saw Emily and Brooke eyeing her with curiosity. She gave a little shrug and returned to her half-eaten cake, and though it was delicious, she wasn't hungry anymore.

Not hungry—what was wrong with her? She stared out the window toward the gravel road, and beyond it

Silver Creek, winding its way toward the Roaring Fork River. She'd always believed in the rightness of the widows' causes, and this mammoth dig was no different. She was already signed up to help at the Mammoth Party. But planning a protest for a wedding weekend seemed a little extreme—not that she thought the widows would honestly risk disrupting the wedding. But mistakes happened, like when her mom told her that, in the sixties at the height of the Daniel Boone craze, the widows had worn coonskin caps during their protest over opening a hiking wilderness to hunters. They'd blended in so well, they'd been shot at, and it was lucky none of them were hurt.

Or was Monica's uneasiness about Travis Beaumont? If he was a Secret Service agent, he wouldn't be thrilled with something unexpected when the president was in town.

It wasn't until the party was over that Brooke, Emily, and Whitney were able to corral her alone in the parlor while the widows and Heather worked in the kitchen.

"Okay, what was up in the library?" Brooke demanded. "Or was my grandma showing you her knitting?"

Monica dropped a paper plate into a garbage bag. "Mrs. Ludlow said it was *her* knitting, and she was showing me—"

"We don't keep secrets," Emily interrupted her. "Come on, out with it."

That was pretty forceful for Emily, Monica mused. And Emily seemed to realize it because she raised her chin even while she blushed. After a heavy sigh,

Monica told them about the widows and their need to stop the archaeological dig, thinking their best chance to get noticed was while the president was in town.

Brooke blinked at her for a moment. "Well, they have a point."

Monica groaned. "Think about what could happen. Isn't it for the best if we talk them out of this?"

"You're just touchy because of what happened to you," Brooke said gently.

Whitney eased into the nearest chair. "You all need to sit down and explain. What happened to you, Monica?"

Monica pulled up a dining-room chair, even as Brooke and Emily took the couch. Monica saw that Emily was just as eager as Whitney and realized that she'd never talked about this with either of them. She'd thought it was in her past, after all.

"I . . . Missy and I . . . used to participate in a lot of activist protests in college," she began, her voice sounding tired. "I was—am—a firm believer in envi-ronmentalism: Keep old forests, farm organically as much as possible, don't expand natural-gas drilling, that kind of stuff."

Emily gasped. "But your dad's job—"

"I know, I know, but he understood my principles and didn't interfere."

"What about you, Brooke?" Whitney asked.

Brooke winced. "My dad needed me on the ranch."

"You look guilty—stop," Monica ordered. "I made my own choices." She glanced toward the kitchen, then lowered her voice. "The widows often joined in the protests. You know how they are when they believe in something. One time, we were in Denver protesting the government, which was making overtures to sell a huge chunk of wilderness in the Rockies for another resort. And you won't be surprised, but we timed it for the president's being in town for a campaign stop in his reelection. It got pretty heated, and somehow I was in the front, marching and yelling. What I didn't know was that someone was burning the US flag behind me. A photographer captured me all red-faced and screaming—"

"She looked positively *fierce,*" Brooke said proudly.

Monica felt her face heat, thinking, *If you only knew.* "Yeah, well, I wasn't promoting flag-burning, but that's how it looked. Some environmentalists saw the photo and circulated it, as an example for their cause."

"Imagine Josh's viral fame," Brooke said to Whitney, "except with activists."

"Don't forget the people on the other side," Monica pointed out. "A lot of people were appalled by the flag-burning, but I could hardly whine that I honestly didn't know about it. And now the widows are gearing up all over again."

"And you're not sure you want to risk it?" Emily said gently.

Monica frowned. "It's not that. I . . . I don't know why I'm so uneasy. I should trust them to do something appropriate, but . . ." She trailed off.

They all nodded and looked thoughtful, while Monica felt a little bit panicky, as she always did when that photo came up. What would happen if everyone found out it *wasn't* her, that she'd taken the rap for her sister, who was frightened it would damage her future in journalism? Monica had never even told Brooke.

Back in college, it had been so easy to step up and insist the girl in the photo was her, not Missy. Her sister's shock and teary relief had been all the thanks Monica needed. It hadn't been a big deal to her at the time, and though they were only fraternal twins, they looked enough alike that no one had been able to tell the difference in the slightly grainy shot. When the fame of that photo spread across the country, when Dom was furious with Monica, Missy had been horrified, insisting that the truth come out. Monica had refused to back down and was still glad for the decision she'd made.

"Speaking of inappropriate," Brooke said at last, breaking their thoughtful spell, "Tony told Nate who told me that our Monica here had a good time with a group of strangers at his tavern last night—and didn't invite us."

"Hey, isn't this baby shower about Whitney?" Monica protested. She wasn't about to tell them her suspicions about Travis being a Secret Service agent. He could be a well-dressed criminal.

"If it's all about me, then tell us what happened, Monica," Whitney said eagerly.

"Nothing much, I swear. Yeah, Travis was there, and about all I got out of him was that he's working, can't talk about it, and is an ex-Marine."

"Really?" Brooke asked. "I'll have to tell Adam."

"That's it?" Emily sounded disappointed.

"You haven't even been married a year," Monica

said. "Don't tell me you already need to hear the exciting stories of a single woman's life. I should write a blog: 'The Last Single Girl in Valentine.' But honestly, I danced, I played darts, I had a good time."

"Nothing else?" Brooke asked. "Tony says Travis walked you outside."

They all leaned toward her, and Monica smiled as if some drunk hadn't accosted her. No point scaring everybody. "Nothing happened, which was just fine with me. I admit I'm curious about Travis, but that's all."

They shared groans and disappointed smiles.

"Oh, please. Back to the kitchen, let's go help."

She was relieved when they grumbled but complied. She was starting to feel surrounded, the past coming back to haunt her, and her fascination with a possible Secret Service agent confusing.

But there was only one way to deal with Travis Beaumont.

Chapter Four

The next morning, Friday, Monica drank her coffee, browsed her e-mail—and saw one from the widows, inviting the "protest group" to the boardinghouse Saturday evening to discuss the Mammoth Party and other "important events." All the emphatic quotes made her smile, even as she shook her head. She saw her mom's e-mail address included as well, and frowned, but she did send an offer to pick her mom up.

She usually took an early-morning run since the flower shop didn't open until ten. But after a restless night thinking about the president's approaching arrival, she had to know the truth. Was Travis really involved? She locked her shop door, hesitated, then spontaneously decided to skip her run. Wearing shorts, a t-shirt, and loose jacket, she marched across Main Street toward the Hotel Colorado.

To her surprise, the door opened before she even got there, and Travis came down the stone stairs. He was wearing another pair of casual pants, shirt, and jacket. Did that jacket hide a gun? Those black sunglasses certainly hid his eyes, but he saw her because he paused a moment, then came directly toward her. Once again, it was as if she couldn't quite take a deep enough breath.

Monica strode between the parked cars and stopped in front of him, hands on her hips.

"Good morning." He quirked an eyebrow and waited. "You okay?"

She knew what he referred to but just gave him a smile. "I'm fine, thanks." She looked both ways for eavesdroppers, then said quietly, "I hear the president will soon be making an appearance. Maybe you know something about that."

He didn't even pause, just took her arm and began steering her back across the street. "Is your store unlocked?"

"Of course not. I was going for a run."

"Unlock it."

Amused at his bossy tone, she unzipped her jacket pocket and produced a key. Once they were inside, he turned and locked the door himself.

Was this a good idea? She didn't really know him, after all, and she'd just confronted him about his supposedly "secret" job. But . . . she'd never felt afraid of him and wasn't going to start now. And he'd put himself in danger to protect her.

He walked past her and swung the door open to the workroom. "No one else is here?"

"As you can see, no."

He came back to her, removed his sunglasses, and spoke seriously while piercing her with those blue eyes. "What I'm about to tell you can go no further, at least not for a while. Yes, I'm a special agent with the Secret Service." Pulling out a wallet, he flashed an ID and a badge.

Aha! She'd been right. She took it before he could put it away and made a point of studying it—although it was mostly just to get a reaction out of him. "Looks real."

"It's real," he said shortly. "I'm the lead agent preparing for the president's visit for her son's wedding."

"I heard all about the wedding from the bride's grandma," Monica admitted, smiling at his discomfiture. "Don't worry, she didn't give dates or anything, and we all understood this was under wraps for a while."

"The wedding is two weeks from tomorrow."

"What?" The shock next gave way to panic. "You can't be serious. They've asked me to do the flowers for the wedding, but we haven't even had a meeting. There's so much involved! I have to present ideas—*presidential* ideas. And design kick-ass window displays."

"Just listen. Yes, I've been surveying the neighborhood because I need an observation post to monitor the front entrance of the hotel when the president is in town, especially when she gets in and out of her limousine. I'd like your permission to use your store, with its perfect sight lines."

"So you use flirtation to soften women up for an observation post?" she cracked.

He frowned.

"Never mind, you didn't flirt. I was teasing. You would have asked to use my shop even if I'd been an eighty-year-old grandma."

"Do we have your permission?"

"Of course you do. I'm honored to help. What's involved?"

"My agents won't bother you until the day of the president's arrival. We'll set up cameras, binoculars, rifles—"

"Rifles?"

"We'll have snipers along Main Street while the president is staying in the hotel. Most will be on rooftops."

"Oh, of course," she said, suddenly realizing what a big production this wedding would be—and not just for her. The entire town would be affected. Perhaps it would even be detrimental to business—for all she knew, they'd shut down streets to pedestrians. But there was no point worrying about what she couldn't control.

"I appreciate your cooperation," he said politely.

"So . . . is it true you guys would take a bullet for the president?"

He blinked at her. "We don't exactly sign an oath saying that."

"I remember seeing clips of when President Reagan was shot—an agent stepped right in front of him and almost died."

"A brave man," Travis admitted. "A legend."

Without a doubt, she knew he'd do the same.

There was another awkward pause, and she couldn't

resist her most pressing question. "You could have chosen any store on either side of this one. Why did you choose me—my store?"

Saying nothing, he looked her in the eyes, and suddenly it was as if national security, her flower shop, none of it existed. They were just two people alone in a room, and his eyes, so mysterious to her, for just a moment seemed to . . . smolder.

Her breath caught and faded away, and she felt an urge to lean toward him, to press against him.

They both took a step back.

"You are the most obvious choice, Monica, being across the street. And we do background checks, as well—"

She froze, imagining what that might have turned up of her past. Not that she'd been convicted of anything.

"—and you passed that. We'll be doing background checks of every store owner on the street, and every employee who might come in contact with the president."

"Wow," she said a bit breathlessly, still recovering from that moment of lust. "It's a big production."

"It is," he said solemnly. "We prepare for the worst and hope for the best."

She heard a faint buzzing; he pulled his phone out of his pocket, glanced at it, and put it away. Should she feel flattered he hadn't taken the call?

"And we take our duties very seriously," he continued. "If you ever hear of anything, or know anyone, who could disrupt this wedding weekend, let me know."

Disrupt? she thought, feeling a twinge of queasiness

at the thought of the widows and the archaeological dig. Somehow, Monica had to convince them that Ashley's wedding weekend wasn't the appropriate time for one of their extravaganzas.

"I—I will," she said. She cleared her throat and forced a smile. "The bride and I are old friends. But, of course, you probably think everyone in a small town knows each other."

"I know better—small town in Montana, remember?"

"Oh, right, forgot. So anyway, you say this is supposed to be a secret as long as possible—how am I supposed to explain you and your men, and woman, if you're seen coming out of here? People have already begun to talk."

"Let them think what they want," he said, slipping his sunglasses back on his face and turning toward the door.

For just a moment, she thought he winked at her—but no, she had to be mistaken.

"At least your job should be pretty easy here in Valentine," she said, following him across the showroom.

He glanced back. "We never underestimate the enemy. I'll be in touch."

She shivered even as he went out the door. She didn't want to be his enemy. And she thought maybe he needed a friend.

The next morning, Saturday, Travis headed out for an early run. He wasn't alone in that—his fellow agents all had to stay in the best shape to perform their duties, but he usually liked to run alone. In D.C., it was difficult enough to feel peaceful when there were people everywhere exercising on the Mall at the same time, but here in Valentine Valley, other runners were few and far between and respectful of his privacy. Only a few shops were open, catering to the breakfast crowd. Other than the occasional car, he heard little but the sounds of birds singing and the peal of church bells at the top of the hour. The mountains rose above him, silent and majestic, the higher peaks still frosted in white above the tree line. The air smelled of the outdoors, trees and flowers, and was a little thin with the altitude. He didn't push himself, knowing he didn't need a case of altitude sickness.

Heading down Main Street toward the mountains, he scanned the streets, unable to ignore his training even off duty—and then he caught a glimpse of Monica a half block ahead. He only saw her from the back, but he couldn't help recognizing her. She was wearing tight black shorts that hugged her ass, a tight hoodie, and her dark curls bounced at the back of her head where she'd held them off her forehead with some kind of band. She had the long, muscular legs of a runner.

He flashed back to that moment in her shop, when she asked why he'd chosen her for the OP, and something in him had just wiped out every thought unless they were hot and lusty. He could have put her right up on her counter, stepped between her thighs, and—

He had to stop these thoughts, or running was going to be uncomfortable. But he couldn't help admiring

Monica's form. He'd examined her background report a little more closely than necessary and seen that she ran in college. This little obsession he had with her wasn't wise—hell, choosing her store wasn't wise, not with the way he was attracted to her. It was tempting fate, especially when he was close to being recommended for the next job up, the Presidential Protective Detail. He tried to focus on that, to tell himself *he* wasn't going to be manning the OP, after all . . .

And then Monica took the corner across from town hall and happened to glance to the side, as if she meant to cross the street. Their gazes met, and she slowed to jog in place, waiting for him to catch up.

"Good morning," she called.

Her smile tugged at him, so bright and teasing and intrigued. She was too curious for her own good. "Good morning," he said, trying to sound stern. Instead, he sounded like an old stuffed shirt.

She laughed. "Grumpy in the morning, are we?"

He shrugged.

"I know your big event"—she air-quoted the last two words—"is at the Sweetheart Inn. You heading up that way? I could show you the grounds."

He opened his mouth to politely refuse, but actually, that was a smart idea. There was already a site agent in charge of the hotel, but it wouldn't hurt for him to get a look himself. "Sounds good."

If possible, her smile brightened even more. It was so strange for someone so stunning not to have a cooler, wary persona, but she truly was a cheerful small-town girl with a model's face . . . and body.

Side by side, they ran the couple blocks north toward the Sweetheart Inn, the old-fashioned mansion nestled on the lower slopes of the Elk Mountains. Baskets of impatiens hung between the columns of the wrap-around porch, and yellow forsythia bushes dotted the grounds.

"Am I holding you back?" Monica asked, only a little breathless.

"Not at all. You're pretty fast. But, then, I know you ran in college."

She made a wry face. "We're not going to ever be able to have a discussion because you already know too much about me. I feel a little . . . invaded."

"Don't. It's just an outline, where you went to school, the jobs you've held, any problems with the law you might have had."

"And my track scholarship."

"That was part of school. You're a lot more than your background."

"Is that a compliment, Special Agent?"

"Just a fact," he said, turning up into the parking lot that led behind the inn. "Let's circle the property."

"There are a lot of hiking trails up behind, too. I imagine you have to keep watch over it all."

He nodded, taking in the stone terrace behind the banquet wing that had been added to the original mansion. A pool and hot tub had their own landscaped grounds, and, in the distance, he could see a gazebo, and even a bridge over flowing water.

"Show me the hiking trails," he said.

She led him past an arrow sign that said HOT SPRINGS,

and they followed the trail as it wound its way along the bank of the stream. The slope steepened, but she still kept up with him easily. He was impressed.

The hot springs were something you'd expect in low-key Colorado, a rock-edged pool, surrounded by trees, which gradually emptied into the cooler water. Steam softly rose from the surface, a rustic bench rested nearby. There were no other guests. Monica slowed to a stop.

"We're going to have an interesting event here in the next few days," she said, shaking her head. "A group photo shoot for the 'Men of Valentine Valley' calendar."

He frowned, but before he could ask a question, she laughed, and he enjoyed the sound far too much.

She raised a hand. "I know, I know, it's ridiculous, but it's to benefit the Valentine Valley Preservation Fund, and they do good work. The calendar has eleven participants, so they decided to do a final group shot here, bare chests and all. You know," she added thoughtfully, "there are some pretty good chests in the bunch. Anyway, the arrival of the president spurred them to finish it up, so it could be available all around town in time for the wedding weekend. I'm sure I can get you a copy if you'd like." Those chocolate eyes sparkled as she teased him.

"That won't be necessary," he said mildly.

"Will a manly calendar 'disrupt' your wedding weekend?"

He heard the emphasis she put on "disrupt," and knew she was echoing his words back to him. "No, it won't, but I appreciate your warning me."

He glanced around the hot springs, and when he looked back at her, she was studying him.

"If you ever need a hand getting a feel for Valentine, you can let me know. Spent my whole life here, but for college. We have a little bit of nightlife here, too. I'd hate for you to hang out just with your coworkers twenty-four hours a day. As you said, you can't really let loose with them."

"Thanks for thinking of me," he answered.

Her smile faded, and they had one of those strange moments where he felt almost . . . attached to her by some sort of invisible rope that kept drawing tighter, pulling them together. She gave him a slow, gorgeous smile that made him flush with warmth. God, she was sexy.

"Gotta go," she suddenly said. "See you later."

And then she turned and ran back down the trail, treating him once again to a view of her ass cupped in those tight shorts.

Why hadn't he discouraged her? He didn't have time for a flirtation with a beautiful woman.

But she made him want to, and that wasn't good.

Chapter Five

After a busy, satisfying day at work, Monica dropped in at her parents' place a good hour earlier than the widows' protest meeting was supposed to start. The Shaws lived a few streets off Main, where the houses were built in the twentieth century rather than the nineteenth, a regular four-bedroom colonial that you could find anywhere in the US. But inside, Janet had decorated with mountain décor, twisted twigs in a tall vase in the corner, a fireplace made of stone, antique skis hanging on a wall next to a landscape of snow-covered mountains. In the family room, she'd grouped framed ski posters from the forties and fifties. It all felt like home when Monica dropped in until she caught her mom eating dinner in front of the TV, a *huge* no-no when she was growing up.

Janet visibly brightened when she turned and saw Monica dump her purse on a chair. She jumped up, setting her plate on an end table to hug her daughter.

"You're early!" Janet exclaimed, appearing perfectly happy about it.

"When I saw you at the shower, I realized I hadn't been home in a while, and if I was going to take you to the meeting, we might as well chat first. Dad here?"

"In his office."

Monica blinked. They hadn't eaten dinner together?

"I'll call him up. Have you eaten?"

"Nope. Any extra?"

"Of course! Let's head into the kitchen."

The kitchen was only separated from the dining room by a column, after her mom had had a wall torn down for a more "open" look. The cabinets were pine, the window curtains white, and everything seemed so cheery.

Except her mom, although she was doing her best to fake it.

As Monica washed her hands, Janet opened the basement door, and called, "Ben, Monica's here!"

"I'll be up in a minute!"

With tongs, Janet spread a plate with spaghetti. Though she used sauce from a jar, her meatballs were homemade and incredible. Back in high school, Monica and her teammates used to debate whose team meals were number one, and each was convinced their own mom made the best meatballs. Monica knew the other girls were all wrong.

"I probably shouldn't be eating all this pasta," Janet said ruefully as she placed Monica's plate next to her own on the kitchen table. "I seem to be putting on a few pounds."

Janet had always been a little chubbier than her

daughters but not seriously overweight—and she wasn't now.

Monica frowned at her. "Mom, you look fine. Why would you think that?"

"Well, if I don't diet occasionally, the weight keeps creeping up."

"You're still taking that yoga class, right?"

Janet nodded, but she seemed distracted as she poured a big glass of milk and set it down on the table, along with silverware.

When her dad came through the door, Monica hugged him but looked him over curiously, considering her mom's unusual behavior of late. He was a tall, lean man, with the broad shoulders Dom had inherited but a little belly above his belt. He wore a closely trimmed beard and mustache threaded with gray though he wasn't one of those guys making up for a balding head.

He always had a big smile for her. "Good to see you, baby girl."

She smiled at the childhood endearment. "Thanks, Dad." She looked down at the empty plate he set on the counter. "You're not eating with us?"

"Already did, sorry."

She thought he avoided her mom's gaze. What the heck?

"Sit down with us anyway," she urged.

As Ben slid out a chair, Monica dug in to her spaghetti. The two women ate silently for a few minutes, Janet taking smaller bites and chewing a long time.

"Very exciting about Ashley Ludlow marrying the president's son," Janet said.

"What?" Ben said, looking between them in surprise.

"Oh, we're not supposed to tell anyone," Janet explained. "I must not have showed you the wedding invitation that just came in the mail. You don't care all that much about weddings, anyway."

"Maybe not," Monica said, "but since this one will be taking place in Valentine Valley, and the *president* will be attending, this might be one wedding to capture your interest."

"Wow," Ben said mildly.

"But you really can't tell anyone," Monica amended in a serious voice. "They're trying not to make this a circus."

"Fine by me."

"But Ashley wants me to do the flowers for the wedding!" Monica said excitedly, and they talked for a while about her plans and how the business had been going lately. Thank goodness, nobody asked about the stranger lurking around her shop.

At last, her dad excused himself to go work on his vintage Mustang in the garage since she and her mom would be leaving for their meeting soon. He didn't ask what the meeting was about. Monica watched Janet's eyes follow him out, and there was no disguising her troubled expression.

"What going on with you and Dad?" Monica asked.

Janet gave her a phony smile. "Nothing at all, so don't you worry about it. Every marriage has the occasional patch where you don't get each other. We'll be fine."

This seemed more serious than that, and Monica felt a little lump in her stomach although she told herself she'd just eaten too fast. "Is whatever"—she waved her hand toward the garage door—"the reason you're suddenly so interested in the widows' latest cause? You disapproved of it when Missy and I were younger."

"I never disapproved of the *causes*," Janet said, pointing at her with a meatball on a fork. "I disapproved of the way the protests were handled, and I disapproved of your youth and how things could backfire and ruin college for you. And after that photo came out, and strangers were calling you or showing up at the door or using that photo for their own purposes—well, it only made me more nervous."

Monica sighed. "That was one bad side effect. It didn't negate the good work we did bringing environmental issues into the public eye."

"I see that. And now that you're all grown-up, I'd like to be a part of it."

"I notice you didn't remind Dad of where you're going—does he know?"

"It's none of his business."

Monica straightened abruptly, no longer hungry. "None of Dad's business? Are you embarrassed?"

"Not a bit! But I want this to be for me. He has his friends in the vintage-car-racing world; I need to develop my own interests. Don't think you're the only one who was inspired by Grandpa Shaw's stories of the marches. I don't remember a lot from those days, but I do remember the occasional suspicious looks when I shopped in certain stores. And, sadly, that *still* happens."

And what was Monica supposed to say to that? "I suggest you don't tell Dom unless you have to," she finally said, taking her plate to the sink and rinsing it off. "He still hasn't forgiven me for that photo."

"Nonsense." Janet opened the dishwasher.

"Oh, we get along, but . . ." She let her words trail off. Dom's reaction had almost made Missy come clean about the whole deception. Monica hadn't allowed it.

"I hope you're not trying to change my mind," Janet said softly.

"I'm not, I promise. I've just been curious about the motivation."

"Understandable." Janet took the rinsed plates Monica handed her and loaded them in the dishwasher. "So let me be curious. I talk to a lot of people at Doc Ericson's all day, right?"

"You're the 'face' of the medical community," Monica agreed brightly. As the receptionist to the town's only doctor, her mom ended up speaking to absolutely everyone in Valentine Valley.

Janet chuckled. "And they like to talk to me, especially about my own children. Someone saw you running this morning with a handsome out-of-towner."

"Of course they did." Monica rinsed the silverware and handed it over. "He's just a guest at the hotel, Mom. We were running at the same time."

"And hanging out at Tony's, too? And in your flower shop?"

"Mom! Honestly, he's just an interesting guy, and

he's flirting." She hesitated, but this was her mom. "All right, there is more, but it can't go any further, right?"

Janet leaned against the counter eagerly. "I may be the face of the medical community, but I don't spill secrets to them, especially not *your* secrets, baby girl."

Monica grinned. "Okay, then. Travis isn't just an interesting guy. He's with the Secret Service, setting up the trip for President Torres. He wants to use my shop for an observation post."

Janet's expression fell. "That's all?"

Monica started to laugh.

"I thought it would be about you and a nice guy," Janet explained lamely.

"Most people would think a presidential trip is a big deal, but not a mother wanting her daughter to settle down."

"I never said you had to settle down—I just want you to be happy."

Monica reached across the dishwasher and gave her mom a quick hug. "Thanks. You've raised me to make *myself* very happy. I don't need a man for that."

Janet groaned. "So I did too good of a job, making you independent and self-fulfilled."

"Guess you did. Are we done here? They'll start without us, and I have a few words to say to the widows."

Janet gave her a speculative look but didn't ask questions.

The sun was already behind the Elk Mountains when Monica drove down the gravel road and followed the drive to the back of the Widows' Boardinghouse. The porch lights were on, and she marched up the steps with determination, organizing all the things she wanted to say to dissuade them. She prayed they didn't have in mind an actual protest at the Renaissance Spa, like chaining themselves to the front door or camping out among the fossils to protect them.

Everyone else had already arrived and welcomed Monica and Janet. Besides the widows, Emily's cousins, siblings Theresa and Matt Sweet were there. Matt, a little younger, had never protested with them, but Theresa had dragged him along. They both had variations of light brown hair, Theresa's a chin-length bob, Matt's sun-streaked because he was in charge of the landscaping at the Sweetheart Inn and spent a lot of his days outside. He'd even taken a part-time job with Josh Thalberg, stitching together his leathercraft creations. Theresa had been as avid a protester as Monica a few years back, but lately she was being groomed by her grandma to eventually help run the Sweetheart Inn. Sometimes, Theresa complained that that only meant too much hostessing at the hotel's five-star restaurant.

Brenda Hutcheson was the last member of their group, a rancher's wife with short, curly gray hair, hands that had seen a lot of hard work, and a brisk manner that made her clip her sentences short.

Soon the eight of them were settled around the dining-room table, each with their own matching pad of paper provided by the widows. Mrs. Thalberg took the lead, glancing at a typed set of notes, then thanking them all for coming. She briefly went over the mammoth dig again, and their original plan for a party to present the archaeology to the public, make it fun for kids, and in general, get the population enthused.

"That's the problem—people *aren't* too enthused anymore," Mrs. Palmer said with a sigh. "After the dig at Snowmass, people feel they've given enough money to support fossils. And one little mammoth seems trivial compared to the thousands of bones found down there. We've been to town-council meetin's, we've met with the museum, and with the spa—although they say they're done talkin'."

It was almost hard to concentrate on her serious words when Mrs. Palmer had a fake dog bone stuck in her blond wig, like Pebbles from the old *Flintstones* cartoon. Monica loved that about her. She wanted to *be* her when she was an old lady.

"Then perhaps we should just stop at the party," Monica suggested.

Everyone turned frowns on her.

"All right, let me say my piece, then you can shoot me down. Yes, this is a presidential wedding, and perhaps making President Torres aware of the dig might do . . . something."

"It's more about making the media aware of the dig," Mrs. Ludlow said patiently.

Monica turned a serious gaze on her. "But it's your granddaughter's wedding weekend. Do you want to mar her memories?"

She almost expected Mrs. Ludlow to stiffen, offended, but she just gave Monica a kind smile.

"I would never permit that to happen, my dear."

"Of course you wouldn't intend to, but—"

"And we would have our demonstration on Friday, before the rehearsal dinner or anything else related to the wedding."

"But won't the Mammoth Party bring just as much attention to our cause?" Monica continued.

"No, it won't," Brenda Hutcheson said firmly. "The posters have been up for a week. When I ask, no one has even read them. We'll get parents and kids. That's it. We need more attention than that."

All around the table, heads bobbed in agreement.

Monica had to make one last attempt. "You don't think people holding signs will be ignored? Especially when everyone's trying to get a look at the president herself?"

"That's why we can't have our *usual* demonstration," Mrs. Palmer said with satisfaction, as if Monica had made her point for her.

With a sigh, Monica sat back and admitted defeat. Her last desperate strategy would be to curb their more insane impulses.

"What's the 'usual'?" Matt, new to the group, asked.

Monica ticked off each point on her fingers. "Picketing, camping out in the way of . . . whatever, organizing an e-mail barrage, chaining themselves to buildings—"

Janet interrupted. "And let's not forget national exposure in what some might term 'offensive' photos." She patted her daughter's hand.

Theresa and Matt exchanged an amused glance.

Monica rolled her eyes. "I'm not saying I've haven't

been side by side with you all. But if you're going to do this, I want you to be reasonable about it."

"The wedding weekend will probably be our last chance," Mrs. Thalberg said earnestly. "The spa is even discussing moving up the construction date."

Solemn looks were exchanged.

"It's hard to be both original and tame," Monica pointed out. "But . . . I have an idea."

They listened politely, and before Monica knew it, the widows had gone beyond her original idea with an over-the-top one of their own. Much laughter and discussion filled the next hour as they began to work, even as Monica promised herself she would steer the group away from anything that might bother the Secret Service.

"Now that we have a plan," Mrs. Palmer said, clapping her hands together, "we need a name for our group, so we can talk among ourselves and people won't know what we're talkin' about. I have an idea already."

Monica saw Mrs. Thalberg and Mrs. Ludlow exchange glances with an air of resignation.

Mrs. Palmer beamed. "Well, we're all defendin' the mammoth dig, so I thought about calling us the Defenders, short and sweet. But if people overheard, they'd be curious—"

"You mean if your grandson overheard," Janet said, smiling.

Mrs. Palmer waved a hand. "Adam can be too curious. So what are we doin'? We're defendin' science and the important memory of a mammoth—we're defendin' an archaeological dig. How about Dig Defenders, the Double Ds for short?"

"Uh . . . the Double Ds?" Monica said. "You do know what that can be interpreted as?"

"Bra sizes!" Mrs. Palmer said, nodding vigorously. "And who wants to talk to an elderly woman about that?"

Monica's snort turned into a laugh, and she was joined by the others. "Fine, the Double Ds it is."

"Now that that's settled," Mrs. Ludlow said, giving them all a tolerant stare over her glasses, "let's put the finishing touches on the Mammoth Party. It will be good to remind people why history is so important and to have children excited, too."

Mrs. Ludlow was a retired teacher, so she always thought about the children.

"I've typed out a list of everything that still has to be done," she continued.

"And if people think this is our last protest?" Mrs. Thalberg said, rubbing her hands together. "So much the better." She smiled at Monica. "Thank you for the wonderful idea."

Janet even patted her back with pride, and they all began to discuss the party. But all Monica could think about was Travis. Though he'd asked for any information on wedding weekend "disruptions," she couldn't betray her friends—or her principles—by telling him about this. So now she wasn't only lying to her friends and family *about* him, she was lying *to* him.

What a mess.

Chapter Six

The next morning, Travis walked out of the firehouse with Sheriff Buchanan, his liaison with the local police. They were on Grace Street, a block off Main, and the firehouse was built of brick, as if it had seen at least a hundred years of Valentine Valley history. The sheriff, a grizzled man in his sixties, had a white crew cut and the stiff bearing of a former military man. Travis felt right at home with him, especially when they each looked discreetly at their phones before putting them away again.

"Thanks for introducing me to the fire chief, Sheriff," Travis said, glancing up at the overcast sky to see if it looked like it was going to rain. "I think it'll make a great safe house should we have an emergency while the president is on the route through town."

"Both Bud and I are proud to be of help, Agent Beaumont," the sheriff said.

Standing on the street, they casually discussed routes to the medical clinic and the hospital in Aspen, making plans to go over maps together. The sheriff had

already agreed to make detailed notes on any vulner-
abilities along the planned motorcade routes.

"Any known dissent groups in the area?" Travis
asked.

"None that would harm the president," Sheriff Buchanan said, then took another sip of the coffee in his
styrofoam cup. "Around here, the majority of the activism is about wilderness conservation, and even then it's
been a while."

"I saw posters protesting the closing of an archaeological dig." He wondered if Buchanan would enlighten
him more than Monica had. She'd seemed a little protective when telling him about it.

The sheriff shook his head. "Yes, sir, there's a group
of people wishing that owners of private land could be
forced to change their construction plans. Ain't gonna
happen. I mean yes, dinosaurs are big about now, what
with the huge find at Snowmass Village. Hell, I even
bought some Dino Dirt up at the farmer's market in
Glenwood Springs."

"Dino Dirt?" Travis echoed curiously.

"The scientists removed a lot of dirt as they uncovered the fossils. Someone got the great idea to sell it,
and I tell you, it did wonders for my vegetable garden."
He cleared his throat. "There's a certain element behind
most of our local demonstrations, but I don't think
you have to worry about them. They're the widows of
the Widows' Boardinghouse, but one of them is the
grandma of your bride."

"The Widows' Boardinghouse? Sounds like the
nineteenth century."

"That's why they like it. They live in a renovated house on the Silver Creek Ranch. They're the major force on the committee for the Valentine Valley Preservation Fund—supporting historical houses and promoting small businesses and such. They're pretty proud of this town and determined to protect it. They've done some demonstrating in the past, and now they've taken the spa dig as their new project. Kind of surprised about it, myself—they're getting up there in age. But these women are passionate—they once chained themselves to a brothel because it was part of women's history in Valentine. Kept them from tearing it down, they did."

"They *sound* passionate. I'd like to meet them."

"You can sign up for a tarot reading," the sheriff said dryly. "They do that, too."

Travis hid a smile. "No, thanks. Mind if we take a ride together? I'd like to get a feel for what's outside the town, the ranches, maybe even the spa that's getting so much attention."

Monica was relieved when Ashley Ludlow came to town on Sunday afternoon, settled into her mom's house, and wasted no time in getting down to business. Monica, Emily, and Heather got a text from her, apologizing for the last-minute notice, and asking if they could meet that evening at the Sweetheart Inn. Like any of the three women minded.

Because the rain clouds had at last departed, the women walked the few blocks to the inn, where globe lights lit the grounds as dusk descended. Spotlights highlighted the three floors of Queen Anne turrets and porches adorned with sunburst trim. The lobby was the original front parlor, still decorated with stained-glass lamps resting on mahogany furniture, and a wide staircase led up to the next floor. The front desk must have been the bar in an old saloon because it was massive and intricately carved. The only modern thing was a huge family portrait showing the living generations of Sweets. The next photo they took, Emily would be a part of it, Monica thought, smiling with contentment, Eileen Sweet's long-lost and newly found granddaughter.

Ashley Ludlow rose from the sofa in front of the fireplace and rushed to hug Monica.

"Congratulations on your engagement," Monica said, giving her a squeeze.

"Thanks!"

They separated and looked at each other for a moment, still holding each other's upper arms. Her hair was blonder than Monica remembered, cut in a short, shaggy style that looked casual but probably took more time to style than it seemed. She still had a curvy figure that made you think old-fashioned movie star and cute glasses that managed to remind you that she was a serious lawyer.

Mrs. Ludlow rose slowly with the aid of her daughter-in-law, Donna Ludlow. They watched the reunion with fondness, even as Donna still looked a little dazed and wide-eyed. Who could blame her, having to plan a wedding in less than two weeks' time? Still young-looking, with wavy brown hair and a slim figure, she wore a suit, as if she was ready to impress the president from the beginning.

"Practicing law in D.C. seems to suit you," Monica told Ashley.

"And so does being in love—don't forget that. Jeremy is an incredible man—I can't believe I'm lucky enough to be marrying him!"

Monica introduced Emily and Heather. Heather glanced through the open French doors into the restaurant, with its ambiance of candles and fine linen.

"I'm not sure why I'm here, Ashley," Heather said with regret. "The inn has a delicious menu."

Mrs. Ludlow walked around the couch, leaning on her walker. "I'd like you to cater the bridal shower, Heather. Emily tells me wonderful things about your cooking."

Heather blushed as only a redhead could. "Thank you, ma'am, and I'd be happy to help."

Ashley led the way into a conference room off the main lobby. It had obviously once been a spacious dining room, complete with wooden columns, an intricately carved fireplace, and a long, stained-glass window running along the top of the other windows. Theresa Sweet was waiting for them, pouring coffee and straightening bottles of water and soda. There was a big spread of cookies, along with a tray of cheese, vegetables, and fruit. The elder Mrs. Sweet was already seated, stirring a cup of coffee. Monica wasn't surprised that the owner took a personal interest in such an important wedding.

Theresa smiled at them. "Ladies, please help yourselves to some refreshments first."

As they began to fill their plates, Monica asked Ashley, "So, will you have Secret Service protection, too?"

Ashley made a face. "When we're married, yes. Children of sitting presidents have to. I guess they can be pretty good at fading into the background, but still . . . it'll be difficult not to just hop in my car without running my plans by someone else at first."

Monica wondered if Travis had done such protective duties already, and she had a hard time imagining anyone thinking he "faded into the background." She'd caught the occasional glimpse of him leaving or entering the hotel since she'd last seen him yesterday morning, but that was it.

Mrs. Ludlow sat down next to Mrs. Sweet while her daughter-in-law brought her a coffee cup and a plate of goodies. As much as the widows as a group did not always get along with Mrs. Sweet, Mrs. Ludlow was a bridge of sorts, and now the two women talked softly together.

Everyone soon took a seat but Ashley, who perched one knee on her chair as if she were too nervous to sit down. "I knew months ago that we were going to get married in Valentine. Mrs. Sweet let me know when one of the reservations for a banquet room canceled, so I could have it. I still can't believe the president was able to alter her schedule for us. It's been really strange not to have more time to deal with all this."

Nodding, her mom, Donna, took too deep a gulp of her hot coffee and coughed into her napkin.

"Poor Mom," Ashley said, wincing. "I wanted to

elope, or get married in a very small ceremony in D.C., I really did, but frankly, I couldn't hurt both sets of parents. You can't believe how excited the president is for her son's wedding."

"He's her only child," Theresa reminded them.

"Yes," Ashley answered, "and she just wants to be like a normal mother of the groom. Well, normal might be relative," she added ruefully.

"How did you two meet?" Emily asked.

Ashley's smile softened. "Typical singles in a bar. I didn't know who he was—most people didn't. He's not been in the public eye all that much since he doesn't live in the White House. Dating has been an interesting adventure, but when I'm with the Torreses for a family dinner, they're really just like everyone else." She turned to Monica. "I have to tell you, I've been keeping up with everything online, reading the *Valentine Gazette*. I was so excited to see how well you'd launched Josh's craftsmanship. Your flower shop really must be doing well!"

"Thanks, I'm pretty happy with how it's going," Monica admitted.

"My future father-in-law is a big fan of Josh's, and he really wants to see your display of his work. Would you mind if he stops at your place when he gets into town next week?"

"Of course not. Maybe I can even arrange for Josh to be there if you give me advance notice."

"I'll do that!"

After promising not to be a bridezilla, Ashley got down to business, looking through Emily's binder and

Monica's PowerPoint presentation. Emily stuck out her tongue about the computer demonstration, making Monica laugh. Plans were made, the Sweet ladies consulted. Heather and Mrs. Ludlow kept their heads together discussing the bridal shower.

As the meeting broke up, Monica felt energized and challenged and thrilled about the work. She'd be putting fresh flowers in the president's suite at the hotel and at St. John's Church, as well as the banquet room at the Sweetheart Inn. Her mind was already buzzing about how to keep the whole schedule straight, but she didn't panic. She'd always had a cool head under pressure.

Out in the lobby, Theresa pulled her aside while the others began their good-byes.

"Did you hear anything from the wi—the Double Ds?" she asked in a quiet voice.

Mrs. Sweet watched her granddaughter with faint suspicion, and Theresa made it worse by looking guilty.

"Nothing," Monica answered. "But it's only been a day."

Theresa nodded and seemed to dart away as if she were hiding a crime.

Once Monica, Emily, and Heather were outside, Emily shot Monica a suspicious look.

"So what's going on?" she asked. "You and Theresa looked too cozy."

"And Mrs. Sweet noticed," Heather added. "She scares me a little."

Monica sighed. "Theresa used to go to protests with me in college and helped me do the research for the grants I used to write—heck, so did Ashley, but she gave it up a long time ago. Anyway, as I predicted, the widows haven't given up their idea of protesting the closing of the spa dig, especially now that the president is coming. They've settled on the morning of the wedding rehearsal. They want national attention for their cause, and I couldn't talk them out of it."

"Well, if anyone can keep a lid on things, it's you," Emily said at last.

Monica felt a twinge of unease. She hoped she proved worthy of the trust.

Late afternoon on Monday at the flower shop, Monica heard the door jingle and looked up from her computer behind the front counter. Travis Beaumont was already removing his sunglasses as he walked toward her. It had only been two days, and she was surprised at the feeling of anticipation that welled up inside her at just the sight of him. She found herself smiling, and to her surprise, the corners of his lips turned up a bit, his first almost smile.

"Hi, Travis," she said pleasantly.

"Monica," he said with a nod, "I need to meet the pastry chef next door since she'll be supplying food at several of the wedding events. I thought you could introduce me, so I could get a feel for her."

Business. Monica wasn't surprised since he seemed like a focused kind of guy. She wondered if there was a way to get him to realize there were more hours in the day, a way for him to relax.

"We should get one thing straight," she said. "Do you still need your secret identity? I've already met with Ashley about the wedding."

"Secret identity—you make me sound like a comic-book character."

"Didn't you always want to be a superhero when you were young? My favorite was Spider-Man."

"No, I just wanted to be a soldier. I was focused, even then."

"Were you any fun to be around, Beaumont?"

He looked like he was giving that serious consideration. "I guess it depends on whom you ask."

She rolled her eyes. "A vague answer."

"But in answer to your main question, I'd rather wait until the news of the president hits the paper. Anonymity makes it easier to do my job. But I will introduce myself to vendors as necessary and hope I can count on their discretion."

"Emily is very trustworthy. Let me tell my sales associate, Mrs. Wilcox, that I'm leaving."

When they reached the street, several people were turning into Sugar and Spice. Monica peered through the window and saw even more customers at the counter and seated at the scattered tables.

"You know what, it's the end of the workday, and she's very busy. And I'm starving. How 'bout you buy me an early dinner in exchange for my help? And then we can have dessert with Emily, when her business has slowed down."

To her surprise, he didn't even look through the window himself, only nodded.

"That makes sense," he said. "Where would you like to go?"

She rubbed her hands together, trying to think of restaurants while wondering if he wasn't quite as rigid as she'd thought. He didn't seem reluctant to change his schedule, after all.

"What are you up for?" she asked. "Mexican? Japanese? Italian?"

"You choose."

"A polite man," she said, sliding her arm into his without thinking. "Oh, sorry. Forgot who I was with."

"No problem."

In that brief moment before she let go, she felt the warmth of his body, the hard muscles beneath his casual jacket and shirt, and inhaled another intoxicating whiff of his citrus aftershave. "You must think that an old-fashioned thing to do, take a man's arm."

He studied her. "Maybe. Makes you seem like an old-fashioned girl, and I haven't gotten that impression so far."

She laughed. "I'm not sure that's a compliment."

He blinked at her. "I certainly didn't mean to disrespect you."

"Now who's old-fashioned? Honestly, I'm not offended. And I guess I'm not old-fashioned, owning my own business and being single. Said like that, I seem like a modern woman. How about you?"

"Am I a modern woman?" he shot back.

Surprised and delighted by this glimpse of a sense of humor, she took his arm again. "I think I'm starting to like you, Travis Beaumont. I'd say let's have a good steak, but you've probably eaten in the Main Street Steakhouse plenty of times since it's right in your hotel."

"You would be right."

"Then let's go to the Halftime Sports Bar. It'll be crowded, but if I bore you, you can watch a game."

He shook his head. "Monica, you don't bore me."

She gave his arm a squeeze and smiled up at him.

It was early enough that they got a table right away although their waitress, Linda, gave Travis a second look and Monica a wink. The building had been a saloon for over a hundred years, and it still had the original carved wooden bar. The walls were paneled and covered in sports memorabilia between flat screen TVs. Neon signs filled each window.

Monica wasn't certain she'd have Travis's attention in such a busy place, the way his eyes continually scanned the crowd, but she imagined his behavior was ingrained after the military and now the Secret Service. He probably had to be paranoid all the time.

"If you like BLTs," she said, when they had their menus and ice water, "you'll want to try theirs. It's their specialty."

He closed his menu. "Done."

She did the same, smiling at him. "You know, Travis, you've done a background check on me, so it only seems fair that you talk about yourself."

"A background check doesn't tell you any details about the person, mostly about what she *hasn't* done."

"I'll answer questions if *you* will."

"You can try," he said.

He almost sounded . . . teasing. She enjoyed looking into those deep blue eyes across a table, knowing she had his complete attention. But, then, he was very good at that.

"So do you have family?" she asked.

"An ex-wife, if that counts. No kids. She's in the Secret Service, too."

"That must be awkward."

He gave that faint smile. "I don't think that was the reason we failed. But I do have closer family, three sisters, all younger than me."

"You must have played the overprotective big brother really well." She gave an exaggerated shudder.

"Two of them wanted that from me. The other one wanted to do everything I did, even when it meant building army forts in the woods near our house. And she's four years younger than me, so you can guess I didn't enjoy her most of the time."

Monica grinned. "I like her already. So you played a lot of war games when you were young?"

He shrugged. "I like to be in command."

She shivered and pressed her thighs together at the sexual thoughts that simple sentence aroused in her. Not the time for it, so she went back to a safe topic. "Maybe your sister didn't like following your orders. What's she do now?"

Travis seemed to straighten with pride. "She's in the Marines."

Her mouth dropped open. "Wow! She really did want to be just like you."

He lowered his gaze to the table briefly, and she

thought there was some kind of pain inside him that he didn't want her to see. She didn't press it, not when he was finally revealing a bit of himself to her.

They paused to give Linda their drink and food order, and Monica wasn't surprised he had a Coke rather than a beer. She was lucky he deigned to have dinner on the job, let alone a drink.

"Well, Kelly's not just like me," he continued. "She enlisted right out of high school although I thought she should go to college like I did. Being an officer just makes everything easier."

"Girl who knows her own mind. Is she still in?"

"She is. That made it tough for me to leave when my enlistment was up, but she'd have been furious if I didn't follow what I wanted to do because of her."

"And I agree. Why did you leave the Marines—I mean, why did you want to join the Secret Service?" She lowered her voice on the last words.

Again, he gave her that faint, barely noticeable smile, but it was almost a grin on him. She felt proud every time she could get any sort of reaction out of such a carefully guarded man.

They both leaned back while Linda put down their drinks. Monica had ordered an iced tea.

"I felt like something was missing with my life in the Marines," he continued after taking a long sip of his Coke. "You won't be surprised, but my revelation had something to do with the former president. He was almost assassinated when he was visiting my battalion in Afghanistan. It was downplayed."

"And I bet you helped save his life."

"Details are classified," he said.

But he didn't quite meet her eyes, and she knew he'd probably risked his life jumping right in to help.

"That was when I realized I didn't just want to protect the country but the commander in chief himself. It was a challenge I couldn't stop thinking about. When my enlistment was up, I resigned and applied to the Secret Service. Not that they take you right away, I still had to jump through hoops and prove myself."

"Even with your record?"

"Everyone is rigorously tested and interviewed."

"Makes sense. What was your first assignment?"

"Nothing exciting. I was in the Denver Field Office for a couple years, handling bank fraud and computer-related crime."

She was in Denver at least a half dozen times a year—she could have passed him on the street. No, she'd have remembered him.

"Then I was transferred to CAT—counterassault team—which was a lot more like my work in the Marines. I can't say much about it except CAT are the guys carrying weapons in black SUVs in the presidential motorcade. CAT agents distract if the president's detail needs to get him away."

Distract? Now that could mean a whole lot of things.

"And now I'm with the advance team."

"Preparing for the president's trips," she said. "So is the next step of your career guarding the president herself?"

He nodded. "Presidential Protective Detail. I'm hoping my work here will get me one step closer."

She took a deep breath, glad for Linda's interruption with their giant BLTs. If she thought too much about the widows' protest, she might feel guilty, and she had nothing to feel guilty about. The Double Ds were allowed freedom of speech, and Monica herself would make sure nothing bad happened that would interfere with Travis's job.

After swallowing a mouthful, he said, "Great BLT. But now let's talk about you."

She took a quick bite of hers, wondering how she could compete with his exciting life. Her small-town world was the life he'd escaped after growing up.

Chapter Seven

The sports bar was warm with people, the sound of laughing voices, and the background drone of sports on TV, but Travis didn't have any problem concentrating on Monica. He had a problem concentrating on anything *else* when he was with her.

She was too easy to talk to, too easy to confide in, and he'd had to remember his various oaths before revealing too much. That was a rarity for him since he'd spent his adult life keeping the secrets of his country.

Her beauty was a distraction, those large eyes that saw too much, the way her hair was as free and uncomplicated as she seemed to be. He liked the curve of her lips and thought too often about kissing her.

She interrupted his thoughts with, "But you haven't told me about your other sisters."

And that made it obvious she didn't want to talk about herself, which intrigued him even more.

"One is a teacher and the other an architect. The teacher is married with a two-year-old, and the architect has a girlfriend, but Montana frowns on gay marriage. My parents are both alive and healthy. Your turn."

"You know, you're a hard act to follow," she admitted, setting down her sandwich and eyeing him.

"I have such an exciting family?"

"You've had such an exciting life. Mine must look absolutely dull in comparison."

He found himself leaning toward her and speaking honestly in a low voice. "Monica, there's nothing dull about you. I wish there were."

She leaned toward him as well. "I think that's another compliment. Although every compliment you give is pretty unusual."

He stared into her brown eyes, and he could only think of the warmth of hot coffee on a cold winter's day. She'd be just as welcome and even more satisfying. There was something so genuine and fun-loving about her, and that kind of woman never tolerated someone like him for long. But he wouldn't be in Valentine for long.

He straightened and lifted his sandwich again. "You're procrastinating."

"It's just a pretty basic story, nothing with exciting highs and lows, like yours. I have a brother named Dom who's a food broker, and fraternal twin sister, Missy— Melissa—who's a correspondent on CNN. Have you seen her?"

"I don't watch a lot of TV, but I imagine I would have noticed someone who looks like you."

"We're not identical."

"But you're sisters."

She blinked. "Yeah. Close sisters. She's my best friend—along with a couple girls in town, one of whom is Emily at Sugar and Spice."

"You're getting distracted from your family."

"You're really nosy."

He eyed her intently. "So it's only nosy when other people do it?"

She blushed. "Well . . . you have me there. But you've heard all the major stuff about my sister and brother. Dom still lives here, so you might end up meeting him. And as for my parents"—she hesitated a little too long—"they're alive and healthy just like yours. They live here, too."

He stared at her a moment, tempted to ask more, then took a bite of his sandwich. She released her breath. He could tell she really didn't want to talk about her parents, and he wasn't about to pry into something that made her uncomfortable.

He washed his sandwich down with a swig of Coke, then said, "So why choose flowers as a career?"

"They're beautiful, they make people happy," she said, her shoulders lowering as she relaxed. "And I'm lucky enough to have a gift for design—enhanced by all the classes I took, of course."

"But how did you know you liked working with them? You could have grown a garden if it was just about looking at them."

"A lot of it was because of my Grandpa Shaw. He moved in with us after my grandma's death when I was a little girl because he was too ill to live on his own. He was a pretty cool guy, and he lived until just before

I went off to college. He'd been a bellman at the Hotel Colorado, and my grandma a maid. They met there. He didn't just believe in equal rights—he marched for it. Great guy."

That made him think of the local protest against the hurried spa construction. But that was different, of course, and it was about old women, not young ones who owned their own business and probably had to chase guys away. He urged her on with his sandwich.

"Can you believe they saved enough to put my dad through college?" she asked. "Pretty impressive. But anyway, we read to each other, played cards and board games. Missy would write him stories, and I would draw him pictures of flowers because he used to garden before he became ill. He told me all about plants, long discussions about them. As I got older, I did start my own garden, just so he could advise me. He'd watch from the window although on some days he made it to the back porch."

He watched her expression soften, her gaze lose focus, as she looked into her happy past. Their child-hoods hadn't been too different although they'd focused on different things.

"In the winter, we potted so many plants inside that Dom used to say it was a jungle in the house," she mused. "Anyway, as I went through high school, I wondered what to do about my love of flowers and thought maybe I should go into interior design, as if beautifying homes was what I wanted. Thank goodness I took a lot of business courses, too, because it didn't take me long to realize it was only the flowers I wanted to beautify with, nothing else. So that's when I knew. Luckily, the previous owner of my shop took me on each summer. When I graduated, he was ready to retire, and I bought the business—or I went into major debt for the business," she corrected herself, wearing a crooked grin. "Not as exciting as saving the president's life, I bet."

Without thinking about it, he put his hand over hers. "But satisfying to you. You're happy. I think I keep waiting for the next thing, hoping it will finally make me happy."

Where the hell had that come from? Monica's eyes grew large. He released her immediately, and she didn't try to hold on. He signaled for the check. The silence could have been uncomfortable, but Monica seemed fine with it.

After Linda left it on the table, Monica said, "So now you know all about me."

"I don't think so, but I guess I'm not entitled to more since I'm only treating you to a meal for my own benefit." But he'd touched her, and her skin had been so warm, so soft, and it made him wonder if the rest of her skin would feel the same.

"What benefit is that?"

He put a couple bills on the table. "I'm going to use your knowledge of local contacts for the good of the country, after all."

She stood up. "All right, have it your way. Oh, speaking of flowers, I thought of a question, but I'll ask you when we get outside."

They weaved through the tables that had grown crowded while they'd eaten. Travis saw all the curious gazes he drew, the recognition when they spotted Monica, the smiles, the waves, the arched brows aimed from her to him. Small towns, he thought, shaking his head. He didn't miss that recognition. He liked anonymity in his job.

Out on the street, they walked side by side for the block it took to reach Sugar and Spice. The sun had already set behind the mountains although nightfall was still several hours away.

"Travis, you know I'll be doing the flowers for the wedding, right?"

He nodded.

"It's going to be a massive job, all done at the last minute. I spent a lot of today making plans, and, soon, I'll be ordering the flowers. Can you make sure your other agents stay out of my way while I'm working? I imagine they'll be in the front window, of course, and—"

"The front window on your second floor. Do you work up there?"

"Oh. I live there." She blinked at him in surprise, as if it hadn't occurred to her they'd be invading her personal space.

"I'm sorry I didn't explain in detail. When you do this for a living, you start assuming everyone realizes you need a higher vantage point for this kind of observation post. Will you still give us permission?"

"Of course. I just have to rearrange what I was thinking." She looked thoughtful.

"Don't worry, I'll make sure it's painless for you." He anticipated needing to stop in at her apartment, and the thought of squeezing another appointment into his crowded schedule didn't bother him as much as it should.

As he opened the door to Sugar and Spice for her, Monica said, "I'm not one of those girls who skips desserts, and Em makes the best. She's totally self-taught although she had some guidance from our friend, Heather Armstrong, who was trained in culinary school in San Francisco. You might meet her, too—she's doing the catering for the wedding shower."

"I'll meet her on paper anyway," he said.

Monica smiled. "Background checks. Right."

The smell of cinnamon was powerful as they entered the cheerful bakery. Travis saw small tables and chairs to the right, a long counter to the left with glass display cases below, showcasing cakes and pastries. Large glass coolers at the back displayed even more tempting desserts. A rear door probably led to the kitchen. Springtime flowers decorated strategic spots, and he thought Monica might have had a hand in that.

There were only a few customers, and two elderly women waiting on them from behind the counter, one whose hair was obviously dyed red and the other with the biggest blond wig he'd ever seen outside Nashville. They wore aprons that said, WE PUT THE HEAT IN SWEET, and he raised an eyebrow in surprise.

Monica leaned close to him, and he looked down at her.

"Those are some of my surrogate grandmas, Mrs. Thalberg and Mrs. Palmer. They live in the Widows' Boardinghouse."

"I've heard of them."

She did a double take, and he thought she looked . . . nervous. Interesting. Of course, their protesting past wouldn't be any secret to her.

"I can't believe the widows need background checks," she said.

"No, not yet anyway. But a bridal shower held in their home is on the schedule. Even though the president won't be here in time to attend, we will be looking into everything that has anything to do with the wedding."

Then the door to the kitchen swung open, and a young, pretty woman entered. She had strawberry blond hair pulled back in a ponytail and eyes that perfectly illustrated "bright blue." She was short, but with great curves, and she, too, wore one of the signature aprons over khakis and a pink top.

She smiled warmly at Monica, and Travis immediately sensed the bond between them. He might not be a man who showed his emotions, but he felt them in others.

Monica hesitated and glanced at the women behind the counter, as well as their customers.

"Travis Beaumont," she said, "meet Emily Thalberg, owner of Sugar and Spice."

Monica had remembered not to reveal his whole identity in front of a crowd, and he appreciated it. Emily took his hand in a firm grip, smiling up at him guilelessly but with interest, too. She glanced again at Monica with some unseen form of communication. "So nice to meet you, Mr. Beaumont."

"Travis is fine," he said.

She nodded. "Did you two eat dinner already?"

"Just came from the Halftime," Monica said. "BLTs."

Emily briefly closed her eyes as if the memory needed to be revered. But then his sisters seemed to worship their food, too.

"Sounds delicious," Emily said. "But I bet you could use dessert."

Monica rubbed her hands together. "Definitely. Travis, Em has lots to choose from. Let's go browse."

Browsing put him in proximity to the older women, who didn't hesitate to introduce themselves, letting Emily step in to take care of another customer.

The redhead wore tasteful makeup to help disguise her age, but her hands looked like she'd worked hard her whole life.

"I'm Rosemary Thalberg, Emily's grandma-in-law." She shook his hand with a firm grip.

"So you're associated with the Silver Creek Ranch?" he asked.

Her eyes brightened with pleasure. "You've heard of it?"

"Yes, and I took a drive near it when I had some free time. Beautiful countryside."

"Thank you. My son and his wife and kids run it now. Though I may be retired, I like to work part-time for Emily."

She turned to the other old woman with the blond wig, who, beneath her apron, wore a dress covered in colorful cupcake images. He didn't think he'd ever seen that kind of pattern before.

"This is Renee Palmer," Mrs. Thalberg said. "Her grandson Adam works on my son's ranch."

Mrs. Palmer took his hand in both of hers and held it extra long while she studied him, wearing a broad smile. "I'm so glad to meet you," she said, her Western accent strong. "It's been a while since Monica's brought a fellow around. The pickin's were slim around here when she was younger—she had to resort to lookin' for rich young men in Aspen."

Hiding his smile, he glanced at Monica, who closed her eyes and gave a soft groan.

"I was a teenager, Mrs. Palmer. Everyone does stupid things when they're a teenager."

"Renee, leave the poor girl alone," Mrs. Thalberg said.

"So what stupid things did you do with the opposite sex, Mr. Beaumont?" Mrs. Palmer asked slyly.

"You don't need to answer that," Monica quickly said, then sent a beseeching glance at Emily. "We just want to pick out dessert."

But he gave the widow's question serious consideration. "I grew up in a small town, too."

"Look what you have in common," Mrs. Thalberg said to Monica.

Monica's grimace was supposed to pass as a smile, he guessed. He didn't mind if people thought he was interested in her—it might prove helpful as he got a feel for everyone. And spending time with her was hardly a hardship.

"I played soccer rather than football," he said, "so I

tended to have to go against football players to date the pretty girls."

"Monica was a cheerleader!" Mrs. Palmer gushed.

Monica sank into a chair and waited with resignation. He was kind of enjoying watching her embarrassment. She didn't get angry or leave in a huff—she took it good-naturedly because, obviously, all these women were important to her, and she'd never hurt their feelings.

"I was interested in this one girl, and I saw her talking to a football player who knew about my crush, and I was pissed—upset, pardon me, ma'am."

"So polite!" Mrs. Thalberg said in a not-very-quiet aside to Emily at the cash register.

"I lost my temper and kicked my soccer ball at him just to make him look like an idiot. Instead, I hit her."

All the women shared an audible gasp, then a wince. Monica, eyes sparkling, clapped her hands over her mouth to hide laughter.

"Needless to say, that girl lost any interest in me. So you're right, Monica, we all did stupid things in high school."

He wasn't quite sure why he'd felt the need to reveal that, but she'd seemed so . . . good-naturedly picked upon that he'd taken pity on her. To forestall any other reminiscences, he glanced at the cooler in the back of the room. "So what's the best cheesecake?"

He ended up at a little table with Monica, eating triple layer cheesecake while she dug into a slice of carrot cake. Emily brought their coffee and pulled up a chair, and the two women waved good-bye as the widows took off their aprons and headed home for the evening, turning the sign in the front window to CLOSED as they left.

Monica was focused on her cake, but she spared a glance for Emily. "Damn, you can bake."

Emily grinned. "Thanks." She eyed Travis for a moment. "So you're from a small town, too. Nearby?"

He swallowed a bite, then wiped his mouth. "Montana."

"So why are you visiting Valentine Valley? We can't be too much different than where you're from."

"I grew up in a small town, but I live in Washington, D.C., now. I'm here on business." He glanced at Monica and gave a nod, then enjoyed her pleased expression.

"I didn't reveal his title in front of everyone else, Em, but this is Special Agent Travis Beaumont with the Secret Service."

Emily's eyes widened, and she lightly smacked her forehead. "I can't believe I didn't make the connection to the presidential wedding. At least now I know why you were examining Valentine Valley like a tourist—a tourist who stuck out in our laid-back town, I might add."

With his fork, he pointed at her. "But you didn't figure it out."

"True, very true," she admitted with teasing regret.

The door opened, and the frown Emily turned on it suddenly melted away as a tall man entered, removing his Stetson. He wore jeans and a t-shirt with a faded jacket over it.

"Nate!" she said, rising to walk toward the door. "I didn't know you were coming. You just missed your grandma." They shared a quick kiss and a longer hug, then she turned back to their table. "Travis Beaumont, this is my husband, Nate Thalberg. Nate, Travis is with the Secret Service." She shot a troubled look at Travis. "Was I allowed to mention it to my husband? I noticed Monica didn't reveal your identity to the others."

Travis stood up, and they shook hands. "I'm sure your husband can keep quiet until the wedding is public knowledge."

Nate had wavy black hair creased by his hat and green eyes that studied Travis shrewdly. Travis knew small-town grapevines well, and figured everyone was curious about the stranger with Monica. Everyone who cared about her anyway, and he guessed just from the few days of knowing her, that that was the whole town.

"Nice to meet you," Nate said. He turned back to his wife. "Just thought I'd keep you company while you closed tonight, but you didn't need me."

She slid her arm in his and leaned against his shoulder. "I always need you."

Monica tilted her head at Travis. "They can be sickening sometimes."

Nate pulled up a chair, too.

Travis turned to Emily. "I'm starting to meet all the vendors who'll be associated with the wedding. I'm the lead agent, but you'll probably be hearing from the hotel agent assigned to the Sweetheart Inn. I'm just trying to get a feel for the town and the people involved. We will do routine background checks, and an agent will be assigned to watch you bake desserts meant for the president."

Emily's eyes were getting wider and wider.

"But I'm getting the impression I don't have to worry too much about you," he assured her, then looked down at the cheesecake smeared on his fork and resisted the urge to lick it. "And since this is incredible, I'm sure the president will be pleased with your work."

Emily blushed even as her husband squeezed her hand.

To put the woman at ease, Travis started asking Nate about the ranch. He learned that local ranches grazed their cows up in the White River National Forest, and during the late-spring season, they were busy preparing for their hay harvest, so the cows would have food come winter. Travis asked Emily about opening her bakery, and heard the story of how she'd first come to Valentine Valley only temporarily, clueless about her future as a pastry chef.

Monica enjoyed her carrot cake and listened to the flow of conversation. Travis was still pretty formal in his responses and mannerisms. She knew he was asking questions to gauge reactions, but she guessed Emily didn't mind. It was all part of the high honor in being involved in a presidential wedding.

As for his first introduction to the widows—Monica had been a wreck during that. She herself had told Travis about the protest against the Renaissance Spa's handling of the dig. There was no reason he'd connect the widows to the environmentalists, but he did seem awfully interested in them. Of course, they probably needed background checks, too, because they worked in the bakery. She wasn't quite sure what those reports would turn up . . .

Travis's story about hitting the girl with a soccer ball? At least he didn't take himself seriously all the time, and she wouldn't have thought him capable of that before. It made her feel . . . lighter, somehow. Maybe there was hope that a more carefree man lurked inside the dutiful special agent. She wasn't quite sure why it felt important to her, but she'd always trusted her instincts.

The hour in the bakery almost felt like a double date; at least that's how Nate and Em were treating it. And for the first time, Monica felt a twinge of sadness at the thought of Travis's departure. She'd forgotten what it was like to be part of a couple, chatting with another couple. Not that they were a couple, of course, she hastily reminded herself.

She excused herself to use the restroom, and when she returned, Travis was standing near the door with Nate.

"Come on out to the ranch anytime," Nate said. "I'd be happy to show you around."

"Not sure how much time I have, but I appreciate the offer."

They shook hands.

"I'll get out of your way," Monica said to Emily and Nate, as Travis opened the door for her. "Have a good evening!"

Out on Main Street, the sky was dark, the street lit by old-fashioned lamps. Many couples strolled by, off to a late dinner or maybe the film festival at the Royal Theater. Travis didn't have far to escort her. Her door was already closed and locked, only the faint night-light on inside. She fished her keys out of her purse.

"Would you like to come in?" she asked.

With streetlights behind him, his face was shad-owed, and she couldn't quite read his expression. But the pause was long enough that she wondered if he was considering it—and wondered what she'd do if he took her up on her impulsive offer. She felt so aware of him, her body coming to life, her mind intrigued though she kept warning herself off. But . . . he was just so interest-ing, so different than most of the men she knew. And he needed her help—in more ways than one.

He shook his head. "I've put off my paperwork long enough. But thank you for the introduction to Emily and some of her employees. Meeting the people feed-ing President Torres helps me feel confident going into the wedding."

"I don't blame you. Very interesting that agents watch the food prep. It really is a huge production, isn't it?"

"It is. Have a good night, Monica." He nodded and turned toward the street.

He looked both ways, then crossed at a brisk, con-fident pace. She leaned back against the door, unable to help watching the way his shoulders moved beneath the windbreaker. She felt a sense of regret that he'd de-clined her invitation though it was probably better that way. Helping a man relax and lighten up didn't mean the two of them had to be alone . . .

He disappeared into the hotel, and, as she unlocked the front door, she heard her phone chirp. After digging in her purse, she found an e-mail from the widows, letting the Dig Defenders know that their next meeting was tomorrow evening. She sighed and locked the door behind her for another quiet night. She had a lot of those lately, now that her best friends were all either married or engaged. She could have hung out with any one of them with just a phone call, but tonight . . . tonight she'd rather be alone and eat ice cream. A second dessert. Yeah, that would hit the spot as she thought about Travis. She'd just run an extra mile tomorrow.

And maybe she'd see him in his running shorts.

Chapter Eight

Inside the hotel's front doors, Travis found himself turning to look through the glass at the flower shop across Main Street. Normally, he'd have waited on her doorstep until the woman he'd spent the evening with was inside and safe, but he'd been worried he'd join her in that darkened shop and kiss her like he wanted to— like *she* wanted him to.

Gritting his teeth, he turned toward the lobby, old-fashioned with red-patterned wallpaper, antique gas sconces on the walls. A round plush ottoman dominated the center of the lobby, across from the registration desk, with a huge vase of flowers rising up through the center.

A young woman came toward him, and although they'd never met, he recognized her immediately from photos: Ashley Ludlow, the bride in this huge "production," as Monica had called it.

She put out a hand. "Special Agent Beaumont?"

She was obviously waiting just for him. He shook her hand. "Good evening, Miss Ludlow."

She smiled and blushed. "Please, it's Ashley. And you know me by sight already? Guess I'm not surprised, with all that the Secret Service does."

"Please call me Travis. Did you need my help?" he asked.

"I honestly don't know if you *can* help. I'm having a problem with one of the president's junior staffers. I've been dealing with her about the wedding schedule— she's sort of my liaison. Anyway, she's been a little . . . difficult to deal with. Have you heard of her, Samantha Weichert?"

"I've heard the name, but have had no dealings with her."

"You probably will. She just arrived yesterday, on the same plane as me. She even insisted we sit together. I had to plead exhaustion and pretend to sleep just to get her to leave me alone."

"Sorry about that. I can tell you the type—often from a wealthy family, went to an excellent college, smart enough to land a position in the White House, and believes she's better than everyone else."

Her tense expression relaxed into relief. "Yes! You captured her perfectly."

"That type tends to think the Secret Service is the hired help and often asks us to carry luggage."

Her eyes widened. "Wow, that's presumptuous. I know there's not a lot you can do about her, but if there's some way to get her to back off about the wedding itself, like she's my wedding planner and knows best, I'd really appreciate it."

"I will make a point of meeting her."

"Thank you. Will she give you a wedding schedule, or do you need that from me?"

"One from you would be great, then I can confer with the president's staff as well."

"There's one other thing." Almost nervously, she glanced around to see if anyone was listening. "I have reason to believe there might be some kind of protest during my wedding weekend—not against the president!" she amended quickly.

And her grandmother was one of the notorious widows, so she might have reason to suspect. "I have heard that people are upset about the closing of an archaeological dig."

"They are strongly concerned about the environment around here, and when I was younger, I was also involved in that kind of concern, so I get it. And I'm not even upset about it. I just don't want *you* to be taken unawares."

Travis wondered if she wanted a possible protest stopped but couldn't quite bring herself to say it. Or perhaps she was simply trying to protect everyone involved by bringing him into the loop.

"You might wonder how I know about this," she continued, blushing. "My grandmother is one of the 'rabble-rousers' "—she used air quotes around the words—"but she's a wonderful person and is even throwing me a wedding shower. The president won't be there, so maybe that doesn't have anything to do with you."

"No, but my work will probably intersect, so thanks for the advance notice."

Ashley seemed almost lighter as she waved good-bye and headed out onto the street. It couldn't be easy being a bride who had to do everything at the last minute—and on a world stage.

As Travis took the stairs to the third floor, he thought about Monica's closeness to the widows. Did she know what was going on? Could she even be involved? It was a troubling thought. He didn't want to see her get in any kind of trouble.

Hanging out with her might have the side benefit of figuring out if she was involved, or maybe even stopping the protest altogether. That was his job, after all, smoothing everything out for a presidential visit, keeping everyone safe. He made a mental note to go order background checks on the notorious widows.

After spending much of the morning working on presidential wedding plans, including trying to convince a harried wholesaler that Monica needed exotic flowers guaranteed quickly—without revealing details—she took a break to attend the "Men of Valentine Valley" photo shoot at the Sweetheart Inn hot springs. This was the last shot necessary to complete the calendar, one big group photo for the month of July. It had been her idea to surprise the men, and Brooke, Emily, Heather, and Whitney had all gone along with it. Whitney was thrilled just to be moving around because Josh often "encouraged" her to remain at home or at Leather and Lace—like she was an invalid, she complained. The women had ordered subs from the Mountainside Deli, cookies from Sugar and Spice, and now carried the bags and pulled a couple coolers full of water and soda.

When the girls walked up the path, they came upon eleven of their favorite men in various states of undressing, and the middle-aged photographer from the Back In Time Portrait Studio, Carolyn Covich, watching them all in bemusement. She saw the women approach first, and to Carolyn's credit, Monica couldn't tell whether she was annoyed or relieved.

"Do we have an audience?" Carolyn called.

Monica had to laugh as Chris Sweet, in the process of pulling off jeans to reveal swim trunks, actually stumbled and had to catch himself on the bench.

His girlfriend, Heather, snorted through her nose as she tried to stop her laughter, before saying, "Good thing he only had to read by the fire for January. He might have broken a bone doing anything more athletic."

He gave her a good-natured grimace.

"Aren't you guys going to be cold?" Monica called. "It's still spring weather around here."

"It's a *hot spring*," Josh Thalberg called.

His wife, Whitney, gave a groan at his joke, and he left his shirt half-unbuttoned to run to her.

"Are you okay?"

She smiled up at him and put his hand on her swollen stomach. "I'm more than okay, and this little one agrees. I just came to watch her daddy pose in the nude."

"We are not posing in the nude," Josh said mildly, his gaze unfocused as he moved his hand around on Whitney's belly. "She's pretty active."

"It was a long walk up here," Brooke told her brother.

"Maybe you should get the clothes off the bench and let your wife sit down."

Several of the guys cleared off the bench while Josh led her to it.

Emily perched next to Whitney and looked at the group of men expectantly. "Don't let us stop you!"

Some of the men seemed a little more reluctant, and others, like Emily's brothers Will and Daniel, quickly stripped off their shirts and jeans to reveal swim trunks. Since there wasn't room for all of them to be in the tiny hot spring, Carolyn began to arrange the men the way she thought best. Monica had never seen so many gorgeous torsos—except for poor Howie Deering Jr., he of the receding hair and freckled face. Now that he had a wife and two small kids, it was pretty obvious he'd let go of any kind of exercise besides walking to the houses he sold. Monica worried he felt truly out of place. But she'd seen pictures of his March photo shoot on a snowmobile, and Carolyn had done a great job, letting him wear a vest and capturing the feel of having a good time in winter.

To Howie's credit, he stripped off his t-shirt, let a towel drape around his neck, and knelt behind the group of guys already in the hot spring. Monica cheered for him, and he grinned.

"Did we miss it?"

That was Mrs. Palmer's twang. Monica turned to see the three widows making their slow way around the curve in the path—even Mrs. Ludlow, with her walker, a sweater draped around her shoulders, moving almost briskly.

"Grandma, you aren't exactly helping!" called Adam Desantis. He was waist deep in the hot spring already, frowning.

Mrs. Palmer gave him a big grin. "But this is our idea, Adam! O' course we want to be here for the final picture-takin'. Just pretend we're not here when you look sexy."

He shuddered, and Nate tossed a towel into his face.

Mrs. Palmer turned around. "And we had a kind gentleman give us a hand."

Monica felt a little thrill start in the pit of her stomach when she saw Travis at the tail end, carrying lawn chairs for the widows. He was once again dressed casually, his sunglasses in place, hiding his eyes. She wondered if he wore the jacket to conceal his gun. It wasn't that she felt he was dangerous, but there was always the possibility that he'd have to *do* something dangerous.

"He came," Emily said in a low, satisfied voice.

Monica whirled to face her, and whispered, "You invited him?"

"Sure, while you were in the bathroom last night. He said he'd consider it." She smirked. "Guess he considered it."

Monica tried to look serious, but a smile broke through. "You're bad."

"I know," Emily said, chin raised in satisfaction. "But he needs to have some fun, doesn't he?"

"That's exactly what I was thinking—although I'm pretty sure watching a bunch of guys pose for a calendar isn't all that fun for a straight guy."

"You're sure he's straight?"

Monica chuckled. "I'm sure. My gaydar is pretty good."

"No other reason you'd know he was straight?"

"Of course not," Monica chided, but she kept her eyes on the Secret Service agent. He just . . . drew her gaze.

After Travis finished setting up the chairs, Mrs. Thalberg gave him a little push toward Monica. "Introduce your young man, my dear."

Monica waited for him to contradict her, but he didn't. She suspected Travis was using the widows' assumption to his benefit to meet more residents of Valentine Valley.

She turned and swept an arm wide, encompassing everyone. "Men of Valentine Valley, meet Travis Beaumont, a guest at the Hotel Colorado."

A few of the men called out a greeting, some eyed him with curiosity, but her brother, Dom, leaned his dark, muscular arms on the rock ledge surrounding the spring, and said, "A guest at the hotel? What does that mean?"

Monica shrugged. "Just what I said." She put her hands on her hips and leaned down toward her brother. "You got a problem with it?"

Several people "oohed," but Dom only shrugged. "Guess you know what you're doing. Just be careful."

She put a hand on her chest. "Such protectiveness. I'm speechless."

"You're never speechless," said Josh.

She stuck out a leg as if she'd trip him on his way back to the spring. He laughed and pretended to jump.

"Hey, can we finish this up?" Carolyn called. "I've got an appointment with a baby." She eyed Travis. "You want to join in on this photo shoot? I'm sure the women of Valentine wouldn't mind."

"No, thanks," he said politely.

Monica and the other girls backed away, Travis helped the widows set up their chairs, then Carolyn took control of her photo shoot. For a half hour, she posed the men in various positions, some in the hot spring, some surrounding it. Sometimes, she just let them have fun choosing their own poses, and she continued to snap pictures throughout the whole thing.

From her place standing behind the bench, Monica couldn't help glancing at Travis, who'd taken up what was almost a military stance beside the widows, as if protecting them from roaming terrorists. She found it kind of cute. She was pretty sure he met her gaze from behind his sunglasses and arched an eyebrow, wearing that faint almost smile that was growing on her. And then he pulled his phone out of his pocket to check the screen.

"You just can't stop looking at him," Brooke said quietly.

Monica turned back to the photo shoot but gave Brooke a rueful smile. "I know. He's easy to look at."

"Seems exciting to have a guy like that trying to get close to you."

"Well . . . I think that's overstating his interest."

"He's here, isn't he?"

Emily looked up and back at them from her seat on the bench. "Because of me, remember!"

Whitney eyed her. "She's not likely to forget. Now, Monica, why don't you forget about us and go talk to him?"

Monica grinned at them all and turned away. Travis met her a little way from the widows' viewing place. They turned to watch the photo shoot together, and Monica felt a stir as he seemed to deliberately brush shoulders with her. Or was it an accident?

"So why didn't you tell me you were coming?" she asked quietly.

"I didn't know if I could get away. It *is* a workday."

"Which made the photo-shoot coordination hard. Everyone agreed to take the morning off because it's for such a good cause. But you seem to make your own hours."

"That, and it's not easy to outright refuse Emily Thalberg," he said with the seriousness given state negotiations.

Monica laughed. "She is pretty strong and persuasive. And now she's full of herself, too. Thanks for that. You do know that since only a few of us know you're here to spy, everyone else thinks you're interested in me."

"Spy? That's pretty harsh. I happen to be taking advantage of a new friendship to meet more people."

"Friends? Is that what we are? So you don't mind what others think? I warned you what your secrecy would lead to, after all."

He glanced down at her from behind his sunglasses. "I'm okay with it if you are."

As his voice rumbled tantalizingly, her amusement faded away to be replaced by delicious tension. "Are you saying it's okay to make me look so hard up for a date that I'd hang out with a guy only temporarily in town?"

"Your words, not mine."

She punched him lightly in the arm. "Not very gentlemanly of you, Beaumont. I may have to sic my brother on you."

"It's not like you introduced me."

She looked away, feeling a twinge of discomfort. "I introduced him with the crowd."

"I see."

And she thought maybe he was seeing too much. Helping him let loose was one thing—he didn't need to know about private family problems. And she didn't like being transparent.

The photo shoot ended, the guys got dressed, then enthusiastically dug into the subs.

"Hey, Monica!"

She turned to find Josh approaching her and Travis. She made the introductions.

"When I talked to Ashley," Monica said, "she told me that the First Husband is a big fan of yours and plans to drop in to the flower shop. I told her I'd try to arrange for you to be there."

Josh blinked. "That's flattering. Of course I'll come. Unless Whitney's in labor, I'm yours."

"I won't be in labor!" Whitney called from where she was sitting with the widows. "Not this early," she continued in a mutter.

"Thanks, Josh," Monica said. "Did you need me for something?"

"I just wanted to let you know I have some frames almost ready for you."

To Travis, she explained, "Not sure you noticed, but I take local crafts on consignment. Needless to say, Josh is my best seller."

"I'm sorry I've been so busy," Josh said. "And when the baby comes, I might have even less time. I hate affecting your business in a bad way, so I'll do my best not to."

"Don't worry about it," she insisted. "The baby is more important than your fans."

He grimaced, and she knew he was remembering the fan who threw a rock through Leather and Lace's window out of jealousy over him last year. As for herself, she'd found the perfect way to combat her worry that Josh's fame had more to do with her business success than her own flowers. She'd prove that she could decorate a presidential wedding as well as the best florists in the big city. Ideas were bursting in her brain, the chance to use the most exotic flowers in intricate designs she seldom had the opportunity—or the budget—to try.

Gradually, all the subs were consumed, sodas drained, cookies devoured. Everyone started departing by twos and threes, and Brooke gave Monica a head gesture in Travis's direction, and mouthed, "Stay!"

Monica hesitated, then nodded. What else was she supposed to do, especially since Travis was letting people think what they would? She walked to the edge of the spring, sat down, took off her shoes, and lowered her feet in. Might as well enjoy the day—maybe Travis would join her. She gave a sigh of contentment, leaned back on her hands, and let the sun filtering through the trees bathe her face with flickering light. The last voices faded away.

It was still quiet behind her. For all she knew, Travis had left, but . . . she thought she would have sensed it. Or at least he would have said good-bye. She finally snuck a peek over her shoulder and found him, arms crossed over his chest, his expression impassive beneath those sunglasses.

"That must be your bodyguard face," she said, smiling, kicking her legs gently in the hot water. "Is that what you're doing, guarding me? Or keeping up your story?"

"*My* story?"

"Of course! You're the one who told me to let people think what they want. And they're thinking it, believe me. Meanwhile, it sure helps you get to know all my friends, dangerous criminals that they are."

"I do my job thoroughly."

She thought he spoke with a hint of relish, and she got a different impression than what he might have meant. Or was she was reading him right . . . "Or maybe you came prepared to use the hot springs."

He glanced at the pool, heat steaming off it. "I actually hadn't thought of it."

She stood up. "I did. I have my suit on. Do you mind?"

Without missing a beat, he said, "Not at all."

That surprised her, intrigued her, but she tried not to think too much about it as she pulled her shirt off over her head.

She saw him inhale swiftly at the sight of her white bikini top, which she thought made her skin look incredible. His expression stayed impassive, but he didn't look away. She slid off her cropped pants to reveal the little string-bikini bottom.

"Want to join me in the water?" she asked.

"I can't, but thanks."

"Right, you're working." She stepped down in near the edge, then waded up to her waist and found one of the rock ledges built to sit on. She let her arms rest wide along the rim of the rock wall and hoped he was checking her out from behind those sunglasses. She wanted to chastise herself—it's not as if a flirtation could go anywhere, but . . . she was having fun.

He started moving toward her, and she found her breath trapped in her lungs with anticipation. She couldn't read his expression as he walked slowly around the spring to the far side, forcing her to tilt her head back to follow him, but he never looked away. Then he walked back again. Her body was strung so tight, it was like foreplay, and he hadn't even touched her.

He moved back toward her again, like a jungle cat, all pretty on the outside but powerful and dangerous on the inside. He stopped right behind her; she tilted her head back and squinted up at him.

He pulled his sunglasses off, and she was startled yet again by the sharp blue of his eyes. Slowly, purposefully, he bent down, put his hands on her face, and kissed her, an erotic, upside-down kiss. His lips moved over hers possessively, parted but not wide, framing hers, capturing them one at a time, his nose brushing her chin. She moaned when he tilted his head and kissed her more deeply, his tongue meeting hers like a conquering hero. She found herself straining upward toward him, desperate for this to go on and on, starving for the taste of him, wishing she could touch him—

And then suddenly he was no longer touching her. He straightened up and ran a hand through his perfect hair while she turned on the ledge to get a better look at him.

"I hope you're not angry about this," she said.

"Not at you. But it was a mistake. I should go before I do something else." He started to turn away, then paused, saying over his shoulder, "Go ahead and dry off. I'll wait for you."

"So you can escort me home?" she asked, amused. "Don't worry about me. You're obviously on the clock at this photo shoot. Sorry to distract you."

He hesitated, then said in a wry voice, "I don't think you're all that sorry."

She chuckled. "I can't be sorry for that kiss. It was pretty hot."

He shook his head as he turned away and strode down the path, disappearing behind trees as he followed it along the curving stream.

She sank lower in the spring and grinned like it was Christmas Day.

Chapter Nine

Travis barely remembered driving the few blocks back to the hotel, that's how much Monica's kiss had affected him. If he'd let himself, he could have been feeling up a sexy woman in a mountain hot spring, where anybody could find them. How long had it been since he'd had a date?

Too long.

God, he couldn't even remember. Sometimes he had to work for weeks at a time without even a day off, and that didn't sit well with most women. His ex-wife, who was also an agent, did understand that—and it *still* hadn't helped their marriage survive.

He couldn't blame himself for seeing Monica in that white bikini and losing it. But even when she'd been fully clothed, it had taken everything in him to resist the lure of her. He could have lost it in front of all her friends—and her brother—that's how close he'd come to his control evaporating.

Lately, he'd been nothing but the job, the job that had given his life purpose for so many years. He knew he was doing important work, and it satisfied his need to help, to be involved. But the job also made him serious and paranoid and exhausted. And suddenly it seemed . . . a hollow, lonely way to live.

Monica got a call from Brooke just before lunch Wednesday.

"Come on over to Leather and Lace," Brooke said. "I've got some of my mom's chicken to share—and something to confront you about."

"What are you talking about?" Monica demanded with amusement.

"You'll see."

"I can't just drop everything. I'm in the middle of—"

The phone was already dead.

Mrs. Wilcox, white hair in a bun at the back of her head, glasses sliding down her nose, gave Monica a look. "No problem, I've got this covered. You should get away from here for a while. I don't think you've ever made so many phone calls in one day."

Monica reached under the counter for her purse and gave the old woman's shoulder a squeeze. "Thanks. I'm placing a lot of big orders for this wedding, and our usual wholesalers are having trouble getting enough of the more exotic flowers Ashley wants. But I always make it work. And I'll keep my cell handy—just call if you get busy. I'll only be at Leather and Lace."

"Lately, you're so focused on this wedding, I'm at this counter more often than not."

"Good thing Karista comes in after school to help. I'd really feel guilty."

Mrs. Wilcox smiled. "You go on. You work too hard anyway."

Monica waved a hand, then headed through the workroom toward the alley to walk the block to Whitney's store. Leather and Lace showcased upscale lingerie in a beautiful old Victorian. Whitney had kept the gorgeous woodwork and carved banister, even as she'd opened up the floor plan and used antique dressers to display her clothing. Brooke found the girls on the back terrace, surrounded by a landscaped garden that invited customers to think of peaceful tranquillity even when they just glimpsed it through the French doors.

Whitney was relaxing on a lounge, and Monica looked her over. "Swollen ankles again?"

Whitney wrinkled her nose. "The doctor says I might have to cut back my hours to rest more. This is such a pain. Good thing there's a wonderful outcome."

"And good thing you have assistants—and good thing I do, too, because I left Mrs. Wilcox alone during the lunch rush because Brooke insisted."

Monica turned to find Brooke and Emily seated at the glass-top patio table, spreading out a feast of fried chicken and salad. Monica's stomach growled audibly.

"See, I knew you needed lunch," Brooke said. "Thought you might need to see this, too." She pushed a folded copy of the *Valentine Gazette* toward the end of the table.

The giant headline stood out: "PRESIDENT TORRES TO VISIT VALENTINE VALLEY."

"Well, we knew it would come out," Monica said. "Now the rest of the town knows."

She exchanged a glance with Emily, who said, "Look beneath the fold."

Frowning, Monica unfolded the paper and saw a photograph of the front of the Hotel Colorado, a group of sunglasses-wearing men standing together, Travis at the center. They were trying to look casual but only succeeded in looking like soldiers ill at ease in civilian clothes.

"Secret Service. And you knew," Brooke accused with fake disappointment. She gave Emily a mock frown. "And I think you knew, too."

Monica grinned. "Yeah, we knew. He didn't want anyone else to know, only vendors to be used in the wedding."

"I can finally tell Heather, too," Emily said with relief.

"President Torres wanted to keep it secret for as long as possible, so that's why no one could know." Monica gestured at the paper. "This'll make Travis's job harder."

"Oh, we're name-dropping the president now?" Brooke asked.

Monica laughed and would have sat down, but Whitney raised an imploring hand.

"I can't get out of this damn lounge chair," she grumbled.

Monica pulled her to her feet, and, together, they sat beside Brooke and Emily at the table. Chicken and salad were piled on paper plates, and Whitney was the first to dig in.

After they'd all had a few bites, Brooke said, "The article doesn't have a lot to say, just that the top two floors of the hotel will be taken over for the president, so they're in the process of planning the removal of the last guests now."

"Good thing it's not the height of the summer season," Monica said, then speared more mixed greens and ate them.

"And special agents are interviewing businessmen—businesspeople, whatever we're called now." Whitney blotted her lips with a paper napkin. She sighed. "No one from the government wants to talk lingerie—although Ashley Ludlow did stop by to introduce herself and buy some honeymoon stuff. Did Travis want to interview you?"

"Eventually. I kind of . . . forced our first meeting, remember."

"Because we saw him going store to store," Emily reminded them all.

"But the Secret Service did choose my store to be an observation post when the president arrives—well, not my store, but my apartment."

"You're going to have handsome men in your apartment all hours of the day?" Brooke said, her smile growing. "Travis?"

"Well, he's in charge, so he says it won't be him."

"So he says." Emily pointed at her with a drumstick. "But I saw him when he hung out at my bakery that evening. He was watching you, Monica—and he certainly didn't have to come to a photo shoot on behalf of the president."

"You look embarrassed!" Brooke gaped at Monica. "What happened?"

Monica chewed her chicken slowly, enjoying the mounting eagerness and tension. "Well, I happened to have on my bathing suit underneath . . ."

"That white bikini?" Brooke said. "The man killer?"

Monica laughed. "Yeah, that one. So I stripped off my clothes . . ."

They all leaned forward.

"And got in the hot spring."

"Did he get in, too?" Emily asked breathlessly.

"Nope. He paced around me for a bit—and then he kissed me. Upside down, like the Spider-Man movie."

They collectively "oohed."

"Then what?" Brooke demanded impatiently.

Monica sighed. "Then he said it shouldn't have happened, and he left."

Shoulders sagged.

"Really?" Whitney asked in disappointment.

"I don't mind. It's not like I want to date him, but I am enjoying the challenge of getting him to relax a bit," she added, grinning.

They all began to grin back.

"And was that kiss relaxing?" Brooke asked.

"Not exactly . . . And though I hadn't meant it to happen, it sure was nice. We even went running again today—not that anything else happened, and we didn't talk about the kiss. We were like exercise buddies."

"Exercise buddies?" Whitney echoed, making a

face. "Surely, you can get him to have more fun than that. What are you going to do next?"

"I don't know. I'm taking it as it comes. I'll probably keep running into him. He asks for my help about townspeople. We had a great meal before he met Em the other day, and he actually opened up about his childhood and his career."

"Since you two discussed your pasts," Brooke said, "did you tell Mr. Special Agent about your activism in college?"

Monica winced. "I did not. I don't think that has to come up."

"So you didn't tell him about the widows' current protest?" Emily asked.

"How could I? It would feel like I was betraying my grandma! I can make this work out, I promise. I can keep the widows low-key, and Travis won't be upset."

"I hope so," Brooke said doubtfully.

While they finished up their lunch, Monica still felt they were studying her.

"Okay, what is it?" she finally asked.

"Well . . ." Brooke began, "you do seem like you're having a good time with Travis."

"Okay, I'm a little fascinated by him," Monica admitted. "But the wedding's a week from Saturday. Not sure when the president is arriving—"

"That sounds so cool," Emily interrupted.

"—but I think once the president arrives," Monica continued, "Travis'll be busy, then he'll go back to Washington. I keep telling myself I should just step back now, but . . . I don't want to."

"Then don't," Whitney said, leaning toward her. "If you're having fun, and you're not hurting anyone, then enjoy yourself without looking to the future. Sometimes things turn out the way they're meant to be."

Monica looked at her three closest friends, all of whom had found love when they hadn't been looking. They'd all taken chances, risked their happiness and their hearts. Why couldn't she take a chance—not on love or anything long-term like that, she assured herself. Just . . . fun.

Travis and Royce entered the flower shop, and an old woman behind the counter glanced at them—and then glanced again, eyebrows raised. It had to be that newspaper article. Travis didn't know how the hell they'd been captured unaware by a photographer, but all morning, people had stared, pointed, and whispered—when they weren't approaching outright about the president's visit. He'd had to brusquely remind more than one person that the president had a press secretary to announce her schedule, not the Secret Service.

The white-haired old woman raised a finger as if gesturing for them to wait a moment, then finished ringing up the single rose that a teenage boy had purchased. He was flushed when he ducked past the men and out the door without meeting their eyes.

"That was adorable," the woman said, looking at them over her glasses. "Just when you think teenage boys are clueless, some of them get it right." She studied them. "You two look familiar. Have you been in here before?"

"I have," Travis said, "but I spoke with Monica. Is she here?" He tried to keep his tone flat and impassive rather than ringing with eagerness.

"Oh, *I* know where I've seen you. The newspaper! You're with the Secret Service to prepare for the president's trip here." She put a hand to her chest. "It's so exciting. To think the first female president of the United States is coming here, to Valentine Valley. If anyone will understand and support the romance in our community, it's a woman."

Support? Travis thought skeptically. He wasn't going to ask. "Mrs . . ."

"Mrs. Wilcox," she said, blushing. "Can't believe I didn't introduce myself. And you are . . . ?"

"Special Agent Beaumont," Travis nodded toward his friend, "and Special Agent Ames."

Royce flashed his white smile. "Pleasure to meet you, ma'am."

His deep Southern drawl always made the ladies swoon—except Monica, Travis remembered, feeling a little too satisfied.

"Is Monica available?" Travis asked again.

"Sorry, no, she's out to lunch. Can I help you?"

He frowned. "We'll be using Monica's building as an observation post when the president is in town—"

Mrs. Wilcox gasped. "*Really?* It's so exciting to be part of something so important."

"Agent Ames needs to look over the room where we'll be stationed. Monica says she lives up there.

We've promised not to intrude too much, but if we could just go upstairs . . ."

"Of course! Let me just see your badges—you can't be too careful."

Travis found himself relaxing. At least Monica's employee wasn't going to let just anybody in her boss's apartment.

She handed back their badges and smiled. "Give me a moment to put the BACK IN 5 MINUTES sign in the door." She locked it as well, then bustled past them. "Follow me. The entrance is off the alley."

She led them through what was obviously a workroom, with spools of ribbon lining one wall, a big cooler filled with flowers and greenery on another, and lots of worktables. A door led out into a little hall, with a door opposite to the alley and another entrance to the left.

She sorted through keys, tried one, then another before grinning. "Got it."

After she led the way upstairs, they moved through a long hall with scattered framed photos of family, friends, and scenes of Colorado. There were doors off the hall.

"Bedrooms and a bathroom," Mrs. Wilcox explained, then added in a teasing, singsong voice, "and none of your business."

There was a galley kitchen, then one room that encompassed both a dining area and the living room.

"This is good," Royce said. "Room for a couple of us to move around in."

Travis let Royce look out the window, while he studied the room where Monica lived. There were deep, upholstered chairs beneath the big picture window, and a love seat perpendicular against the wall. A huge potted plant of some kind rose almost to the ceiling in that corner. The opposite wall had floor-to-ceiling shelves filled with books and knickknacks, lots of potted plants, and little woven square baskets that must hide stuff while still looking neat. It seemed like a girl thing to do, and Monica was definitely a girl. There were books scattered on a coffee table, magazines, some papers, but overall, she kept a neat place.

"I hope you don't need to be here much longer," Mrs. Wilcox said, glancing down at the sidewalk through the window and frowning. "If a customer comes, I don't want to keep them waiting."

"Hello?" Monica called from the stairwell, uncertainty in her voice.

He was surprised at the little jolt of desire just the sound of her voice gave him. He remembered her low moan, too, when he'd kissed her. That kiss had continued to haunt him, and more and more he couldn't regret it. When they'd gone running that morning, he'd tried not to look at her because, otherwise, he'd have dragged her behind a tree.

"We're up here, Monica!" Mrs. Wilcox called.

Monica appeared at the back of the hallway. "We?" And then she did a little stutter step as she saw them.

His heart did its own little stutter in his chest as he tried to shove down his intense, physical reaction to her. He'd heard of desire clouding a man's thinking, but he'd never believed it. He did now.

Her expression smoothed into pleasant lines, but Travis thought perhaps he should have waited until she could escort him into her apartment. She'd given permission, so he hadn't thought she'd need to give it again.

"Hi," she said as she entered the living room.

She was wearing cropped white pants and sandals, along with a sleeveless blue top that showed off her supple arms. Though he tried not to think about it, the image of her breasts in that white bikini flashed through his mind. Royce was no better. Travis almost felt like elbowing him since he seemed to be staring a little too worshipfully, the afternoon sunlight glinting off his bald head.

"Monica," Mrs. Wilcox began tentatively, "I hope you don't mind that I showed these gentlemen up. They had badges and said you'd given permission to use your living room?"

"I did. Don't worry about it. Why don't you go back downstairs and open up? Thanks."

Mrs. Wilcox gave the two men another grin, then hurried to the staircase.

"This room will be perfect, Monica," Royce said. "Come on over to the window and let me show you the sight lines."

Travis stood for several minutes and watched as Royce explained the observation post, the rifles, the binoculars, the cameras. She listened patiently until at last Royce seemed to run out of things to say.

"Thanks, Royce, you can take off," Travis said. "I have a few more things to talk to Monica about."

Royce gave her a regretful smile. "I've been at Tony's a couple times but haven't seen you there."

"Yeah, I've been pretty busy lately, what with the big wedding."

"Of course. I'll look forward to seein' all your flowers."

As he walked between Travis and Monica, Royce shot Travis a semiserious frown. Travis knew he was going to have to listen to another evening of how "fine" Monica was.

When he was gone, Monica's pleasant expression remained but with none of the warmth and sparkle he associated with her.

"I wish you'd have waited for me, Travis. This feels like an invasion of my privacy."

"I'm sorry. You'd given permission, and I assumed that included a walk-thru."

She nodded, looking around warily.

"Worried we stole something?" he asked with faint amusement.

"Worried about what personal things I might have left out."

"We didn't enter your bedrooms, and we didn't touch anything, either."

She eyed him, but there was more warmth now, and that made his pulse pick up speed. He could think of something he wanted to touch. And suddenly that kiss was between them as if it had just happened. It took everything in him not to look at her mouth, not to step closer and take what he wanted—what she wanted.

"So glad you're conscientious in your duty, Special Agent Beaumont."

He nodded, relieved she'd spoken lightly, hoping that would break the spell between them.

She set down her purse and held up a newspaper. "Did you see this?"

He didn't need to take it. "Yes, and I'm now regularly stopped on the street, and the mayor is bugging me to schedule an event with the president, so she can give her a key to the town." He arched an eyebrow. "And what about you? Were your friends upset you didn't tell them the truth about me?"

She shook her head. "They were rather fascinated, the girls, anyway. Haven't talked to any guys this morning. And I . . . already told my mom about the Secret Service infiltration. Hope you don't mind."

"That would be a superhuman feat, to keep it from your mom."

Her dark eyes were alight with humor and relief. "Could you have kept it from *your* mom?"

He hesitated. "It would have been very difficult."

"Men and their mothers." She rolled her eyes, then gave him an adorably lopsided grin. "Can I get you a drink? Water, coffee?"

"No, thanks."

She went into the kitchen, and as she poured a glass of water, called through the pass-through in the wall, "Although I am glad to hear that you're close to your mom. It must have been hard on her when you and your sister went into the Marines."

"She thought it was inevitable, as far as I was concerned. But Kelly's enlistment? I think it was a shock for both my parents although my dad was immediately proud of her. We were raised hearing that our ancestors fought in every war back to the American Revolution."

"Wow. Your dad, too?"

"No, my dad didn't qualify for medical reasons. And it was hard on him. Especially since *his* dad loved to recount tales of Korea."

"My brother tried to join and was denied, too."

She walked back into the living room with a tall glass of ice water. "For him, it was asthma. And he's such a patriot, too. I felt bad for him. Hope your dad didn't push you too hard because he couldn't join up."

"He didn't." It was what he'd wanted for himself. "So . . . did you mention anything else to your mother about me?"

She gave him a slow, sexy smile. "Did I tell her you'd kissed the heck out of me? No. But she'd heard about you, of course, since you'd showed up at the hot springs and ignited gossip."

Her voice was a little deeper, a little throatier, and if he wasn't mindful of his thoughts, he'd soon have to adjust himself. They stared at each other, on the precipice of making a move they couldn't take back.

"Regardless of what I wanted, I shouldn't have kissed you. But that bikini—" That came out too much like a growl.

Her grin smoldered with delight. "I'm so glad you approve."

He cleared his throat. "Monica, I don't know what you expect of me, but—"

"I don't expect anything," she interrupted, her expression turning serious. "I'm just enjoying the ride.

But if you don't mind my saying, I think you work a little too hard and could loosen up a bit. If you want to see more than Tony's Tavern some evening, give me a call. Maybe I'll be able to help you get to know our fair town."

"That's a nice offer—I think."

"You think?" she said, arching an eyebrow.

"Well, it's not every day a woman I've just met tries to dissect me."

"I do sound awfully presumptuous," she said with mock seriousness. "I hope I'm not offending you."

He resisted the urge to smile. "Maybe we can call it even since I might have presumed when I entered your apartment without permission."

" 'Might have'?"

"Okay, okay, I presumed. Even?"

"Even."

"Then I'll let you get back to work."

"Have fun with Valentine Valley, now that your secret identity is revealed."

She was smiling up at him as he walked past, and she looked so beautiful that he had to forcibly restrain himself from taking her in his arms and kissing her.

Chapter Ten

That night at the Widows' Boardinghouse, Monica was met by the very eager and expectant faces of the widows and the other Double Ds. She answered questions about the Secret Service and how they were going to use her apartment for an observation post.

"Well, I can't believe he came to the hot springs yesterday just for business," Mrs. Ludlow said briskly. "He's interested in our Monica."

Monica put up both hands. "Let's not go there, ladies. He'll only be here another ten days or so."

"So?" Mrs. Palmer shot back. "If you like each other, things might change."

"Enough of that. I don't want a *second* daughter moving to D.C.," Janet insisted in a huff.

Monica hadn't even thought of that—couldn't imagine chasing a man across the country and leaving behind the business she cherished—the family she loved. Missy lived in D.C., and had once been very depressed that Monica hadn't moved to be with her. But even her twin sister hadn't been able to persuade her to move away from Valentine. She'd loved her mountain home too much.

They got down to business, discussing the calendar, then the Mammoth Party, assigning people to booths, splitting up lists of supplies, and figuring out what still had to be made. Monica concentrated as best she was able, trying not to dwell on Travis. She was at war with herself, mostly thinking that this protest was none of his business, that everyone had the right to speak freely. And the other part of her thought he would consider this a "disruption" of his Friday schedule. They'd do it well before the wedding rehearsal, she told herself. But she still felt uneasy.

When she and her mom got back in the minivan, Janet said, "Oh, I forgot to tell you! Missy pulled some strings and is flying out here to help cover the wedding for CNN!"

"That's great!" Monica loved her sister and was always so happy to spend time with her, especially since they had reconnected two years before. Everything was just like it used to be.

"I met Travis today," Janet said in a pleased voice.

That captured Monica's attention, and she glanced at her mom curiously before returning her focus to the road.

"I must say—he's gorgeous."

Monica laughed. "Mom! But yeah, he is. How did you meet him?"

"He had a meeting with Doc Ericson about the medical needs for a presidential visit. Although the president travels with a doctor, they need to know routes to the nearest clinic and hospital."

"You're pretty well-informed," Monica said with a smile.

"Travis told me. Not that I got to be in on the meeting, of course, but we chatted. He recognized me right away, said you and I looked alike."

"What a flatterer."

"You *should* be flattered to look like me."

They exchanged a glance and started laughing.

"Oh, I'm flattered, Mom."

"Good," Janet said, although her voice still shook with amusement. After a moment, she turned serious. "Monica, does he know about the protest?"

She sighed. "No, I haven't said a thing, and I feel a little uneasy about it."

"About participating?"

"No . . . yes. I think it's a worthwhile protest, don't get me wrong. But . . . Travis has talked a lot about his mission here, smoothing the way for the president, planning everything down to the last detail. He even asked me to let him know if anything comes up to disrupt his weekend."

"Ooh," Janet said with sympathy.

They pulled up in front of her parents' house. "Yeah, that's what I mean. I really believe we can pull this off with little bother to anyone—except for closing down Main Street for a few hours. And the Renaissance Spa needs to know we aren't just a few crazies. I plan to do everything in my power to keep the widows in check."

"Not an easy thing to do. But Travis won't like it."

"No, I don't think so, but I can't worry about that. My position is clear, but . . ." She trailed off on a sigh.

"But you feel guilty."

"I do, like I'm keeping a bad secret. Do you think I'm doing the right thing, Mom?"

"I can't tell you what to do, baby girl, but I appreciate the position you're in. I think you'll make the right call."

"I can't tell him—he might try to get the whole thing canceled. I would feel like I betrayed the widows, betrayed what I believed in."

"So you've already made up your mind to keep quiet."

"I hope he doesn't hold it against me."

"Sounds like you care," Janet said softly.

Monica felt her mother studying her. "Why should I care that much when we've only had one dinner together and various run-ins?"

"I don't know, you tell me."

Monica tightened her jaw. "I'm socially conscious—I always have been. The government isn't always right, and sometimes people can only make changes by speaking up."

"There's my girl!"

They exchanged grins.

The next morning, Travis was sitting in front of a computer in the room he was using as the command center. Behind him, Royce was talking to a couple other agents about how enjoyable the OP would be with Monica nearby. Travis was trying not to listen, telling himself it didn't really matter that Royce thought Monica was "hot"—to use his words.

It was like Travis couldn't escape her, especially since his own thoughts kept wandering in her direction. More than once, he glanced out the window and thought he saw her in the shop, just a flash of her as she showed something on a display table to a customer. He thought she'd be able to sell oil to an Arab.

Would he see her today?

Oh, this obsession was getting out of hand.

He checked his e-mail and was glad for something to distract him. It was the background checks he'd ordered on the widows. Pretty soon he was wishing they hadn't been necessary. Seemed like the grandmother of the bride had a criminal record for trespassing at a nuclear power plant during a protest. He might have tried to excuse her if she'd been young and immature, but she'd been sixty. Apparently, the widows were more serious protesters than he thought.

He was debating on how to figure out if a large-scale protest was in the planning stages when an agent from the Forensic Services Division called him about a photo match from a past demonstration against a president, this one in Denver. The name popped up, and they'd done facial recognition to confirm: Monica Shaw.

Demonstrating against a president? She'd just convinced him that she'd been following her passion for flowers. Apparently, she had a passion for violent demonstrations, too. He felt a clenching in his gut at the thought of her in danger. He clicked on the photo and stared in disbelief. She was much younger, probably college-age, but it was Monica all right. Her fist was raised as she shouted something, her expression fierce and determined—while behind her burned the American flag.

Travis wanted to wince, but he kept his expression impassive. No point alerting Royce. He wanted to look into these new facts all by himself. He was bothered that she hadn't told him about it, especially when she knew he was doing background checks. But, of course, it hadn't come up there because she hadn't been arrested. He might think she was just trying to forget about her past—if it wasn't for his nagging suspicion that the widows weren't about to let slide this perfect opportunity to get the archaeology dig more recognition and support. And Monica was close to the widows. He had to find out what was going on and prevent them from getting into serious trouble.

On his way out, he ran into a woman with short, silver-white hair, wearing a business suit and a determined expression.

"Special Agent Beaumont?" she asked.

"Yes?"

"I'm Mayor Galimi."

He withheld a sigh as they shook hands. "Good morning, Your Honor. What can I do for you?"

"I've been told you're in charge around here, Agent Beaumont. I'd like to make an appointment to see the president when she arrives, to welcome her and offer a ceremonial key to Valentine Valley."

"That's gracious of you, ma'am, but the president's schedule will be extremely tight because of wedding festivities. Frankly, I don't even have the full schedule yet. And this is not a public visit."

"We both know the president is in the public eye, Agent Beaumont. We both know she will be shutting down major streets for her motorcade and inconveniencing many citizens, as well as taking up the valuable time of public servants. We are all glad to accommodate her. I believe she'd probably like to thank us personally."

Travis couldn't help admiring the mayor's no-nonsense firmness. "I promise I will give the president's staff your request and urge them to do what they can, Your Honor."

"Thank you."

And then she gave him a smile and a wink and started walking down the hall. Travis waited until she got on the elevator, then he took the stairs down himself. After walking through the ornate lobby, he headed across Main Street to Monica's Flowers and Gifts.

When he ducked inside, she was already busy with several customers. Mrs. Wilcox manned the cash register, while Monica moved among the display tables, discussing the various crafts with two middle-aged Asian tourists with expensive cameras around their necks. She wore a green sundress with a little white short-sleeve sweater.

Travis hadn't exactly paid attention to what she sold besides flowers—he'd been far too interested in looking at Monica. But now he scanned the one side of the flower shop, full of potted plants, terrariums, and little gift baskets. On the other side, various crafts were displayed on tables and boxes and shelves, pottery pieces, knitting, quilting and a few leather goods—from Josh? He didn't want to get too close to check them out because he didn't want to disturb her.

And then he noticed a little wrought-iron table and two chairs, an apple cobbler on display, and a sign that read, PLEASE HELP YOURSELF. He sat down and took advantage of a midmorning snack. Emily Thalberg could certainly bake. He was so busy enjoying the cobbler that he didn't even notice that the tourists had left until Monica sat down across from him.

"Please cut me a slice, Special Agent."

He did, and she dug in, then closed her eyes and moaned. His groin tightened, and he took a deep breath.

"I could so easily get fat on this stuff," she said reverently. "Thank God I run. I didn't see you out there this morning, Travis. Are you avoiding me?"

"No, but I'm curious that you haven't been ignoring me from the moment you suspected who I am."

She blinked at him. "What? Why would I ignore you?"

He lowered his voice, leaned toward her, and spoke with concern. "You had to figure your protesting days would come up eventually."

She stiffened, then sighed and took another bite before speaking. "Yeah, I guess I'm not surprised. I assume you saw the photo?"

"I did."

"For what it's worth, I didn't even know the flag was

being burned behind me. I just somehow became the face of radical environmentalism for a year or two."

"We always take our own photos at protests against the president. We use facial-recognition software to see if the same people are showing up from event to event."

"Well, you can't accuse me of that."

"You're here, aren't you?" he said wryly, spreading his hands.

She snorted. "I live here! And the criminal trespassing was supposed to be wiped off my record."

"Criminal trespassing?" he echoed, unable to hide a worried frown.

She winced. "Oops, it *was* wiped off my record, I guess."

"If this was in your past, I assume you ceased because you regretted what you'd done?"

"Nope."

She enjoyed another forkful of cobbler. He could swear she was making that enraptured face to distract him.

"People need to stand up for the environment," she continued earnestly. "I had more time then, of course, but I haven't changed my beliefs."

"So you don't regret your actions then—or what you're doing now?" Was she truly that unconcerned for her own safety or playing that for his benefit?

"What I'm doing now?" she repeated, her expression innocent. "I don't know what you're talking about, Special Agent Beaumont."

He stared at her hard, but she didn't break. She was going to deny it, he realized. And she wasn't even sorry about anything, which was hard for him to grasp.

Even if she hadn't known about the flag-burning at the Denver protest, she hadn't left when things got ugly, when she could have been hurt.

He knew he was frowning, saw the way Mrs. Wilcox kept glancing at him from behind the counter with worry in her eyes. Even a couple customers still browsing looked their way with interest.

"You know the irony of all this?" Monica continued, pointing her fork at him. "Guess who first got me involved with activism in college—Ashley Ludlow."

He didn't bother revealing that Ashley had alerted him to a possible protest from her own friends. "The widows have obviously been protesting long before we were born. Mrs. Ludlow—grandmother of the bride—has a criminal record."

Her eyes went wide. "Really? I didn't know that! It must have happened after she retired from teaching because, otherwise, that would have affected her job." She tilted her head, curls bouncing against her neck, and studied him. "So this is how you prepare for the worst? Threaten the rights of grandmas?"

"You know there's more involved than that," he said with sincerity. "Whatever you're up to—do you care if there's fallout to your business, to your livelihood? What if your customers decide you're wrong to protest against the president?"

"I would never protest against the president," she said with conviction. "Travis, you're making a big deal of this for nothing."

"If it's no big deal, then you won't care if I interview the people who might be involved."

"Go ahead and do your job." She hesitated, pushing aside her empty plate. "So tell me—does my past fame mean you can't be seen with me anymore?"

When she lifted her chin, a stubborn gesture, suddenly he knew if they'd been alone, he'd have kissed her, kissed away that defiance and shown how much he cared about her. She must have sensed his thoughts, because she licked her lips in a slow dance until they glistened. She could have punched him in the gut, that's how powerful he felt the impact of her sensuality.

He tried to gather his thoughts. "I'm going to figure out what you're hiding, Monica, and I'll put a stop to it."

"I don't know what you're talking about." She gave him a slow, naughty smile.

They might have sat there a long time getting lost in each other's eyes, making fools of themselves, but the door opened again, and the bell jingled noisily.

Monica startled, as if awakening from a dream. His blue eyes were captivating, so powerful and direct and demanding. She wished she could run her hands through his short auburn hair, more red than brown when the sun caught it just right. He wanted answers, but he wanted her, too, and it was obviously getting harder and harder for him to hide it. She was flattered and aroused all at the same time.

But she was also straddling a line between him and the widows. She had to admit—she was enjoying herself, even if all her past mistakes had to be laid out in front of him.

"Monica?"

Her brother, Dom, walked toward them, holding out his hand, wearing a broad smile. She and Travis stood up.

"We weren't officially introduced, Agent Beaumont," Dom said, shaking Travis's hand, a light of interest in his eyes. "I'm Monica's brother, Dom."

Monica wanted to roll her eyes. Her brother, Mr. USA, was going to enjoy knowing a member of the government.

"Good to meet you, Dom. I'm Travis."

"How was I supposed to introduce each person at the hot springs?" Monica asked. "It would have been overwhelming for poor Travis."

Dom glanced down at the two empty plates on the table, then looked between them with not quite a frown. "Did I interrupt a meeting?"

"Only some routine questions," Travis said.

Monica held back a smile. There'd been no questions when they'd been staring at each other.

"My mom tells me you're going to use Monica's apartment for an observation post," Dom said.

Travis glanced at Monica. "I would appreciate if that didn't get much further."

"I'll make sure my friends don't tell," she said lightly.

"Well, if you need anything else," Dom continued, "I'd be happy to help. Although seeing my little sis cooperating with the government sure is strange."

Monica narrowed her eyes at her brother, biting her tongue to hold back the anger even as he elbowed her to emphasize his little "joke." She had nothing against the government, just some of its policies—and Dom knew that. But he'd let that flag-burning photo start a schism between them, drawing other petty grievances into its wake over the years. He seemed to see everything she did through the prism of her supposed rebellion. She could have told him a long time ago that it was Missy, not her, but she didn't want him turning his renewed disappointment on their sister when she arrived. With Travis determined to investigate everything, Missy might crack under the strain of what she thought of as a cowardly lie on her part. Monica didn't see it that way.

Travis was watching her face with a little too much focus, and she tried to keep her expression neutral.

"I'm not sure anyone can help," Travis said. "I'm getting some pressure from the mayor—you wouldn't know her personally?" he asked Dom.

"Sure I know her. Her brother's diner is one of my clients."

"The True Grits Diner?"

"Yep."

"I've eaten there several times. Very good. So he's related to the mayor . . ."

"The mayor's cool," Monica said, "but not so much her brother. He protested against Whitney's Leather and Lace before it opened, claiming it was pornography."

"This town likes its protests," Travis said dryly, "if it gets upset about lingerie."

Dom shot Monica a quick frown, then turned back to Travis. "A bunch of the guys are meeting at Tony's Tavern tomorrow night for a poker game. We call it Robbers' Roost, just having fun. You're welcome to join us."

To Monica's surprise, Travis hesitated, as if he was actually considering it—considering how he could use it to his advantage as far as his job was concerned. She wasn't sure she'd ever met a more focused man.

"I might have to work," he finally said, "but I appreciate the invitation." Then he looked back at Monica. "Thanks for answering my questions. I'm sure we'll talk again."

"Sure." She gave him a friendly smile as he walked out of the shop, then rounded on her brother. "Really! Really, Dom? You had to make it sound like I'm some kind of wacko who hates the government? Dom!"

"I was kidding!" he insisted, spreading his hands.

Mrs. Wilcox, dealing with a customer, frowned at them both.

Monica lowered her voice, leaned in to her brother, and spoke firmly. "Maybe you think you were kidding, but I think you're kidding yourself. You were trying to piss me off. Get. Over. It."

She brushed past him and went into her workroom, where it was time she stopped mooning over Travis Beaumont and concentrated on the most important wedding of her career.

Chapter Eleven

A couple hours later, Monica was looking at her spreadsheets, tracking her flower orders, when Emily came into the workroom.

Monica smiled. "Hey, Em!"

Emily smiled distractedly, then pointed a thumb over her shoulder. "Have you been outside?"

Monica blinked at her in confusion. "Uh . . . I went for my run this morning. And you?"

"Yes, I ran," she said almost impatiently, "but I mean, have you looked outside on *Main Street*?"

Monica got to her feet and followed Emily back through the showroom. To her surprise, Mrs. Wilcox had a box open on the counter, red, white, and blue bunting dangling out of it.

"Mrs. Wilcox, what's going on? Those are our Fourth of July decorations."

"That's what I'm talking about," Emily insisted. "All the stores are putting up theirs."

Mrs. Wilcox blushed. "Well, our president *is* coming

next week, Monica. I was going to run my ideas by you first, of course."

Monica waved her concern aside. "I didn't doubt it."

Emily grabbed her elbow and tugged her to the door. "Come on!"

Monica went outside, where the day was overcast, with a chilly breeze more reminiscent of late winter then late spring. She hugged herself—and stared.

Up and down Main Street, people had their ladders outside, attaching red, white, and blue decorations from bunting to flags. On the door of Sugar and Spice, Mrs. Thalberg was hanging up a wreath made of tiny US flags. Someone was walking from door to door, putting pinwheels in all the planters. At the Hotel Colorado, a worker was putting red, white, and blue stars in each window on the ground floor. Those who hadn't finished their flower-planting were doing it now, and windows were being washed until they gleamed.

"Wow," Monica said, bemused.

"I know! But since the news of the president's arrival broke this morning, this town has gone crazy. You can't believe the orders I'm getting from regular customers whose relatives all decided to visit to catch a glimpse of President Torres or the wedding party. And this is on top of the wedding cakes I'm already baking!"

Emily looked a little wild-eyed, and Monica gripped her upper arms.

"Okay, let's calm down," Monica said in a genial voice. "You can only do what you can do. You've been training your sister to bake, right?"

Emily nodded, breathing in and out deeply.

"Then you can concentrate on the wedding stuff, and Steph can do the smaller, easier orders."

Another deep breath. "Yes, yes, you're right. I just had . . . a moment. Thanks for talking me down. Are you getting hit?"

"Just by the wedding, and regular orders. Although did I tell you I have another wedding that day?"

Emily gasped.

"It's okay, it's okay, I give you permission to breathe. I'll probably end up calling in some seasonal employees to help, especially making bows and doing deliveries. We'll all be fine."

"You're so confident and calm—and you have a man to deal with at the same time."

"Maybe that's why I seem calm because flowers are easy compared to him."

They shared an understanding look.

"Excuse me, are you Monica Shaw?"

She turned around to find a woman walking between parked cars and coming up on the sidewalk.

"That's me. You look familiar."

The woman smiled. "We've seen each other in the grocery store or the diner, but I was a few years behind you in school. We've just never had an opportunity to meet. Strange, huh, in our small town?"

The woman, dressed business casual, looked to be in her midtwenties, with long blond hair that curled in waves down past her shoulders. With a pang, Monica realized she could no longer identify herself in the same way, as "in her twenties."

She was being ridiculous.

The woman put out a hand. "I'm Jessica Fitzjames, a reporter with the *Valentine Gazette*." After shaking hands, she turned to Emily expectantly.

Emily smiled and shook hands, too. "Hi, I'm Emily Thalberg."

"Oh, you own Sugar and Spice," Jessica said. "You've done a great job."

Emily grinned. "I thought you looked familiar."

"I'm a regular—way too often," she said, patting her tummy. Her expression turned more serious though still friendly. "You two must have seen the article in our paper this morning."

Nodding, Monica began to feel a little wary.

"I understand you both will be involved in Ashley Ludlow's wedding."

"It's not like we're in the wedding," Monica pointed out. "But yes, we've been hired." It couldn't hurt to get *that* in the paper.

"It must feel pretty incredible, being involved in the biggest wedding to ever hit town."

"We're thrilled," Emily admitted.

"Any details you can share with the rest of us?"

"You've gotta know we've been sworn to secrecy," Monica said with amusement.

Jessica sighed. "I had to try." She studied Monica. "But I have seen the Secret Service guys, and I hear you've been seen in Special Agent Beaumont's company."

Monica shrugged. "You know the Secret Service prepares for the president's arrival. I'm not the only one to be scrutinized. They have to be careful."

"They're going to watch me bake," Emily said, then

glanced wide-eyed at Monica, as if saying, *Was I allowed to reveal that?*

"Watch you bake," Jessica mused, nodding. "That's an interesting detail. Guess I'll have to do more research." Again her assessing, but still-friendly, gaze came back to Monica. "Someone spotted you and Agent Beaumont running together one morning."

"We met up accidentally, and he was too polite to leave me in his dust," Monica answered smoothly. She didn't want to be fodder for the gossips, not after she saw the toll it had taken on Josh last year.

A smile played on Jessica's mouth. "Was it accidental at Tony's, too?"

"Is someone following me?" Monica asked, only half-amused.

"No, but you know people love to talk in Valentine Valley. And apparently those Secret Service guys get noticed everywhere they go. Have you met the big bald guy? Pretty hot."

Monica almost spilled Royce's name but held back. "I didn't know they'd be there," she said mildly, "didn't even know they were Secret Service then."

"When *did* you know?"

"Now you know I can't reveal classified information, Jessica," she teased. "And before you ask, it was only a business dinner at the Halftime Sports Bar. You can't believe the hoops I have to jump through because my flowers will be at the same venues as the president of the United States."

Jessica arched a brow. "I hadn't heard about the Halftime Sports Bar."

Monica hid a wince and saw Emily biting her lip with great innocence at her predicament.

"Is that when you talked him into appearing in the 'Men of Valentine Valley' calendar I've heard rumors about?"

Monica gave a choked laugh. "Are you kidding? I can barely get that guy to remove his sunglasses as we talk, let alone his shirt for charity. You must already know that the Sweetheart Inn will be the site of the wedding. He was exploring the grounds and ran into our big party."

"He didn't quite fit in," Emily admitted, spreading her hands.

Jessica sighed. "Well, I appreciate your answers. Hope you don't blame me for doing my job."

"Not a bit," Monica said. "That's all we're doing, too."

"I have to laugh," Jessica continued, shaking her head. "Even Leather and Lace is getting more interest because of a presidential romance. The owner says she's glad the uptick in customers is due to lingerie rather than her baby. Finally, people seem to have found something else to gossip about besides Josh Thalberg's becoming a daddy. His and his wife's celebrity never quite dies down, does it?"

"No, it doesn't," Monica agreed, then happened to catch sight of Emily's wistful expression. She felt a pang of sad sympathy. To the reporter, she said, "Why don't you give me your card in case something occurs to us."

Jessica brightened, reached into a side pocket of her

purse, and pulled one out. "Thanks! Nice to meet you guys."

After she'd walked away, Monica pulled a startled Emily to a seat on the bench beneath the flower shop's display window.

"You okay, Em?" Monica asked.

Emily frowned her confusion. "Okay? I don't mind being interrogated by reporters. I have a lot less to say than you do."

"I . . . I saw your expression when she talked about Josh and Whitney's baby. You okay about it all?"

Emily's first marriage had broken up after several miscarriages, a doctor's diagnosis of infertility, and her ex insisting he had to have a biological child.

Now Emily gave her a tender smile. "I am so happy for Josh and Whitney, and I can't wait to hold my niece. Honestly. But it's sweet of you to be concerned."

"Have you thought about adopting? Well, that's a silly question—your husband was adopted."

Emily laughed. "We've discussed lots of things. But right now we're just enjoying being together. We have all the time in the world."

But when Emily left her soon after to go back to work, Monica found herself frowning with a concern that wouldn't go away so easily.

Late Friday morning, in the command center, Travis got off the phone after his first conversation with Samantha Weichert, the junior presidential staffer who'd been bothering Ashley Ludlow. The clipped, arrogant tone of her voice was enough to annoy him, and he hadn't even met her. No, she did not have the president's schedule, she'd assured him impatiently, and he couldn't rush the president. Travis had a feeling that if President Torres knew that the Secret Service was being inconvenienced, there'd be another outcome. But he'd give Ms. Weichert the chance to fix things herself first.

Royce dropped the *Valentine Gazette* in front of Travis, who was working at his computer.

"You're a celebrity, man," Royce said, grinning. "Been seen all over town interviewin' people—but especially that hot Monica Shaw. Maybe someone's tailin' you."

Travis frowned and scanned the article in the local section of the small paper. It read like a "look what your neighbors are up to" piece and talked about the local businesses being used for the wedding, and how the Secret Service had to investigate everything. It did sound like he was focusing on Monica although it was all pretty harmless.

Travis pushed the paper back at Royce. "No big deal, and in this small town, what else do they have to gossip about?"

Royce grinned and walked away, and as Travis frowned down at the paper, the hotel phone rang.

"Special Agent Beaumont," he said.

"Uh, hello? Are you the agent in charge?"

"I am. May I have your name, and how I can help you?"

"I can't tell you my name, Agent Beaumont," he said with a stubborn edge, his voice making him middle-aged or older. "And I ask you not to try to figure it out. People depend on the postal service for privacy, and I already feel guilty enough calling you to report something. But . . . I couldn't live with myself if something happened, and I'd said nothing."

Travis felt his pulse slow, his senses sharpen. "Then tell me what you know, sir, and we'll discuss your identity later if it's important."

"Okay. See . . . we got the word that with President Torres coming and all, we were to tell our bosses if we noticed anything unusual, if a customer acted suspiciously, you know, stuff like that."

"And we appreciate the care you take with your job, sir," Travis said patiently. "Something came to your notice?"

"It did, and I told my boss, but he told me I was nuts, and that this was nothing. It probably is, but since I didn't grow up in this town, I don't really know everyone all that well, you know?"

"I know." Travis tapped his pen on a pad and waited.

"Today someone received a shipment of three ghillie suits. Do you know what they are, Agent Beaumont?"

Travis straightened, focusing on the phone as if he could see the man on the other end. "I do, sir, but you tell me what you think."

The man sighed. "Well, just so we're on the same page, hunters use ghillie suits to sit in the woods and wait for deer during hunting season, right? You know, the suits make you look like you blend into the background, from your toes to the tip of your head, all covered in string and rags that match the color of the woods. Heck, I know guys who have a ghillie covering for their rifles."

Travis felt a chill. Ghillie suits were used by hunters—but they were also used by military snipers.

"Sir, does the person who ordered these suits hunt?"

"I asked my boss that, and he said he thought so. But I don't know the man, and when my boss said he's a Vietnam vet, I just got . . . suspicious. Why order three ghillie suits in May? He could just be preparing for hunting season while he has some free time before the hay harvest, but, with the president coming and all . . ."

"So he's a rancher?"

"Yes, sir." The man took a deep breath. "His name is Deke Hutcheson. I feel sorta bad telling you, but I'd feel worse if something happened. He owns the Paradise Mountain Ranch. His family's been here forever, so I'm told, and my boss says he's never been in any trouble. I'm probably making a mountain out of a molehill, but still . . . Was I right to call you?"

"You were right. Thank you, sir. I can take it from here."

"You won't say where you got the information?"

"No, and I don't know your name, regardless. But if you'd give it to me, I could contact you with more questions." He could also use the hotel's phone records to trace the call, if necessary. But after watching so much TV, most people knew not to call with their own phone if they didn't want to be found.

"I don't know anything else for you to question. Look, I gotta go. My break is up. Hope this is nothing."

The line went dead. Travis stared at the hotel phone,

then put it back in its cradle. He pulled up his computer file with all the ex-military living in the area. One of them was Adam Desantis, whom he'd met at the calendar photo shoot. Adam was engaged to Monica's best friend, Brooke Thalberg. He probably knew where Adam would be that night—at Tony's Tavern, with Dom Shaw and . . . what had he called their poker group? Robbers' Roost?

Friday night at a tavern might be the easiest way for him to pick Adam's brain about any fellow vets.

And maybe he'd see Monica . . .

Travis and Royce arrived at Tony's Tavern Friday night and headed into the back room. He spotted Dom, Nate, and Adam. Adam had sandy hair not exactly worn like a jarhead anymore. Travis ran a hand through his own short cut and knew he'd stayed much closer. The military image helped with the job.

Dom turned his poker hand down on the table and grinned as he stood up. "Agent Beaumont, glad you could join us."

"Travis is fine. This is Royce Ames."

Royce shook hands all around. He could be a menacing man, but when he wore his big grin, it was hard to take him seriously.

"So you boys must be used to towns 'dressing up' for the president," Adam said, as they all sat back down at the table. His brown eyes were intelligent and shrewd as they studied Travis. "We must all look like a bunch of greenies to you."

Travis smiled at the reference to new Marines. "I noticed all the red, white, and blue," he said. "It happens, usually in the smaller towns." He sort of liked the pride of a small town, didn't even mind the nosiness.

"They don't get much smaller than this," Royce said. "At least not where presidents are concerned."

"Unless it's campaign time," Travis retorted, nodding.

"So do you two walk around with the president?" Dom asked.

"No, we're on different teams," Travis said. "We can't discuss much."

"The *Valentine Gazette* certainly wants you to open up," Nate said. "A reporter interviewed my wife, Emily—she's worried she might have said something to offend you."

"Not at all," Travis said. "The article was pretty harmless."

Adam shot a glance at Dom. "It mentioned Dom's sister quite a bit."

Dom frowned. "I hope she's not bothering you."

"Bothering us?" Royce said before Travis could. "Monica's a fine woman—we're not bothered in the least."

Travis wanted to roll his eyes. "Subtle" was not in Royce's vocabulary. "How would Monica bother us?" Travis asked curiously.

But Dom was either being loyal or embarrassed about his sister's past because he shrugged. "She was interviewed by that reporter, too. She was mentioned more than Emily."

"Probably because I've met with her more," Travis said.

Both Nate and Adam studied him as if they sensed something unspoken, but Dom seemed too caught up in whatever beef he had with his sister.

Adam rose. "We need more drinks, and I don't see Nicole. I'll go order some."

"I'll help," Travis said.

Together, they walked back to the main room and stood side by side at the bar. The owner, Tony, held up a finger that said he'd be a minute. The bar was pretty jammed, and he was the only bartender.

"So are there a lot of ex-Marines in the Secret Service?" Adam asked.

"You know what the deadliest weapon on earth is."

Together they said, "A Marine and his rifle," then both grinned.

They spent a few moments getting acquainted, discussing what platoon they'd each served in, some of the action they'd seen.

"So now you're working on the Silver Creek Ranch?" Travis asked.

"I went from a Marine to a cowboy. Good thing I was used to hard work and long hours," Adam said, shaking his head. "But I like the life, I like being outdoors."

"And the woman who comes with the ranch?"

Adam grinned. "I like her enough to marry her one of these days."

"Do you know a lot of the other vets in the area?"

"I didn't think I'd want to be around other guys as

messed up as I was for a while, but an old Vietnam vet named George McKee talked me into helping remodel houses for disabled vets. He was my high-school football coach, the guy who straightened me out when I was a teenager."

"Have you heard of Deke Hutcheson?" Travis asked.

"Sure. He's another rancher, a friend of Brooke's dad. I've only met him once or twice. Seems like a gruff but good guy."

Adam eyed him but didn't question his curiosity.

"I hope he came out of that war better than some other guys did," Travis said.

"From what I hear, Vietnam changed him to a man who wanted nothing to do with guns and killing things. He doesn't hunt at all, which is rare among some of these old-timers. Kill a coyote hassling his herd? Well, that's different, of course, and I heard his ranch is having problems with them recently."

They were interrupted by a harried Tony, who took their order and retreated back down the bar. Cool mountain air blew past them, and Travis looked up to see a group of people come in the front door, Monica among them. He immediately zeroed in on the skirt she wore, so short that her legs looked mile-high and sexy. Her shirt was sheer and clingy over a spaghetti-strap top underneath. She was accompanied by her usual group of friends, Emily, Brooke, Whitney, and her protective husband, Josh, and some other people Travis had seen in passing. They walked the length of the bar toward the back room, and Monica could have been walking down a runway, the way the high heels made her strut.

They might be small-town girls, but they were confident in their down-home charm and sexiness.

Adam was watching Travis's face, his eyes full of amusement, until Brooke called in a voice meant to be heard, "Hi, Travis! Did you know my fiancé there used to date Monica in high school?"

Monica rolled her eyes and just kept walking, while Adam sent Brooke a grin but didn't follow her.

Then Adam eyed Travis. "I barely got to first base, if you're wondering. But you probably don't care who Monica dated in high school."

"You obviously couldn't keep up with her," Travis said lightly.

"No, I couldn't," Adam agreed, taking a sip of the beer Tony placed in front of them.

Tony saw the group heading into the back room. "Should I order a round for the newcomers?"

"Yeah, we'll wait," Adam said.

Adam glanced through the open door, and Travis thought he was watching Josh help Whitney into a comfortable chair.

"Brooke likes to tease," Adam began slowly, "but we're both starting to feel the pressure of setting a wedding date one of these days. Josh is younger than Brooke, and now he's about to be a dad. Gotta feel strange to her. Brooke says we can wait, that she'd rather focus on the new baby for a while, but I'm not sure I believe her." His expression turned serious. "I never had a decent dad, and after all we saw in Afghanistan, how do I know I'll be good enough at whatever gentleness is required? Do you have kids?"

"No, just an ex-wife. But I had a dad who felt the pressure of his dad and grandpa to join the military, just like all our ancestors did. And then he couldn't join himself because of medical issues. Don't get me wrong, he never tried to persuade me, never made me feel like I let him down by not renewing my enlistment."

"But you're Secret Service," Adam said, disbelief in his voice. "How much more service to your country can you give?"

For some reason, that question made Travis pause, but he didn't know why. He shrugged. "But about being a dad, my own taught me to let my kid make his own choices, just like he gave me the freedom to do. Sometimes I think we learn from our dads what *not* to do, you know? That's what my dad said he learned."

"I did learn that," Adam said ruefully. "I joined up to get a chance to start over, to make something of myself—like my dad never did—but the pain of my buddies' dying was hard for me to take. I spent ten years doing my duty, and then . . . had to start over again. Thank God my grandma Palmer tricked me into returning to Valentine Valley."

"Tricked you?" Travis knew Mrs. Palmer was one of the widows actively involved in the protest. What else had she done?

"It's a long story, and she had good intentions. I didn't think of Valentine as home even though I grew up here. Grandma Palmer is in some ways the only real mom I ever had, and I'd do anything for her."

And probably not be objective either, Travis thought, deciding there was no point in questioning Adam about his grandma. Travis would just have to question the widows about a possible protest himself since Monica wasn't talking.

Travis leaned both forearms on the bar. "Sometimes I think it's harder to watch other people suffer than it is to feel it ourselves. My sister, Kelly, also a Marine, was wounded and almost died. I swear it tore something inside me. Even though I knew I couldn't protect her forever, she'd gone into the Marines because I did."

He heard a sound behind him and saw Monica standing there, watching him with wide, sympathetic eyes.

Chapter Twelve

Monica hadn't meant to eavesdrop. She'd come out to the bar to help the guys carry all the trays since poor Nicole looked swamped. But to hear that Travis's sister had been wounded . . . she could only imagine what that had done to a protective man like Travis.

But a sense of remoteness overtook his expression when he saw her, and she guessed it wasn't something he'd wanted to discuss. So, pretending she hadn't heard, she said brightly, "Can I help with the trays? We're thirsty back there."

Tony slid one across the bar toward her. "Thanks, Monica."

She gave Travis and Adam a saucy grin, then turned to take her tray into the back room, hoping that Travis was watching her walk.

She handed out the beer like a waitressing pro, eluding Will Sweet's teasing attempt to tip her with a kiss for her service. Emily's one brother was a lighthearted tease, and the other, Daniel, tended to be the loner of the group. He was playing pinball in a corner and was grateful for the beer she brought him. She returned for another tray and distributed it while Travis and Adam continued to talk. She knew they had a lot in common, both being Marines. Maybe it would be good for Travis to have someone to talk to.

Emily and Heather were seated with Whitney and the guys at the table, while Brooke came to stand beside Monica.

"What do you think Adam and Travis were talking about?" Brooke asked.

Monica shrugged, not wanting to reveal what she'd heard about something so close to Travis's heart. "They're vets."

Brooke leaned closer so her soft voice could be heard over the music. "You know Adam won't say anything about the protest."

Monica frowned. "How much does he know?"

"Some. Mrs. Palmer *is* his grandma, after all, even though she thinks she's keeping it from him."

"And you're his fiancée."

"Yeah, and I talk in my sleep."

They both laughed.

Brooke's smile faded. "You and Travis are closer now. Are you still going through with this protest on his watch?"

Monica nodded and took a deep breath. "And we need your help. It's going to be strange and inconvenient, but I thought it might appeal to you. Can we borrow your indoor riding arena Thursday and Friday of the wedding weekend? And we'd need twenty-four hours of secrecy."

"Secrecy? You know my dad isn't big on Grandma's past protests."

"I know. But can you change your schedule around to help us out? Maybe reschedule lessons so no one will be snooping around?"

"Well, yeah, of course I'll help. But you need to clue me in."

They were deep in discussion for ten minutes until Brooke's eyes went wide, and she finished in a whisper. "Don't say anything. He's coming this way."

Monica turned to face out and put her elbows back on the long bar-height shelf built into the wall. She really enjoyed the opportunity to watch Travis walk, tall and broad-shouldered, with that perfect posture that came from his years in the Marines. Tonight, he was wearing a tight t-shirt and jeans, and she could have gotten weak in the knees at how sexy casual he looked. All he needed were cowboy boots.

He nodded at Brooke, then said to Monica, "Want to dance?"

She exchanged a surprised look with Brooke before saying, "Sure." She saw Royce shake his head regretfully and turn away. And then she realized the song had turned slow, and she felt a quickening hunger of desire flicker to life deep in her belly. He took one of her hands in his and put his arm around her waist, bringing her close. They'd kissed, yes, but nothing had touched but their lips. The brush of his thighs against hers now made her breath go shallow, and his hard, callused, masculine palm made her feel all dainty, something she definitely wasn't. She let her other hand slide up his arm to his shoulder, and the hard muscles rippled beneath her touch.

He was staring down at her, his expression as sober as always, but there was a light in those blue eyes that made her think that, deep inside, something was on fire.

Did he burn for her? Just the thought was intoxicating. Unable to stop herself, she moved a little closer, let her breasts brush his chest once, and the resultant shiver was so overwhelming, she realized she couldn't do that in public again, certainly not with everyone she knew watching openly.

She smiled up at him instead. "So this is a surprise."

"I've been to Tony's before."

"But you haven't asked me to dance. Although maybe you intend to take a spin with all the women here."

"Probably not. That would defeat the purpose of fake-dating."

"Fake-dating?" She blinked her eyes innocently. "I thought we were letting people believe whatever they wanted, to protect your secret identity. Now we all know who you are, Clark Kent."

She loved the way the corner of his mouth quirked when she made him want to smile. She swore she'd get the real thing out of him eventually.

"But I use you for information," he said. "If we're not fake-dating, people will think you've gone over to the enemy."

"Ah, you're protecting my reputation. I appreciate that."

They moved slowly together, their bodies well matched. It was far too distracting.

"You know, I didn't mean to eavesdrop at the bar," she said at last.

He exhaled slowly. "I know."

She couldn't make herself intrude on something he hadn't confided in her.

"You're curious about my sister?"

She glanced up at him swiftly. "Only if you want to tell me. You didn't mention she'd been wounded when we talked about our families before."

"It's not a secret, just not something that's easy to bring up. You could Google her and find out she was injured when her truck ran over an IED—a roadside bomb."

Monica's stomach clenched. "Oh, Travis, how terrible. She must have been glad you were in the same country to be with her."

"Not close enough to help, though, was I?" he asked with a trace of bitterness. "And they airlifted her to Germany pretty fast. She lost a leg below the knee."

Monica pressed her lips together to keep from gasping in horror. "Oh, Travis," she whispered. She knew his little sister had followed him into the military. She could only hope he didn't somehow blame himself.

"You don't have to look so sad. You can't believe how well she's coping."

The pride in his voice wasn't surprising; the faint smile was.

"She wears a prosthetic, goes for long runs, and she insisted on staying in the Marines although that was difficult to do. There was a lot of resistance. But she proved she could do her job, since most of it's now behind a desk."

"Wow, you have a brave little sister."

"I do."

The song ended, and he stepped back, leaving her with the feeling that he was relieved. Whether it was because he didn't want to talk about his sister any more or didn't want to dance with her, Monica didn't know. Instead, when Dom motioned for him to come play poker, he left her and joined the guys and Brooke, who also enjoyed a good game.

"Pool anyone?" Whitney said from the two chairs she occupied, one for her butt, and the other for her feet.

Monica laughed and sat down beside her.

"Maybe you'll be needing my lingerie soon," Whitney murmured, eyeing Travis.

"Very funny."

But to her surprise, a couple hours and one more dance later, Travis was standing beside her when it was time to head home.

"Well, I have to work tomorrow," she said.

"Me, too."

She eyed him with speculation, then said for his ears only, "I think if we're going to fake-date, you have to offer to give me a ride home, and I'm going to be forced to accept."

"Sounds difficult for you. Sorry to put you in this position."

"Thanks for your understanding."

They said their good-byes, and, as they walked toward the main bar, Monica could feel many pairs of curious eyes on them both.

"Well, that was awkward," she said, when they stepped outside into the cool night air.

"Which part? The dancing I forced you into?"

She smiled. "You're really getting into this, aren't you? No, the part where all my friends wonder what we'll be doing tonight."

His pleasant expression grew shuttered. "I know this is sort of a joke between us, but I don't mean to make your friends think badly of you."

"Oh, they're not thinking badly. Whitney thought I might need lingerie—but then she thinks that about everyone, so don't panic. And, of course, none of them know that the last time you escorted me outside Tony's, I was lucky to have you."

"You didn't tell anyone about the attack?" he asked curiously.

She shrugged. "I didn't want everyone to worry. If I thought the guy was a hard-core menace, I'd have let the police know. But I really do just think he was a drunk idiot. Doesn't mean I don't realize you were the reason he probably sobered up fast."

She wished she could see his face, but once again, the shadows left him a mystery. "So tell me, Agent Beaumont, have you had to do that sort of thing a lot since you joined the Secret Service?"

He leaned his shoulder against the brick wall. "Not a lot, no. And, of course, I can't officially mention any protectee by name."

"I'm not asking for names," she cajoled, "but I'd love to hear some exploits."

She saw the faint gleam of his teeth as he smiled. "Exploits, huh? We train so those exploits don't happen. We have a tactical 'village' of sorts, where we run courses as things actually blow up around us, including simulated gas or chemical attacks. We go over it so many times until we react, not think. But that's not all of our mission—much of it is determining the actual threat to the president, for example, breaking down letters to find the villain's identity. You pretty much can't threaten a president by mail and not be discovered. Even the ink can be traced—we have the world's largest collection of samples, dating back to the turn of the *last* century."

"These are all the things you do to prepare, I get that. But what about on the job?" She softened her voice and touched his chest. "Have you ever been hurt?"

"You know I can't talk specifics," he said, lightly touching her hand where it rested on him.

"I don't think that's totally true—I think you don't *want* to tell me details. I'm a delicate woman who needs to be protected, right?"

He cupped her cheek. "Much as I think you're sexily feminine, Monica, I wouldn't call you delicate or fragile. But . . . I honestly don't believe anyone should know about the rare times things go wrong."

She felt disappointed but not surprised. He obviously didn't brag, but he was also *very* protective. It came with the job. And that meant protecting her—as he'd already shown not too long ago.

And he was loyal, too, dedicated to the agency, dedicated to the people he protected. She admired everything about him.

With a sigh, she said, "Come on, fake boyfriend, drive me the couple blocks home."

When he pulled into the alley behind her flower shop, she hesitated as if she couldn't quite unbuckle the seat belt. The tension of being alone in a dark, enclosed place was thick between them. He sat still for a moment, just breathing, but, to her consternation, he finally got out and came around to open her door.

She slid out of the SUV. "Does this mean you're coming in to examine the apartment again?"

"No, just walking you to the door."

Monica slipped her keys from her purse. She expected Travis to stay close to his getaway car, but when she turned around, he was standing right there, a step down from her, so their eyes were nearly level.

"Fake dates should get kissed, too," he said in a rough voice as he drew her against him. "What do you think?"

They stared at each other from an inch away, both breathing heavily, her breasts pressed against the hard wall of his chest, his hands at her waist.

She lowered her mouth and kissed him. He gathered her hard against him until her toes only brushed the stairs. His mouth slanted over hers, and she opened to him, to the taste of beer and man, and the exquisite excitement of his desire for her.

And pressed so hard against him, she couldn't miss the obvious signs of his erection against her stomach.

Their tongues joined the play, and she slid her fingers into his short hair and along his warm scalp, holding him against her. His hands slid down to cup her ass, to knead and press her even tighter. Her toes lost their purchase on the top stair, and he held her against his body as she gradually slid to the ground. God, it was incredible to feel him, the heat of him, the hardness. She wanted to wrap her legs around his body and hold on tight.

Instead, he lifted his head and stared down at her, taking several deep breaths as if to calm himself down. She let her hands slide down his shoulders to his chest, where she could feel his racing heart.

As he stared into her eyes, the corner of his lip quirked, and this time she let her fingers touch it. He turned his head and captured her finger gently between his teeth. She shuddered in helpless arousal.

He released her finger, as well as the grip on her waist. "Good night, Monica."

She hugged herself around the waist and watched him climb back in the SUV and drive away.

Damn, but she liked kissing him. She was trying to understand him, to find the more relaxed man he might once have been, but now he was surprising her, changing things between them. And she didn't know what to think.

After spending Saturday morning working, Monica picked up her mother and drove them both to the Widows' Boardinghouse. Brenda Hutcheson brought the big box that held three ghillie suits, and the Double Ds dug in to examine them.

"Oh, we can make these," Theresa insisted. "Right, Matt?"

He was pulling apart the jute and strips of material, dyed all shades of browns and greens, and looking at how they were sewn on.

"Oh, see, they're just attached to this webbing. We could just tie them on pretty easily. It's a matter of cutting jute the right length to tie in place—we don't need the strips of material. And we want to make sure and not tie them too close together."

"Kind of reminds me of the yarn rugs and hangings I used to make as a kid," Monica said, glancing at her mom. "Remember those?"

Janet brightened. "There's one still hanging on the wall in your old bedroom. You remember, the daisies in a vase? I thought that was pretty."

Monica rolled her eyes as everyone chuckled. "You could take the shrine down now. I'm thirty years old."

"I have another guest bedroom. Yours is my craft room." Janet winced and looked a little sad. "All my children are in their thirties—how did that happen?"

"Much quicker than you ever think possible," Mrs. Ludlow said. "And then they get married."

"To the son of the president," Mrs. Palmer said with relish.

"Okay, okay, enough with the memory lane," Brenda said shortly. "We've all got things to do. I already examined the suits and purchased some supplies, every bit of jute and twine I could find at the feed store, along with some fishing net, and canvas to attach it to. This is enough to get started. We're running out of time. And we still have the Mammoth Party details to finalize."

They spent about fifteen minutes deciding how long to make the jute, then Monica went into the kitchen to use the table since they were running out of space. The widows followed her, ostensibly to find more scissors and bring out the salsa and chips, but Monica noticed they were hovering.

"Something I can do for you ladies?" she asked, head bent over the yardstick she was using to measure.

"How is Agent Beaumont?" Mrs. Palmer asked. "Adam tells me he was at Tony's last night."

Holding the jute tight to cut it evenly, she eyed the old lady. "Did he call just to tell you that?"

"Of course not. But we chat most every day for a few minutes. He said Agent Beaumont is a fellow Marine."

"Was," Monica corrected.

"Adam says you're always a Marine."

"Then I won't dispute him." She put both hands on the table and leaned toward the widows, who'd given up pretending to do other things. "Look, I haven't told him a thing about the protest although he's very suspicious that one might be happening, probably because of the background checks and our concern over the archaeology dig."

"Oh, dear," Mrs. Ludlow murmured. "Perhaps Ashley mentioned something to someone . . ."

"Does she know?" Monica asked sharply.

"No, of course not, but she knows us, doesn't she? I think she suspects something. But surely she understands we would never ruin her wedding."

"Brides get awfully suspicious when their big day approaches," Monica warned. "You should have seen Whitney, convinced some of Josh's teenage fans would break into the church right at the part where the priest says 'if anyone knows any reason these two shouldn't be joined together . . .' We stationed lookouts, and no one spotted anything, but you could practically hear her sigh of relief when the priest said they were married."

"So you've said we aren't protestin'?" Mrs. Palmer asked.

"No, I haven't lied. I said what we did was none of his business. I'm on top of this, don't worry. Now go on and feed your guests. And remember, you wait to sew until we're with you. No point in getting exhausted with the manual labor when we need you ladies to be the brains of this outfit!"

An hour later, Monica's back was aching from leaning over the table to cut jute, so she took a break and went into the parlor for some salsa and chips. She didn't see her mom right away and thought she must be in the bathroom, until she spied Janet and Mrs. Thalberg through the French doors that separated the parlor from the library. Her mom seemed all . . . hunched over. Was she crying? She wanted to burst inside and demand to know what was wrong, but moms shielded their kids, and Janet would probably lie rather than admit anything.

They hadn't closed the door all the way, though, so Monica pretended to be stretching while looking out the big bay window at Silver Creek. She had to listen hard, but at last she could hear a couple sentences.

"He's gone every weekend," Janet murmured, then blew her nose. "Oh, Rosemary, should I just keep ignoring it? What if he's having . . . having—"

"An affair? Don't be silly!"

Monica swallowed against the lump in her throat. She'd known things weren't so good between her parents, but she thought they would work it out. But if her dad's car racing was becoming an obsession, and her mother suspected an affair . . .

That couldn't be true. Her parents loved each other! All through her childhood, friends' parents divorced, and she had to see how the breakups hurt everyone involved. Some girls let themselves be treated badly by boys, all because their own dads weren't so close to them anymore. At the same time, she'd felt happy and relieved and guilty that her own parents still held hands when they walked together.

But at least now she knew why her mom hadn't confided in her. What could she do to help?

Chapter Thirteen

When Monica pulled her minivan into the alley behind her shop, she was surprised to see Travis leaning against her back door, reading his cell phone as he waited for her. She was worried he might have followed her to the boardinghouse and was going to grill her, but his expression was relaxed and easy. More and more he was letting down his guard—at least around her.

Smiling, she got out of her van. "Long time no see."

He shrugged. "I had a break and thought I'd take a walk."

"And I wasn't here right at the moment you need ed me."

He gave her his sexy faint smile. "I didn't mind the wait."

"I'm surprised you don't have your own key already."

"You're a private citizen."

She grinned. "You know you could have waited in the showroom. Mrs. Wilcox would have loved to keep you amused. And there are peanut butter cookies today."

He patted his stomach. "Can only take so much temptation."

Their gazes met and lingered. "Don't tell me you're here because you're avoiding the job?" she asked as she walked up the stairs.

He held up the phone. "The job follows me."

He didn't make any attempt to move away as she fumbled the key in the lock clumsily. She was never clumsy. But it would help if she could tear her gaze away from his handsome, square-jawed face. She kept picturing him in a Marine uniform and mentally swooning. So much for just wanting him to relax. She was getting all caught up in him.

Inside the workroom, she set down her purse and refilled her bottle of water. She offered him one, but he declined, only started perusing the framed photos of the weddings she'd worked on. She wasn't sure what he wanted, but she didn't mind working while she waited. After telling Mrs. Wilcox she was back, she sat down on a stool and got out her list.

"We always seem to meet here," she said. "When are you going to invite me over to the command center? I hear you're slowly taking over the top two floors. And considering there are only three . . ."

He glanced over his shoulder at her but didn't leave the photos. "Yes, it's been difficult. There's a regular guest who doesn't want to move even though we'll pay for his accommodations somewhere else for the weekend. And if he doesn't move, the president won't stay there."

"Really?" she asked in amazement. "No presidential orders insisting he leave?"

"No, not at all. Most people leave, though, and I think I have him almost persuaded. Mrs. Sweet is saving a good room for him, and since the president will be there as well, this guy's curiosity will get the better of him. We're also dealing with a convention of drunken dentists, which is supposed to be gone by Wednesday, the day the president arrives."

"I bet you weren't supposed to tell me that. Not that it was a surprise to me, considering the wedding rehearsal is on Friday." *And so is our protest.* At least the president would be in town to see it.

"I trust you not to tell anyone."

"Gee, thanks."

"You are my fake girlfriend, after all."

He was giving her a slow, sexy smile that about made her heart flip over just to beat faster. She hadn't seen that before, and now she knew it was a secret weapon that he must only bring out for . . . whom? Fake girlfriends? She was starting to think their relationship wasn't simply friendly anymore. Not that she knew *what* it was. But here he was being positively relaxed and chatty, for a guy. She liked it—she liked him. It had taken a while for him to warm up to her, but he was worth the wait. His kisses were, too.

"Have you been doing this advance work for a while?"

"A year now. It means I'm on the road much of the time. No two-day weekends for me."

"That's got to be tough. I may have the responsibilities of owning my own business, but at least I can choose my days off. But still, you must see the world."

He nodded. "Last month I was in Moscow and Hong Kong."

"And now you're in Valentine," she said, smiling. "Things just get better and better for you."

"I don't mind Valentine." He leaned against a work-table, crossed his arms over his chest, and regarded her. "It has its perks. And we don't have to worry quite as much about foreign operatives spying."

"Just nosy neighbors. So when you're at home, what do you do?"

"Do?"

"For fun? You seem to like relaxing with a beer at Tony's Tavern."

"It's not the same in D.C., certainly not as relaxing. There are a lot of people who make it their business to know what you do for a living. My buddies on the Presidential Protective Detail? Women have been known to slip their hotel keycard in their pockets because they saw them with the president on TV."

"The Secret Service has groupies?"

"Just about."

"None of that here, I hope." Although she was tempted . . .

"Jealous?"

And then she was blushing. "Just didn't want you to lump me in with the groupies."

"I wouldn't do that."

They stared at each other again, needing no words to communicate. She gave up any pretense of cutting ribbon.

He was the one who finally spoke first, after clearing his throat. "People have been pretty relaxed with my agents, open with their curiosity, not underhanded."

"It's good to know we have some manners," she said. "But really, what do you do for fun besides have a beer in a bar and dance with your groupies?"

Gosh, she liked the faint smile, probably because she felt special that she was able to bring it out in him. He didn't readily show emotions—the Marines and the Secret Service had buried any easy rapport with people he might have had.

"I run, which you know about. I've been known to watch football and basketball, I read a lot of nonfiction and military stuff, but I don't really have time for anything much beyond that. What about you?"

She felt a little guilty at all she had to choose from. "You know I run, of course. And I read."

"Romances. Saw them upstairs."

"I love a happy ending—don't we all?"

"Keep going. I spilled about myself. Your turn."

"I ski in the winter, but you get funny looks in the Rockies if you don't do something outside."

"Same in Montana although it's been a few years for me."

"I keep a vegetable patch at my mom's since I don't have a yard. Bet that's a fascinating detail about me."

"Everything's fascinating about you," he said quietly.

"Even my activist past?" Maybe she shouldn't have brought that up.

But he nodded, a half smile playing about his mouth.

Did he . . . like that about her? Was he challenged by what he thought she might be doing right now?

And they lapsed into another silent stare. He took a couple steps toward her, and she stiffened with excitement and tension and possibilities.

Then he spoke abruptly. "So Mayor Galimi ambushed me again at the True Grits Diner."

"Her brother's place," Monica admitted, unable to choose between disappointment or relief that he'd decided to keep talking. "Sylvester's probably under orders to call her when you're there. You weren't able to give her an answer about meeting the president?"

"Not yet. It's a private weekend for President Torres, so the schedule isn't set."

"Can she do anything spur of the moment?"

"We frown on that, but like you and me, she runs, and she doesn't mind doing it in public. SS agents are with her, and you'd be surprised how many people walk or drive right by, thinking she's just another middle-aged woman out for a run. But we *know* she'll be running, so the agents prepare in advance. But when she wants to stop at a bookstore or something we haven't approved, well, things get dicey. The president can do a lot of what she wants—we just have to know about it in advance. Unless it's dangerous, then forget about it. We've made a president or two see the error of his ways, but it's hard to dissuade the leader of the free world."

"I can imagine," she said, wide-eyed. "Oh, I forgot to ask—did you see the article in the newspaper? I hope you're not too upset."

He shook his head and came to lean on the table beside her. "The reporter tried to interview me, too, and I didn't make a comment."

"Yeah, but when you're doing the flowers for a presidential wedding, you kind of want potential customers to know. Hope you don't mind."

"Not at all. You did good."

He looked at his phone, whether to check the time or a message, Monica didn't know.

"I've got to go. But I wanted to tell you that the widows asked me over tomorrow. They want to reassure me that nothing will go wrong with the shower they're hosting for Ashley even though the president isn't attending. And since Mrs. Ludlow is such a hellraiser, I thought I'd better drop by and checks things out. So do you want to go? You know them better than I do—I wouldn't want to screw up. They might never talk to me again."

She snorted. "As if *that* would ever happen." Her head tilted to the side, she eyed him. "Is this a fake date?"

"Hardly. I would hope I could do better than that. It's a fake investigation," he pointed out. "Well, I *am* curious to know them better. The entire town respects and admires them, even though they seem to do . . . crazy things."

"Not quite everybody is full of admiration, but they don't have any real enemies, anyway." Then she smiled. "All right, I'll go."

He smiled back, then glanced at the window that separated the showroom from the workroom. Mrs. Wilcox seemed preoccupied with several customers.

Monica caught her breath as he took her arm and led her toward the far side of the room, out of sight. Then he put her up against the wall and held her there with his body.

With a gasp, she let her hands roam up his arms and just enjoyed the weight of him, the force of him, inhaling his aftershave with the faint scent of citrus.

"I shouldn't do this," he said with a groan, leaning down over her. "I told myself I wouldn't." He brushed her lips with his, once, twice. "But I find you irresistible, Monica."

And then he kissed her, and she came up on her toes to meld their bodies even closer, feeling giddy and aroused. His hand ran down her hip and along the outside of her thigh, until, still kissing her, he pulled her knee up and pressed his hips between her thighs.

She moaned against his mouth, suckled his tongue, then let him do the same. He rubbed himself slowly against her, and she shuddered, feeling her real self fall away until she only existed in the sensual world they spun like a web about themselves.

Travis had never had a problem separating his personal life from his professional life, but whenever he was in the same room with Monica Shaw, he just about lost his head with desire for her. Kissing her was like playing in a sensual pond that surrounded him, bathing him with heat and desire. He loved the taste of her, the feel of her body molding to his, the softness between her thighs he was desperate to explore. He pressed harder there, and her answering gasp told him she was just as affected.

He wanted more of her, all of her, as he explored her waist and ribs, then slid his hand up between them to cup her breast. He could feel the hardness of her nipple against his palm as he rubbed, then used his thumb against it until she writhed in his arms.

With a gasp, she broke free from their kiss, tipping her head back, eyes half-closed. "Okay, okay," she said breathlessly. "God, this feels good, but I can't—we shouldn't—a customer could—"

Those last words broke the spell, and he stepped away. This was her place of business, where she had to be professional, and he'd just put her up against a wall like she was his plaything.

"I didn't even think of that," he said hoarsely. "Can't think of anything around you. I'm sorry. I won't—"

She put her fingers on his mouth to stop him. "There's nothing to forgive. I don't remember the last time I enjoyed myself as much as I have since you've come to town. I had to stop you before you said something stupid, like this'll never happen again." She let her hand drop.

He searched her eyes, and she held his gaze proudly, honestly.

"I'll only be here another week," he said softly.

"I know. Let's enjoy it without thinking too much. I'm even getting good at avoiding accidentally touching the gun at your waist."

He tilted his head. "You're a very different woman, Monica."

"Good. I hope to be memorable. You know, like the widows."

He winced, and she cracked up at his expression.

"I have to go," he said, shaking his head. "I'll pick you up around two?"

She nodded, then pointed to the back door because she couldn't stop laughing. Bemused, he sort of waved, then left while she tried to get herself under control.

Mrs. Wilcox ducked through the swinging door. "Is everything all right?"

Monica settled her laughter down with a snort. "Sorry. Yeah, everything's fine. The shop good?"

"More than good. I've called Karista in, we're so busy. Whoops, there she is."

Karista came bopping through the back door, all smiles at the chance to earn extra money for the mountain bike she managed to mention every day. And Monica thought of what the teenager had almost witnessed and started to laugh again. This was going to be a crazy week.

After church Sunday morning, Monica found her dad at the True Grits Diner, in his usual booth. All the booths were upholstered in red, with sleek chrome outlining everything, including the counter. The place was as crowded as ever, and she ducked around tables to reach him. As a kid, she'd come here every Sunday with him, Dom, and Missy, their Daddy-and-kids time, while her mom sometimes had brunch with her friends or Aunt Gloria. Monica and Missy would color their place mats, while Dom and their dad pretended a paper clip was a hockey puck and flicked it with their fingertips through the salt-and-pepper goal.

"Hi, Monica!" called Harriet, the chubby waitress in her fifties. She wore a white buttoned-down shirt and khakis beneath her apron, and a fifties pointed cap in her bright blond curls. "Ben, your daughter's here!"

He looked up from his newspaper, and his blank expression morphed into pleasure. Monica kissed his cheek, felt the reassuring brush of his beard against her chin, and suddenly she was just his daughter again.

"Hi, Dad!"

She slid into the booth opposite him, then turned her coffee cup right side up in the saucer for Harriet to fill. Ben already had a full plate of bacon, eggs, and hash browns. She snagged a triangle piece of toast.

"Know what you want, Monica?" Harriet asked.

"A piece of ham and broccoli quiche, thanks."

"I don't even need to write that down. You never change."

When Harriet left, Ben leaned toward Monica and pointed at her with his fork. "I thought you didn't come here anymore since Sylvester protested against Leather and Lace last year."

Monica shrugged and swallowed the piece of toast. "I've decided to forgive and forget—I have too many good memories of our Sunday mornings here."

They grinned at each other.

"And you can't do without their quiche," Ben said.

Monica licked her lips. "Okay, okay, you got me. The forgiveness was a little harder to manage."

They chatted about the presidential wedding for a while, and it wasn't until Monica had taken her first delicious bite of quiche that she hesitated, thoughts sobering.

"Spill it, baby girl," Ben said, wiping his mouth. "I know that expression."

"I was just wondering how the vintage-car-racing scene is going."

His brown eyes lit up. "Great! I've really been enjoying myself. Once I got the Mustang running last winter, there's always a race within an hour or two driving distance. I don't do it every weekend, but once or twice a month. There are some great guys on the circuit."

She wiped her own mouth to hide her smile. The racing circuit, huh? A bunch of older guys enjoying reliving their youth. Everyone had a hobby. But was that all it was?

"So do you go overnight on these trips?" she asked, trying to sound innocent.

"Sometimes, why?"

"Do you ask Mom to go?" She kept her tone lightly curious.

"She doesn't like cars. It's just not her thing."

He answered easily, without an evasion, and Monica began to feel a little bit better.

"Well, if you're going away every other weekend, what do you do with Mom when you're home?"

He sighed. "Your mom always has her own stuff to do, her charities, her girlfriends, you kids—and now whatever she's doing with you on such a frequent basis," he added meaningfully. "She said it's going to be every night this week?"

Monica gave him a bright smile. "We're just helping

out the widows, Dad. It's really no big deal. But we're trying to keep it a surprise."

He held up a hand. "Fine, fine, I don't need to know. Your mom is busy, and I'm sure that makes her happy. The car is something I do for myself."

"It does sound fun to get away occasionally to new places," Monica mused, after taking another bite of her quiche. "I sometimes think Mom was *always* busy, what with raising us and taking care of Grandpa Shaw, all while working part-time. Not that you didn't take care of your dad, too," she added hastily.

"But your mom did the majority of the work," he agreed. "My father really appreciated her, and so did— do I." But he frowned.

"I guess it's easy for all of us to get too busy and just assume everything will stay the same. I mean, our households become different, right? I've been on my own for a while, and sometimes it's still strange to be alone in the evening. And you two are down to just yourselves, after all these years of taking care of everyone else. I'm glad you've found a hobby to replace some of those hours."

She smiled at him, and though he smiled back, she thought she might have made him think about a few things in a new light.

She leaned toward him and lowered her voice. "Guess what? You can't tell anyone, but the Secret Service is going to use my apartment as an observation post!"

Chapter Fourteen

When Travis picked Monica up, he gave her his usual impassive nod, and she was a little disappointed. Where was that sexy smile that was all for her? Was it because he was visiting the widows for business reasons? Was he trying to restore their supposedly professional relationship? He wore a suit, one tailored so perfectly to conceal his gun. Because the widows were dangerous, she thought, and almost snorted a laugh again. Lately, she wasn't very elegant when she laughed.

It didn't take long to cross the bridge over Silver Creek and turn down the gravel road to the boardinghouse.

"Nice sign," he said, when they pulled past it to drive around back. "Don't people think the Widows' Boardinghouse is some kind of bed-and-breakfast? Or apartments for rent? It is a pretty big Victorian."

"If so, they don't think it for long," she answered, getting out of his SUV. "And it's not right in town, so people don't drive by unless they mean to. Farther down this road is the remodeled cabin Nate and Emily live in." She pointed through the trees. "And you can just catch a glimpse of the Silver Creek Ranch—see those red roofs?"

He nodded, even taking off his sunglasses to see where she pointed.

She touched his arm. "So we're on the clock here? All business?"

He looked down at her seriously. "What else can we be while we're here? The widows expect me to do my job—they *want* me to do my job, I suspect. So I have to be in my Secret-Service-agent persona."

She saw the little quirk in his lip, and it cheered her. "Okay, then."

The back door opened while they were still climbing the porch stairs.

"Agent Beaumont!" Mrs. Palmer called happily, her bright purple housecoat billowing in the breeze. Then she saw Monica and seemed just tickled. "And our dear Monica. Our company has arrived, girls!"

They entered the kitchen, and Monica watched Travis take in the cow-themed décor—the white-and-brown-spotted platters, the horns on which to hang coats, lovely curtains that, if you looked close, had tiny cows printed on them.

Preparations were obviously under way for Ashley's wedding shower that night: platters spread on the counters, some with dip bowls nearby, others with an unopened bag of chips sitting on top. Several unfolded accordion wedding bells perched in the center of the kitchen table, waiting to be distributed around the house. The oven was on, and the smell was incredible.

"Agent Beaumont," Mrs. Thalberg said, "please, let us show you our home."

As they walked around the first floor, there were no ghillie suits, of course. Monica wondered if they were hidden in the basement, or even out in the garage, just in case. She did see a stack of Mammoth Party posters and signs in the first-floor bedroom suite they often used for guests.

When she saw he'd noticed the signs, Mrs. Ludlow leaned forward on her walker and regarded him. "You're coming to the Mammoth Party tomorrow night, aren't you, Agent Beaumont?"

"Please call me Travis, ma'am. Thank you for the invitation. If I'm not too busy, I'll attend."

"We're doing our part to encourage the Renaissance Spa to hold off their construction so the museum has more time for their archaeology dig. A pool can be delayed—"

"And there are other pools people can swim in!" Mrs. Palmer pointed out indignantly.

"—and those fossils are so fragile," Mrs. Ludlow continued in a cool, even voice.

She should be on the stage, Monica thought. As for Travis, she liked how he was making a big production of checking everything out, as if the widows were dangerous, and he took them seriously. It was a sweet thing to do for the old ladies, to make them feel special and important. For an unemotional, ex-military guy, he was surprisingly thoughtful.

The widows had them take a seat in the parlor, offered coffee or iced tea, and brought out little appetizers of veggie pizza: veggies and a seasoned cream cheese on crescent-roll pastry.

Mrs. Ludlow returned to the topic of the Mammoth Party, which was so close to the truth it made Monica a little nervous.

"We've informed the schools about the party since it's all about science. I was once a schoolteacher, you know," she added. "I taught Monica when she was in the second grade. She was such a cute little dear."

Monica gave Travis a hokey smile, but he just nodded and ate another appetizer. He was working the Secret Service angle all the way, and the widows were eating it up.

"We'll be bringin' in archaeologists from the museum in Denver," Mrs. Palmer. "We're just hopin' the spa can see how badly people are takin' their stubbornness. They don't seem to care they might lose customers." She gave a dramatic sigh. "It's our last chance to make them see sense."

"That's very civic-minded of you all," Travis said. "Who else is helping you out?"

"Monica, of course," Mrs. Thalberg said warmly. "She's like one of our granddaughters."

Monica smiled at all three of them, knowing she'd do just about anything for them—and she was going against the might of the US government, too, represented by Special Agent Travis Beaumont.

"Who else?" Travis asked pointedly.

"Theresa and Matt Sweet," Mrs. Thalberg said, "cousins to our Emily. There's Monica's mom, Janet—have you met her?"

Travis nodded. "At Doc Ericson's." He glanced at Monica, no suspicion in his voice as he added, "It's good that a mother and daughter can find things to do together."

Monica gave him a bland smile.

"Anyone else?" he asked.

"Brenda Hutcheson, from Paradise Mountain Ranch."

"That's a good-size group. Sounds like you'll need it to staff the community center."

Suddenly, they could hear the back door open, and Nate called, "Grandma, am I interrupting?"

Mrs. Thalberg's happy blush was almost as red as her hair. "Nate! What a surprise!"

After a moment, he came through the dining room and into the parlor in his socks. He shook hands with Travis, then gave Monica and each of the widows a kiss on the cheek.

"Saw your SUV," he said to Travis, then tossed a couple veggie pizza squares in his mouth, chewed, and swallowed with relish. "Thought you might want a tour of the ranch, like we talked about a couple days ago. You game?"

Travis briefly consulted his phone, then nodded. "I have an hour. I'd enjoy that."

"Us, too!" said Mrs. Palmer.

Obviously, they had the shower preparations well in hand.

Before Monica knew it, she and Travis were driving Mrs. Ludlow and Mrs. Palmer over to the ranch, following Nate and his grandma. In the yard in front of the sprawling ranch house made of logs, Nate gave a little history about the ranch, starting in the silver-mining days of the nineteenth century. He mentioned the herd grazing up in the White River National Forest, and the hay harvest coming in June, for which Brooke and Adam were out moving irrigation dams. He talked about the fire that wiped out the old barn, and how Brooke had recently built an indoor arena for her riding school.

Monica glanced at the arena surreptitiously. To her surprise, there were already a few newly cut tree trunks nearby. She couldn't help wondering what Brooke had told her family . . .

"You know," Nate was saying, as they stood beside the barn, "Monica has her own fame where our mountains are concerned."

She felt a little warm at the way Travis looked at her, blue eyes alight. "Nate, that's a boring story." She hardly wanted to emphasize her activist past.

"It's not boring," Mrs. Thalberg insisted, backing up her grandson. "The Silver Creek Ranch came close to having a high-priced development overlooking us, right in the foothills of our own mountains. If not for Monica, it might have happened."

"And what did Monica do?"

Travis asked the question with interest rather than the censure she might once have thought him capable of.

"There's this beautiful meadow called Bluebell Hill, in the foothills of our Elk Mountains," Mrs. Thalberg said, pointing into the distance, where the mountains rose like sentinels guarding the ranch.

Nate squinted into the sun. "It was always the place my sister and Monica rode their horses when they wanted to be alone and gossip."

"We weren't gossiping," Monica scolded, then had to laugh at herself. "Okay, sometimes. But it's just such a peaceful place, with a stream running through it and beautiful wild bluebells scattered everywhere. When I heard that developers planned town houses there, something inside me just snapped, and I had to get involved."

"How old were you?" Travis asked.

"Seventeen. The summer before my senior year."

"And she spent it going door to door to anyone who'd listen," Mrs. Ludlow said with pride. "She built a website, got petitions signed, went to every town-council meeting. And in the end, she triumphed, persuading the owner to let it be absorbed by the White River National Forest, forever wild."

"You make it sound like I did it all alone," Monica said, her cheeks warm with embarrassment. She couldn't believe Travis was actually looking at her with admiration, when she was so used to his serious concern about the Double Ds' protest.

"No, you weren't alone," Mrs. Palmer said, putting her arm around Monica. "You made us all care—you made the town care. We were so proud."

Monica was surprised to feel a rush of tears that she quickly blinked away, hoping to hide her sentimentality.

And Travis was still watching her, that faint smile so clearly for her.

An hour later, after meeting Nate's parents and getting a tour of Josh's workshop, Travis drove Monica back into Valentine. He wasn't any closer to knowing what she and the widows were up to—although they'd tried hard to convince him the Mammoth Party was all they were throwing.

He didn't believe it for a moment, especially not since he could now connect their little activist group to the ghillie suits through Brenda Hutcheson, he thought with relief. He was glad to know the ghillie suits were most likely in the widows' hands rather than with someone unscrupulous.

Not that he'd seen the suits, or any evidence of what they intended to do with them. He'd keep looking into it because it was obvious someone had to keep these women from making a mistake.

Monica sent him an amused look, as if she were reading his thoughts. "So, did touring the ranch help your job?"

"Not really. The Thalbergs seem too busy to cause a problem for the president." He glanced at her. "You spent a lot of time there?"

"A lot of my childhood. Brooke and I have been best friends since kindergarten. I apparently was crying for my mom on the first day of school—not that I remember actually crying, you understand—and she promised I could visit her ranch and ride her pony. Our friendship was sealed."

"You're easily pleased by material things," he teased.

"Hey, this was a *pony*! What little girl doesn't think they're magical?"

He smiled. "All right, I admit I'm curious about you as a little girl. I think I want to see this Bluebell Hill."

"You're kidding, right?" she said, eyeing him with surprise.

"I'm not. It can't be that far if you rode your horses. Can we drive there?"

"Yes, but . . . aren't you busy?"

"I've got time. And your shower's not 'til this evening, right?"

"Five o'clock."

"Plenty of time," he said with satisfaction.

"But Travis . . . it's a reminder of my antiestablishment days."

"You were standing up for nature, for what you believe in. It's a pretty impressive accomplishment for a seventeen-year-old. Give me directions."

Wide-eyed, she said, "We'll have to turn back around and head southwest, past the ranch."

He turned around at the entrance to the road that led to the cemetery.

"It'll be about a thirty-minute drive."

"That's a short drive in D.C."

They lapsed into a contented silence. He found himself thinking of Whitney, who'd arrived at the ranch just before he and Monica left, and how Josh had come running out to help her inside. Their apartment was on the second floor of the barn, newly renovated by Josh himself.

They were obviously thrilled to be parents soon, and he realized it was something he'd never given much thought to. He'd been building his career throughout his twenties and early thirties, and even when he'd been married, they'd never even had any meaningful discussions about having kids. It was like it hadn't occurred to him. Soon, he might be in the craziest part of the job, the Presidential Protective Detail, when he'd be even more busy than he was now. And he wasn't getting any younger.

He saw pregnant women all the time on the street—why was he suddenly thinking about babies and families? Maybe because the Thalbergs all worked together and didn't seem to get on each other's nerves and loved what they did. And they were all preparing for the first of a new generation.

Monica directed him to turn off the gravel road onto a dirt path with two lanes for tire tracks. They'd been steadily rising higher, the valley floor falling away behind them, but this path became even steeper.

"How old are you?" Travis asked.

She stared at him in surprise. "Thirty. Why?"

"You don't look it."

"Thanks. But why did you ask?"

Do you ever think about kids? No, he wasn't going to ask that. She'd think him an idiot—or get the wrong idea.

"Just curious. I'm thirty-five."

"You don't look it either."

He was driving slowly now, the ride rough and uneven. "Good thing I rented an SUV," he muttered.

"We're almost there."

Not five minutes later, the ground leveled out, and the dirt tracks disappeared into thigh-high wild grass bordering a broad grove of white-barked aspen trees that blocked the view of the valley. The mountains continued to rise behind the trees, jagged against the brilliant blue sky.

"Park right here," she said, then unbuckled her seat belt and got out of the car. "We're coming just at the right time of year," she added, excitement lacing her voice. "This way, through the trees."

He reached for her hand, and she smiled up at him tenderly, giving him a little squeeze before leading him through the tall grass and into the trees.

The ground began to slope down almost immediately. Birds chirped as they swooped from tree to tree. The grasses brushed their thighs; the breeze played through the leaves over their heads.

And then the grass just seemed to change right in front of him, turning blue and purple everywhere the eye could see, as the bluebells drooped their bell-shaped heads on tall green stalks. The sun slanted through the trees, like fingers of light combing through the flowers. For a moment, he just looked at Monica, framed in bluebells, the way her orange-and-white-striped sundress blew against her long legs, cinched in at her waist with a little belt, then angled up her back to the little capped sleeves.

"This is gorgeous," he murmured, unwilling to raise his voice, as if the sound of human speech would change the magical landscape back into the ordinary. *You're gorgeous, Monica.*

"Just wait," she promised, luring him deeper.

At last, the trees began to thin, and he could see the

slope of the hill, slanting down and away from him, covered in bluebells. The long narrow Roaring Fork Valley spread out below, from Aspen in the southeast all the way to Glenwood Springs in the northwest. The sky was azure blue, not a cloud to mar its perfection. And everywhere, bluebells swayed in the sun, clustered even closer together along a stream that flowed from rock to rock down the mountainside.

Still holding his hand, Monica spoke solemnly, quietly. "Now you can see why I had to save this place. As a kid, I thought it was a fairy wonderland in early summer. I used to bring my sketchbook and draw the bluebells, the streams, the aspen trees. Brooke and I talked about . . . everything, our families, our friendship, and, eventually, boys, of course," she added, smiling up at him.

"You rode horses up here—did you have your own?"

She shook her head. "I was a villager, not a rancher. But the Thalbergs generously allowed me my choice to ride. I always picked Misty, a flea-bitten gray, they called her, though she was white as snow. She's still alive. I haven't ridden her in a while," she added, a faint line appearing between her brows. "I should make more time."

"It's so easy to be caught up in work, isn't it?" he asked, drawing her toward the stream and sitting down on a boulder. He pulled her onto his lap, and she relaxed back against his chest without a protest, as if she belonged in his arms. "We talked about our hobbies yesterday, but lately they feel in my past rather than something I do right now."

"I've noticed that about you, almost from the beginning," she said, tilting her head up to meet his gaze.

Her curls tickled his chin, and he used his hand, to gently tame them. "What do you mean?"

"I just . . . I wanted to help you, almost from the moment I saw you—and not just about the presidential wedding. Don't take this the wrong way, but you seemed sort of . . . lost, rigidly disciplined, unable even to relax off duty. Are you offended?" she asked, her gaze turning troubled.

"No, I'm flattered that you care."

"I care, Travis. I sort of made a promise to myself."

"A promise about me?" he asked in disbelief.

"Yes. I promised myself I'd find a way to get you to relax, to open up, to enjoy yourself here in Valentine Valley. It's such a beautiful town, and you were missing it all."

"I didn't miss you," he answered quietly. "I couldn't miss you. You were like . . . sunshine the moment I first saw you." He rolled his eyes self-consciously. "Okay, I don't know where that came from. I'm not a poet."

She smiled tenderly. "Bluebell Hill brings out the poet in everyone, I think. That's how I saved it in the end, you know. I made the owner come up when it looked like this, bluebells everywhere, the valley so distant below, God's sky like a brilliant blue umbrella covering the world." She laughed. "Now I sound like a poet."

"You're a poet with flowers," he said. "Everything I've seen of your work paints a picture, no words necessary."

Her brown eyes were wide with wonder as she stared up at him. Then her hands touched his face and brought his head down until their mouths met. The kiss was as tender as he felt, moving in a way that made his chest ache. From the beginning, they'd both been drawn to each other, brought together by a promise she'd made to herself about him—and to think, without that, he would have missed all of this—would have missed knowing her.

The kiss grew rougher, deeper, and he found himself turning her about in his arms until she straddled him. Hungrily, he let his hands roam up the outside of her thighs so that he could grip her hips and bring her against him, her softness cradling his hardness. In unison, they groaned into each other's mouths. He kissed his way down her cheek and past her ear, burying his face in her neck, inhaling the dizzying scent of her hair, of her skin, the scents blending into all that was Monica.

She tilted her head back as he let his tongue brush the hollow at the base of her throat. Through half-closed eyes, he saw the sun bathe her face, making it glow. He arched her back across his lap, holding her shoulders securely, licking a path down to her neckline, letting his tongue slide beneath until she shuddered in his arms. She tasted sweet and salty, felt so womanly in his arms. He let his cheek rest against her breast and thought of all he wanted to experience with her.

"Travis?" she whispered his name.

He lifted his head and looked into her face, framed against the mountains and valleys of her home, the bluebells like a carpet he could have laid her down on. "I know you need to get back," he said huskily. "I just . . ." And the words didn't come.

She cupped his face in her hands and kissed him sweetly on the lips. "I know just how you feel."

Did she? Even he didn't know how he felt. But he let her stand up with silent regret and walked at her side back up the slope of Bluebell Hill and into the dappled shade of the trees. They never said another word, even during the car ride winding back down into the valley. He didn't need to talk with her; theirs was a silent communion that seemed powerful, even a little awe-inspiring.

In the alley behind her flower shop, he put the car into park just as his cell phone buzzed. Back to the real world—and his job. He glanced at the text message, then did a double take. "Give me a sec."

He called one of his agents in the command center and listened in disbelief. When he hung up, Monica was staring at him.

"Can I ask what that was about?" she said. "Unless it's a national secret, of course. But you look . . . confused."

"Oh, I'm confused, all right. Apparently there's a runaway sheep on Main Street."

She covered her mouth even as a giggle escaped, then tried to speak between her fingers. "What—" Another giggle.

"Do you want to hear the rest or what?"

She nodded, wide eyes beginning to glisten, still holding her laugh inside with her hand.

"It's no ordinary sheep. Someone painted it with words. FOSSILS RULE. Know anything about that?"

She shook her head quickly, then spoke in a quivering voice. "I swear to God, I haven't a clue. The widows are far too busy with the shower tonight and the Mammoth Party tomorrow. But I'm all for the democratic process and free speech, even for a—for a—sheep." She burst out laughing, bent over as far as the seat belt would allow.

He sighed. "You'll be happy to know that no one's succeeding in catching it yet."

"Has it gone . . . underground?" She practically snorted.

He smiled at her. "A bad joke."

She sniffed and dabbed at the corner of her eyes with her fingertips. "Sorry. I'm sure it'll wander back home. Maybe you can assign someone to—to follow it." Her lips trembled as she tried not to laugh.

He leaned across the seat and kissed her, and those trembling lips opened to him on a moan. In his mind, they were surrounded by bluebells.

"Are you done laughing?" he said against her mouth, taking tiny little kisses along the curve.

"No. You might have to stop me some more."

They kissed for a long while, in broad daylight, until the buzzing of Travis's phone interrupted them repeatedly.

He pulled back. "I've got to go. Can I see you tonight?"

She smiled. "I have the shower, remember?"

He harrumphed, frowning.

"But I may be free afterward . . ."

He eyed her. "I'll make sure I'm free, too."

This was going beyond professional, and Travis couldn't seem to stop himself.

"If the sheep takes precedence, I understand," Monica said soberly, her eyes twinkling.

Chapter Fifteen

The shower started at five, and Heather's As You Like It Catering outdid itself with miniquiches, sushi, and lobster avocado spoons. Monica tried not to hover around the dining-room table and eat too much, but that was practically impossible. Close to twenty women milled through the boardinghouse, eating wherever they found a place to perch, and children ran among them. Ashley's sister and matron of honor, Kim Avicolli, had two daughters, Zana, seven—"Short for Susannah," the little girl said in a high, serious voice— and Miri, five. Both girls were dark-haired, with bright, eager eyes as they repeatedly told all the guests that they were going to be flower girls in the wedding. They focused on Monica when they heard she was going to be in charge of the flowers they might carry.

The widows had organized games, of course, like guessing the identity of the celebrity bride from published wedding photos, and matching items in your purse to an immense list. It was no surprise when Mrs. Sweet, matriarch of the inn family, had the most obscure items in her purse, including *two* rosaries. Nobody was beating her.

And running late, just as the games were over, Missy rushed in. Monica had known her twin sister was coming, of course, but she was swept up with a feeling of warmth and love and excitement as they hugged each other for a long minute. They'd seen each other at Christmas, and talked at least several times a week on the phone, but being together was just . . . different.

They grinned at each other, briefly holding hands. It wasn't like looking in a mirror of course—they weren't identical. But they were sisters, and the genes ran strong in them. But where Monica had springy curls that sometimes stood out like a sunburst, Missy wore her hair close-cropped and elegant, her jewelry big and tastefully flashy, her clothes of silk and linen and cashmere. She flew around the world to cover stories for CNN—and now to have her back in their small town more than once in a year was a special thrill.

Ashley gave a little squeak of happiness when she and Missy hugged. "You made it! I'm so glad. It's like college all over again."

Not quite, Monica thought.

Missy rolled her eyes. "We had lunch three weeks ago—and you *still* didn't tell me about your wedding."

Ashley and Missy both lived in D.C., while Monica had never moved away from Valentine, if you didn't count college—she never wanted to leave. But as she watched the two of them talk, she knew they shared a relationship she never would, one of the big city, nights out at different bars and restaurants, fast-paced living where political gossip ruled, not the small-town woes of love lost and—and runaway sheep. Monica smiled, thinking of Travis's expression when he heard about the protesting sheep. She loved small-town gossip just the same.

"How could I talk about the wedding when my future mother-in-law asked me not to?" Ashley said, hands on her hips. "But you found out in time, and here you are."

Missy grinned. "I pulled a lot of strings I didn't know I wielded. But my local connection to the story helped the most." She slung an arm over Monica's shoulders. "And here I am, in the town I know best, with my favorite people."

Their mom came in from the kitchen, and with a cry of delight, hugged Missy long and hard.

As they chatted happily, Whitney came to stand beside them, hand massaging her lower back. "It's eerie how alike you two seem."

Brooke shook her head. "Nah, it's a sister illusion, nothing more. They're pretty different—though still really close," she amended hastily, grinning at Monica. "I was very jealous back in middle school. Missy was popular, and I was worried she'd drag Monica into the cool crowd and leave me behind with my horses and cows."

Monica grinned. "No worries there."

"Hey, you were a cheerleader," Emily pointed out. "Or so I heard."

"A cheerleader who once dated my fiancé," Brooke said with mock sternness.

Monica spread her hands wide. "I had some popular

moments, too." To Whitney, she said, "Missy and I may look alike, but she's the glamorous D.C. version of me."

After they opened presents and were sitting around having Emily's delicious vanilla cake with sea-salt-caramel filling, Heather took a break from the kitchen so she could watch Ashley open presents. She sat down next to Monica with a slice of cake.

"I had another talk with your special agent," Heather said.

Monica smiled even as she avoided Missy's raised eyebrows. "Let me guess—background checks."

"How did you know? Yeah, I'm doing some of the catering in the presidential suite. I have to say—he's really handsome."

"We like to call him yummy," Emily said, leaning around Monica so she could meet Heather's amused eyes. Her own gaze dropped, and she gasped. "Is that a diamond?"

Heather's eyes went wide, and she shot a glance at the bride, sitting with the older ladies. "I meant to take this off," she whispered, yanking on the ring. "This day isn't about me."

"Did my brother ask you to marry him?" Emily hissed, grabbing her hand before Heather could get the ring off. She eyed it with delight.

Heather gave a fiery-redhead blush. "Yeah, he did. I was shocked. We were out riding yesterday and took a break, and he actually dropped to one knee."

There were oohs and aahs, and although Monica was thrilled for Chris and Heather, that was one less single girl in Valentine. It was like some kind of countdown.

Missy met Monica's gaze. "You should come to the big city, Monica. You know there are a lot more career-driven girls there. You'd fit right in."

Career-driven? Was that what she was? Weren't career-driven women all about the job, with no time for a social life or a husband? Monica didn't feel that way. She had lots of friends and activities—just no man.

"We've had this discussion before," Monica reminded her sister. "I haven't changed my mind about where I belong."

Missy gave an exaggerated sigh. "I had to try."

When Ashley was done opening gifts and began to mingle again with the guests, Missy excitedly asked her, "So how's the planning going for a presidential wedding?"

Ashley shrugged, wearing a brave smile. "It's quick, but I'm marrying Jeremy, so I'm happy. I only wish . . . no, never mind."

Her mom, Donna, who'd been helping Miri and Zana color pictures of flowers and wedding bells, looked up sharply. "I *knew* it. What's going on, Ashley? You sound frustrated more than happy lately."

The women's conversations died, and Ashley looked around uneasily as she became the focus once again. "I'm happy!" she insisted. "There's just this presidential staffer, Samantha Weichert, who seems to think my wedding is her big project, the way to prove herself to President Torres. Just to keep her happy and out of my way, I allowed her to deal with the wedding favors, and now it's like she's my wedding planner."

"Do you want me to speak with her?" Donna asked.

"She might listen to me," Mrs. Ludlow said.

Donna gave her mother-in-law a patient smile. "Mom, I think—"

"I'm handling it," Ashley insisted tightly. "I know her type—no one in authority ever said no to her, including her parents. I have no trouble saying no." She turned a bright smile on Monica and Whitney. "My future father-in-law is still talking about seeing Josh's work."

"And Josh said he was flattered," Whitney answered.

"And he'd come to my shop anytime the First Husband would like," Monica said.

Ashley continued to diffuse the tension by happily looking at all her gifts with the older ladies.

Missy pulled Monica aside, turning her back on their mom before speaking in a low voice. "What the heck is going on with Mom and Dad? I was only home for a couple hours, and they were all smiles, but . . . something's not right."

Monica sighed. "I don't know. They seem to be . . . growing apart or something. Dad's into his cars, and Mom has decided she needs to find something else to do to fill her time. She was so busy when we were growing up."

"I thought they'd find stuff to do together," Missy said worriedly.

"Me, too."

"Would you mind if I stay with you? It's hard to concentrate on my job with the weight of all that tension."

Monica hesitated, thinking of Travis, knowing he

meant to stop by that night. "Don't hate me, but I have to say no."

Missy blinked at her. "Why? Oh, wait—it can only be a guy. Someone mentioned a Secret Service agent?"

Monica shrugged. "Well . . ."

"It *is* about a guy!"

To Monica's relief, Missy looked excited rather than perturbed. "Well . . . yeah. You promise you won't use any of this on CNN?"

Missy rolled her eyes. "Like I'd talk about my sister's love life to the world?"

Monica laughed. "Just kidding. I've got to tell you, you can tell you're from D.C. You're the first person who hasn't been intrigued so much by what Travis does as the fact that we're hanging out."

"His job's not too much of a mystery to me. I've traveled on Air Force One before. But I *am* surprised you'd go after a guy you know won't be around long."

"I didn't go after him—not to date him anyway. And you haven't seen him yet," Monica reminded her.

"Hot?"

"Hot."

Missy grinned. "So you, Miss Down Home 2014, will settle for a brief affair?"

That took Monica aback. Was that really where this was headed? "It's not an affair," Monica said, glancing guiltily over her shoulder at their mom. "We're . . . having fun."

"So much so that your long-absent sister will get in the way."

"Well . . . yeah."

They looked at each other and shared a grin—and then shared a second piece of cake, taking turns dipping their forks in.

"You know," Missy said thoughtfully, "I wasn't home an hour when our dear brother brought up that awful flag-burning photo again. I honestly think it was accidental—he was talking about how Travis was doing background checks, and his worry sort of slipped out."

"Worry?" Monica winced. "I thought it was because the presidential trip has his patriotic fervor in high gear. Forget about it."

Missy gripped her fork tightly, her expression turning sad. "I don't think I can. He seems to believe that between him and me, we should be able to talk you down from whatever protest you're planning now. And he thinks it's all because of that damned photo!"

Monica leaned closer, and said with serious intent, "No, he's thinking it because there *is* a protest being planned. That photo has nothing to do with it."

Missy's lips trembled. "I don't think I can take it anymore. I want to tell him the truth."

"No!" Monica took her sister's elbow and dragged her toward the picture window, farther away from the other guests.

"But it's not right that he's mad at you! He should be mad at me. I never should have let you take the blame all those years ago."

"The whole picture was an accident," Monica insisted. "And it didn't matter to my reputation like it mattered to yours." She thought of Travis and knew that photo had deepened his suspicions about their protest—but she wasn't going to tell her sister that!

"My keeping quiet *wasn't* an accident," Missy insisted. "I was a coward. And why should it matter if we tell our own brother the truth? He's not about to bring it up again to our friends and family."

"But he'll be all riled up, and for no reason."

"But if I tell the truth, won't it help you with your guy?"

Monica waved a hand dismissively. "Hell, I think that's half the reason Travis is attracted to me—my untamed, protesting past. He's ex-military, so conservative and patriotic he makes Dom look like a wild man."

"And *you're* attracted to him?"

Before Monica could figure out a response that didn't involve waxing romantic about her afternoon with Travis at Bluebell Hill, Emily approached with Brooke and Whitney in tow.

"Did I hear you say something about your protest?" Emily asked.

Brooke's gaze skittered away, and she practically whistled with innocence.

"I need more details," Missy said suspiciously. "You can't possibly protest something and date a Secret Service agent."

"Did you hear about the mammoth dig on the grounds of the Renaissance Spa?" Emily said.

Missy nodded. "Mom keeps me informed." She frowned at Monica. "You've been strangely quiet about it."

"I have it under control. Travis was even out here

today, and he saw the signs and stuff for the Mammoth Party. He's cool with it."

"What's a Mammoth Party, and should I bring a camera crew?" Missy asked.

"That's a great idea," Monica enthused, not daring to meet Brooke's eyes. She wasn't ready for the details of the protest to leak any further yet. She suspected her nosy sister wasn't convinced that's all that was going on, but she could wait, along with everyone else.

The elderly Mrs. Sweet looked between Monica and the widows. "Mammoth Party?" she sniffed. "Why do I get the feeling there's more you're not telling the rest of us, Connie?"

Mrs. Ludlow smiled. "We're keeping the party details secret, so you can be just as surprised as the schoolchildren by what you learn about the mammoth dig, about how important our scientific history is."

Mrs. Sweet shook her head. "You're willing to risk Valentine Valley's reputation for a mammoth that can be excavated another time?"

Mrs. Palmer narrowed her eyes, as if wishing she hadn't needed to invite her nemesis. "They're not just covering it up for a future excavation, like they did in Snowmass Village. This site will be destroyed by the construction. Science is important, Eileen. Or maybe you think dinosaurs are a lie."

"Okay, okay, that's enough," Donna said, stepping into the middle of the room, hands upraised. "This is my baby's wedding shower. I—I can't believe she's marrying into the most powerful family in the country. Honey, how often can I visit the White House?"

Everyone laughed but Mrs. Sweet. Monica glanced between her and the widows—and then saw Missy's suspicious gaze. Things were just going to get more complicated the next few days . . .

But not as complicated as Travis, who'd promised to drop by tonight. Monica shivered and looked away from her family and friends. He was her private fantasy come to life, and she wasn't going to think beyond this night. There would be no promises between them, nothing permanent, no regrets.

Why did she keep telling herself this? She'd always known their relationship was just for fun even if he was surprisingly romantic beneath that stoic exterior. She couldn't have more.

Chapter Sixteen

Travis watched the flower shop from the top floor of the Hotel Colorado, and when the apartment lights went on, he tensed with awareness and excitement, putting a hand on the glass. He saw Monica then, crossing in front of the window, but she didn't close the curtains. In fact, he thought she glanced at the hotel, but he couldn't be certain. Only one way to find out. He headed for the door.

Royce looked up from his newspaper. "Where you goin'?"

"Out."

"You've spent more time lookin' out the window tonight than anythin' else," he said with a smirk. "And you didn't change into sweats."

Travis put his hand on the doorknob. "Your point?"

"I know whose apartment you can see from here. Bet you're discussin' all kinds of protocol for the president's visit with the flower-shop chick."

Travis smiled and felt like a teenager as he said, "Wouldn't you like to know."

"Get on out of here before my jealousy gets the best of me." Royce grinned even as he sighed his disappointment.

Travis practically whistled as he crossed Main Street, the lights of Valentine Valley twinkling all around him. For a small town, there were always people on the street, keeping the restaurants and bars busy. The neon sign of the Royal Theater blinked in three-story glory, advertising a sudden new festival of patriotic movies from *The Sands of Iwo Jima* to *Saving Private Ryan* to *Independence Day*.

He received more than one curious glance, but people were already used to—and bored by—the Secret Service and were itching for the real show, the president.

When he reached the alley and Monica's door, he pressed the bell and waited.

She opened it, wearing a smile, and he was surprised at the warmth of gladness that spread through him just being with her. Damn, he had it bad. And he only had a few days left. Once the president arrived, he'd be lucky even to see Monica in the street. And he wanted to see her; he physically ached for it, had had a hard time putting aside his thoughts of the coming evening while he worked. Memories of her amidst bluebells haunted him.

"Thought you military types went to bed early and rose with the dawn," she teased. "Isn't ten o'clock past your bedtime?"

"I make due on less sleep than you'd think."

She inhaled, her smile faded, and he thought her dark eyes smoldered with awareness.

"Is that a hint?" she asked.

"Do you want it to be?" With him at the bottom of the stairs, she was a little above him in height, and he wanted to take her small waist in his hands and pull her to him. With a husky voice, he asked, "Don't answer that. We have time. May I come in?"

She stepped back and gestured up the stairs. "Of course."

He allowed her to precede him up the stairs, and when the little hallway widened into her living room, he saw that she'd closed the curtains. Good. Not that he thought Royce would spy on them . . .

"Can I get you something to drink?"

"A beer would be fine if you have it."

While she was in the kitchen, he stood at her wall shelves, looking at her collection of books and plants.

He turned when she entered to hand him a bottle of beer and found himself admiring the tight skirt she wore and the silky top with ruffles over her breasts. He forced his gaze upward. "How was the shower?"

She sipped her beer, then smiled. "Good. Ashley received some lovely presents. But she did mention this presidential staffer who's been bothering her."

He frowned. "She mentioned her to me, too. I had my own little run-in with Ms. Weichert, and more will have to be said. We need to keep open exits at the rear of every venue the president is at, but she wanted some big wall of flowers at the back of the church altar, and I had to veto it."

Monica put a hand to her chest and gasped. "My wall of flowers?"

He looked at her until she grinned.

"Okay, the wall of flowers wasn't my idea although I had a great time designing it. I didn't even know where Ashley planned to use it."

"Ashley will be more reasonable than this Weichert woman about where to put it. I'll deal with her."

"Good. Every bride wants to enjoy her wedding. There's always stress, or so I'm told, but it should be the good kind, not the unnecessary kind. When Emily got married last year, it was fun and exciting, and the best weekend of her life. I want that for Ashley, too. It's hard enough to deal with the whole world being interested in your wedding—she shouldn't have this sort of stuff bothering her."

Travis nodded, but he was having a difficult time thinking about the wedding when he was increasingly preoccupied with Monica. He wondered about the softness of her clothes—and how difficult they'd be to remove. He wanted to taste the skin beneath her jaw, lick a line between her breasts. He took another swig of beer, then set it down.

He saw her eyes go wide and dreamy as she gazed into his. He didn't know what he was silently communicating, but she was getting the idea. He shrugged off his windbreaker and tossed it onto a chair.

He saw her register his holster and SIG Sauer on the right side of his belt. She lived in a ranching community, so he thought she might be familiar with guns. She didn't say anything, just watched him slide his belt out from the holster and set the weapon aside on her bookshelf.

She put down her beer. "Stop what you're doing."

He did, feeling frozen. Hoarsely, he said, "Tell me to go, if you want me to, Monica, but do it soon. After today at Bluebell Hill, I could barely function for thinking of you."

She gave a soft laugh. "I don't want you to go. I just don't want you to hurry through the fun parts."

She put her hands on his chest, and just the touch of her made him groan.

He leaned in and spoke against the curls near her ear. "I want you, Monica."

Her hands trembled against him.

"I want you, too. But let me help."

Monica felt as if she had a great beast under her control, newly free of his cage and practically quivering to put his hands and mouth on her.

And, God, it felt wonderful to be so desired. She skimmed the silky feel of his open-necked shirt, unbuttoning it slowly, letting her fingers drift inside and tease his hot skin. He was breathing heavily, his face an impassive mask but for his eyes, which were bright and hot as a sapphire newly revealed to the light. They stared at her as if she were the only thing in his world, the only thing that mattered.

Right now, she reminded herself; she was the only thing that mattered *right now*.

But she didn't care about tomorrow, about the end of the week when he'd leave her behind, when she'd have to pretend he'd meant nothing but a fun fling. Her world had narrowed to just him tonight, and she parted his shirt to explore her prize. He had auburn hair scattered across his white chest, and her hand looked dark against him. She gave another shiver at the very differentness of him. And she liked those differences.

She slid her hands across his shoulders, parting the shirt and letting it drop down his back. On his right upper arm, he sported a single tattoo she recognized as the Marine Corps emblem of eagle, globe, and anchor.

She leaned in to kiss it. "Did you have a wild night and do this? I can't picture it."

He let out his breath, still watching every move she made. "No, my whole platoon had them done before we shipped out."

"Ah, makes sense, deliberate and thought-out. That's what you're all about."

"Not tonight," he said, capturing her upper arms. "I can't think through what this'll mean tomorrow."

She met his hot gaze. "But you thought about it all day, just like I did."

He gave a single nod, then pulled her against him and kissed her.

He must have been showing restraint in their earlier kisses because he let go and took her mouth with wild passion, as if now that he knew they wouldn't stop, he could show what he wanted. And oh, she felt amazed by the power and purpose, by the way his tongue explored her mouth and mimicked sex. If he hadn't been holding her up, she might have just fallen to the floor, pulling him down on top of her.

She put her hands on his pants and managed to undo the fastener even though his kisses seemed to steal away her mind. She let her hand cup the length of his erection through his clothes, and she felt the ripple of his shudder. But he stopped her before she could pull his zipper down.

"My turn," he whispered. "I want to see you. But how the hell do you take this shirt off?"

Smiling, she turned around and pointed to the buttons at the back of her neck. She leaned back against him, letting his hips press in a long, slow motion against her backside even as she felt those long fingers slowly releasing her top. He pulled it off over her head, and, from behind, his hands came up to cup her breasts, covered only in a lacy bra. She threw her head back with a cry, feeling his teeth nibble at her shoulder, his fingers playing with her nipples, his erection urgent against her. Between her legs, she felt hot and full and aching for him.

As if he read her mind, he slid his hands down her torso to her hips, then slowly tugged her skirt upward, his thumbs riding up her stomach. He didn't totally remove her skirt, just reached beneath and pulled her panties down swiftly, his breathing hoarse in her ear before he bent and let them drop to the carpet.

And then he put his big hand flat on her stomach and just held her back against him, moving slowly, sensuously, sliding until she thought she'd go mad if he didn't do something more.

"Travis—" His name sounded broken on her lips. "Please."

And then his hand slid down, cupping her, his long

her elbow to look at him, to run her hand along his abs and up that powerful chest.

And he was so easy to look at, his body sculpted into the perfection of hard muscle, capable, ready to be of service.

And boy, was he of service. She held back a giggle, and he eyed her warily.

"Nothing, really," she insisted. "I'm just . . . happy."

She reached behind her back and unclasped her bra, flinging it somewhere behind her. Her skirt came next, and that required her to stand. He left the bed for the bathroom, and when he returned, he carried his clothes, while she was lying as provocatively as possible, waiting for him.

She frowned. "You're not putting those on."

He tossed them on a chair and held up a condom. "Not yet."

Laughing, she reached for him.

An hour later, she lay curled against his side, her thigh resting over his, her arm across his chest as if she'd hold him there forever. Surely, she was just drowsy and not thinking straight. There'd be no "forever" for them, and it wasn't the first time that made her feel sad.

She tried to remind herself that he traveled all the time, that there were surely "women in other ports," or so the old saying went. It didn't make her feel better. She didn't feel like she was using him, not when they were so open about their expectations. This was just . . . fun. Surely, she could come up with a Last Single Girl in Valentine blog about how you survive a fling. And she would survive it, remembering the good times.

Then again, she couldn't be blamed for questioning things, when she'd never gone into a relationship already knowing how—and when—it would end. It seemed strange . . . anticlimactic, even.

He stirred and drew her closer. "Anticlimactic" was the wrong word for what was happening between the two of them. Travis had been sexy and overwhelming and so good for her ego.

She looked up at his silhouette and touched the slight bend in the bridge of his nose. "So how'd you do that? Afghanistan?"

He glanced down at her with heavy-lidded eyes and gave her a slow, sexy smile. "That would be the heroic answer. But that's not what happened. I was in college, and my fraternity was participating in the Greek games. We might have been drinking beforehand—"

"No!" she said, eyes wide with innocence.

"I was in the chariot race, just one of the guys pulling the chariot someone else was riding in. Ours was made of steel, so we were faster. As we were pulling ahead of the next team, me and another guy started elbowing each other, and I lost the battle. I blame the alcohol."

She winced. "He elbowed you in the nose?"

"No, I went down. First the guys ran over me. I rolled around a bit and got hit in the face by the chariot wheels."

"Ooh, that sounds painful."

"Did I mention the drunk part?"

She felt him kiss her on the top of the head.

"I should go soon. I can't fall asleep here though I'd like nothing better."

She snuggled deeper into the crook of his shoulder. "Sounds wonderful," she murmured.

He tilted her chin until she met his serious gaze. "Are you okay with all this?"

She gave him a sleepy, contented smile and leaned up to give him a quick kiss. "Okay? I'm fabulous. How about you?"

He gave her an endearingly crooked grin. "I don't think I can find the words."

"I don't believe it. You—speechless? But then again, you did just fine with your mouth without words."

He almost growled as he rolled her onto her back and leaned over to kiss her deeply, passionately. When she would have wound herself about him, drew him down into the bed again, he lifted away.

"I have to go, and we both know it."

He stood and walked toward his clothes, and she came up on her elbow to watch him like he was a model on her private runway. He turned and saw her watching and gave her a sexy smile.

"Mind if I take a quick shower?"

"Go ahead. Towels are right on the shelves inside."

When he emerged in his clothes, she was already dressed in a tank top and yoga pants and followed him from the bedroom. She watched the practiced ease with which he donned his belt and the holstered gun, then let his jacket conceal it.

"Now that you got what you wanted, will I see you

again?" she teased and challenged at the same time, not afraid of the answer.

He pulled her against him and kissed her. "Every spare moment I have," he answered meaningfully. "Which won't be many once the president arrives."

"I know. I'll take what I can get. You're coming to the Mammoth Party at the community center tomorrow night?"

"I'll be there. I have to see this protest, don't I?"

He looked down at her with mock suspicion, and she tried for complete innocence in her expression.

He rolled his eyes and stepped toward the door before turning to give her a serious look. "About us in public—"

She put a hand on his arm. "You don't even have to explain anything. You're on duty in the public eye. I get it."

"Thanks."

"Although I'm not going to keep you a guilty secret with my close friends. They can read me too well."

"Just not too many, okay?"

"I promise."

"Good night, Monica."

"Good night, Travis. Say hi to Royce for me."

He shot her a frown, and she laughed.

"What? I can't say his name? How can you be jealous after tonight?"

He shook his head as she followed him down the stairs. He closed the door behind him, and she turned the dead bolt. She headed back upstairs, feeling tired and sexy and happy.

Chapter Seventeen

An hour before her shop opened the next morning, Monica was sitting at her table eating berries and yogurt, reading the *Valentine Gazette,* and trying not to stare for the hundredth time at the sweet text Travis had sent, when her doorbell rang. She was still in her nightshirt, rumpled from a deep night's sleep. Surely, he wouldn't have come by nine hours later. Or maybe he wanted a running partner, while her limbs were still like Jell-O from all their exercise in bed.

The bell rang with more insistence, and she pulled on her yoga pants and went to answer it. Through the peephole, she saw her brother impatiently glance at his watch.

Silencing a groan, she opened the door. "Hey, Dom, what's up? I don't have much time because I still have to get ready for work."

He brushed past her. "I'll be quick."

Gritting her teeth, she followed him up and into the galley kitchen, where he poured himself coffee. She didn't mind—she'd help herself if she were at his place, too.

He was wearing a polo shirt and pants, office casual, so she didn't think he was visiting customers that day.

After a long sip of coffee, he held the mug between two hands, leaned a hip against her counter, and searched her eyes as if looking for something.

She tried not to tense. "What is it? My hair a disaster?"

"No, I'm just trying to understand you. I finally got the truth out of Missy."

She struggled to keep a bland expression though she had a bad feeling. "What truth? Did she once steal your allowance and buy bubble gum?"

He didn't laugh. "She told me the truth about the photo, Monica. You lied to me—you lied for *years*."

She exhaled loudly but didn't bother to deny it. "Surely, she told you why we lied, why no one could know."

"But I'm your *brother*. You knew how upset I was back then. I made no secret of it. It was like you deliberately didn't care how I felt."

"Dom, come on, it wasn't like that at all. Missy was a wreck when she saw that photo. She had all those plans—you remember how she was, how important her reputation was for her 'journalistic integrity.'" She gave him the air quotes.

"That's crap." He set his coffee mug down a little too hard.

"No, it's not! I did it for her, not to hurt you. And if I was really going to go through with it, *no one* could know. We couldn't risk slipping up. Even Mom and Dad are clueless—and you can't tell them."

"Still, you could have trusted me."

"Don't you remember how you were, all gung ho about the navy, especially when you weren't allowed to enlist? You looked down on our activism, as if our beliefs weren't as important as yours."

He flinched at that but kept his lips pressed in a tight line.

"Our sister needed the help only I could give—it was my idea to take the blame, by the way, and she wanted to refuse. But I didn't want her hurt."

"I wouldn't have hurt Missy," he said stiffly.

"No? But you had no problem hurting me." Her voice was soft, full of the sorrow their uncomfortable relationship had given her.

At last he looked away, fingering the mug but not drinking. "I didn't mean to hurt you either."

"Maybe you didn't mean it, but you did it anyway, Dom. You haven't forgotten it; it's carried over into other parts of our lives, and we haven't recovered. Maybe instead of blaming the two of us for keeping it from you, you could try just forgetting about it. It's old news."

"Is it? Or does it matter to Travis Beaumont?"

"He knows all about it—not that it was Missy, of course. And yeah, he can't understand why I'd do it, but he doesn't need to understand. He only has to accept it. Can you accept it, Dom?"

He finally met her gaze. "I'm willing to try. Are you? Willing to put it in the past, I mean, like you say?"

"I am, Dom. It *is* in the past. We have a lot of years in our future." She turned to the stove. "I was going to make a quick omelet. Want one?"

"I can't. I have to work. Thanks for the coffee."

She watched him walk out of her kitchen, not so sure he could get over it, the disappointment in their behavior, what he saw as their mistrust of him. She remembered being back in Valentine after college, the parties he "forgot" to invite her to, how in his eyes she could never do anything right during the holidays. Maybe she wasn't so sure she could get over the past, either.

She called Missy's cell.

"Melissa Shaw."

"You don't even look at the caller ID and recognize your twin?" Monica asked.

"Oh, sorry. I'm waiting for the camera crew to shoot a piece in the lobby of the hotel, and I'm in business mode."

"He just left," Monica said grimly.

"Ooh, Travis?"

"No, *he* left last night. I mean our brother."

Missy didn't say anything for a moment. "You're mad."

"I'm disappointed. And so is he—all over again."

"I'm sorry," Missy said softly.

"Don't be. I knew it was weighing on you, so I'm not exactly surprised. Just don't tell anyone else about our secret switch, okay?"

"I'll try." She sighed. "He was pretty upset—and hurt."

"Tough. I told him his behavior toward me back

then hurt even more. But he'll get over it. We got some things out, and, well, I just wanted you to know he and I'll be okay." *Maybe.*

"I'm so glad. Hold on." She muted the phone a moment, then came back. "I've got to go. Will I meet this guy at the Mammoth Party tonight?"

"Probably. He said he was going to try to come."

"I can't wait. So he was there last night, huh?"

"We rocked each other's worlds. That's all you're getting out of me."

"Unfair. Bye."

After a hectic morning working on the plans for flowers for the presidential suite—much of which she spent assuring Mrs. Wilcox that she had it all under control by displaying her planning spreadsheet—Monica was glad to head to the boardinghouse for an afternoon of sewing. It got a little crazy when Emily and Whitney barged in to discover the truth, trailed by an apologetic Brooke. But in the end, Monica was relieved that her best friends knew all her secrets—maybe not all the details, she thought, feeling dreamy as she remembered her last hours with Travis.

Travis had been glad that work was getting busier, with the president's arrival Wednesday only three days away. But that still didn't stop him from thinking about Monica and texting her a couple times through the day. Her answers had been short and sweet, and he knew she was busy, too.

But doing what? She wasn't at the flower shop—

he'd seen Mrs. Wilcox through the window when he'd walked by once or twice, then the teenager, Karista, after school. Monica could have been in the back, but he didn't think so. He knew she'd claim to be working on the Mammoth Party. He'd gone to her apartment last night meaning to ask her more about it but hadn't been able to concentrate on anything but her.

She was intruding on his thoughts more and more, and he couldn't pretend it was all just about the protest and his concern for her. He kept thinking of Monica laid out on white sheets, her skin like rich caramel he'd had to taste. She was confident in her sexiness, aware and accepting of how they made each other feel.

She made him feel . . . great, better than he had in a long time.

And as he and Royce walked toward the community center that night, he was eager to see her even though being with her would test his promise to remain professional in public.

The Silver Creek Community Center was an old brick factory converted into multipurpose rooms. He'd toured the facility already, saw the rec room with pool table and giant screen for video games, the industrial-sized kitchen for catered events, the big deck with trellises, where people ate lunch during the summer. But tonight, in the biggest event room, a party celebrated the area's emergence as a mammoth stomping grounds.

Hundreds of people milled up and down aisles where tables and booths had been set up. There were huge posters on every wall, with facts about mammoths and pictures of the dig itself: excavation grids roped off in the dirt, open-sided tents over part of the find, scientists protecting a partially uncovered tusk by putting a plaster "cast" over it, men and women in construction hats and reflective vests using wooden boxes to sift through dirt for tiny fossils.

There was food, of course, following the caveman theme: giant, barbecued turkey drumsticks you could walk around and eat without silverware, ears of roasted corn on a stick, and brown cotton candy titled CAVE DUST BUNNIES. He had to clear his throat to keep from laughing out loud at that one.

The widows and their protest committee had done an incredible job, and for the first time, he wondered if he was wrong—perhaps this really *was* the only protest, and Monica had wanted him to be just as surprised as everyone else. He'd be so relieved that nothing bad would happen to her or the people she cared about.

But what about the ghillie suits? Now that he knew more about the widows and their friends, he didn't believe any weapons were involved, but he still didn't know what the suits were for. His gut instinct told him they were important, so he'd keep an eye out.

In the aisles, he saw scientists ready to answer questions as they stood behind dinosaur-bone displays, geology exhibits, a lineup of speeches to be held in front of several dozen chairs set up in a corner, wooden models of dinosaurs for kids to buy, and bins full of dirt for kids to pretend they were scientists and search for bones. That was where he found Monica, on her hands and knees showing a little boy how to use a paintbrush to carefully uncover a plastic dinosaur bone just like an archaeologist would do.

Though he didn't say a word, she looked up as if he'd spoken, and her smile deepened into an intimacy that seemed to make her embarrassed because she hastily went back to working with the little boy.

But he knew what she was thinking, what she was remembering, because he was remembering it, too. It would be easy to get lost in those sensations.

Without looking up again, she called, "Hi, Travis, hi, Royce."

Royce elbowed him, but all Travis said was, "Hi, Monica. If you get a break, come find us. We have a more current wedding schedule for you."

"Sure!"

Then something suddenly hit him hard in the legs, and he bent over and instinctively grabbed—a toddler. The little boy had curly red hair and freckles, a sticky line around his mouth, and mischief-filled eyes.

"Hey, little man, where you going?" Travis asked.

The boy arched his neck back and back to look up at him, and those mischievous eyes suddenly widened and filled.

"I'm out of here," Royce said, both hands raised as he backed away.

Travis barely noticed, doing the only thing he could think of: he dropped right onto his butt, sitting cross-legged to put himself closer to the kid's eye level.

He glanced briefly at Monica, wondering if he could

ask for help, but she had her hands full of dirt, and a frustrated boy who suddenly began to whine because he couldn't uncover a dinosaur bone.

The redheaded toddler held a stuffed dinosaur in one fist and regarded Travis warily.

"Hey, buddy, where's your mom or dad?"

The boy wiped his nose on the dinosaur. *Great.* But at least he hadn't burst into tears.

"What's your name?"

He started chewing the dinosaur snout and spoke around it in a muffled voice.

"Sorry, buddy, I can't understand you."

Travis tried to lower the dinosaur, but the little boy resisted fiercely.

"Hey, no problem," Travis insisted, giving a friendly smile.

"He's Kyle Deering," Monica called, when at last she got her own boy settled. "The red hair gives the whole family away. It makes your hair look positively brown."

Travis looked around. "I don't hear anyone calling for him."

"His dad, Howie Jr., probably hasn't missed him yet. They have an older son, Howie III, who might be taking up their time."

Kyle still chewed on the dinosaur, one lone tear escaping his eye.

"It's okay, buddy, I'm sure your mom and dad are here somewhere." He broke eye contact for just a moment to glance at Monica. "Should I go look?"

He suspected she was holding back a grin. He did

feel pretty silly sitting on the floor, and more than one person did a double take as they passed by. But at least Kyle wasn't screaming.

"You've almost got him settled down," Monica said. "Why don't we play in the dirt for a minute, then I'll sneak away. I know what his parents look like. Can I trust you with two little boys?"

"I'll have you know, I protected two Saudi princes once who weren't much older." To the little boy, he said, "Come here, Kyle, there's a dinosaur buried in here!"

Kyle took a hesitant step, then another, put one chubby hand on the plastic bin, and peered over the edge. When he saw the dirt, he looked back at Travis, his face alight with sudden happiness. Travis felt like a Saudi king as he handed the little boy a paintbrush and watched him stab it into the dirt.

Monica looked intrigued. "So what do you do with Saudi princes, follow them around?"

"I got really good at Wii soccer."

Her smile softened. "You're kidding, right? Secret Service agents aren't babysitters."

He cocked a brow. "Aren't we?"

And then Kyle, in his enthusiastic digging, accidentally flung dirt all over Travis's shirt.

Monica's laughter turned into a snort, and she covered her mouth, horrified. "Oh, I'm sorry."

"Because I got dirty? Please. But maybe you should go find his dad before the poor guy panics." He leaned back into the bin and tossed dirt onto both Kyle's and the other boy's paintbrushes. "So where's the dinosaur buried?"

Monica rose to her feet, but before she could take one step—

"Kyle!" shouted a man.

"Howie, over here!" she called.

Travis glanced up to see a slightly overweight man roughly his own age, with receding brown hair and a worried expression. Then he recognized the man from the group photo shoot at the hot springs.

"You found Kyle," Howie said to Monica, relief lightening his gaze.

"Not me," she said, "but Special Agent Beaumont."

Howie noticed him and paled. "I'm so sorry for the inconvenience, Agent Beaumont. You must be on duty—"

"Not tonight," Travis assured him. "Nothing better to do than dig in the dirt. Right, Kyle?"

The little boy handed him the slightly soggy stuffed dinosaur so he could use both sticky hands in the dirt. They were quickly covered in a layer of filth.

Howie still held a limp Cave Dust Bunny in one hand, so Travis could see where Kyle's stickiness came from. Howie squatted down, and soon enough, Kyle grew bored with the dirt. Monica used a moist towelette on his face and hands, and soon he and his grateful father were on their way.

Right hand gripped by his dad, Kyle managed to look over his shoulder and wave his stuffed dinosaur at Travis, who waved back.

Travis brushed the dirt from his shirt. "Now that was a dinosaur dig."

She was still looking him over as if she didn't know

who he was, but then a little girl joined the boy head-first in her bin, and Monica went back to work.

Travis didn't plan to go far. He was enjoying watching her with the kids, heck, hadn't minded playing himself.

Damn, where did all these kid thoughts come from?

He pretended he was looking at a wall poster when he really was watching her. She shot contemplative glances his way, too. There was something different about her tonight, not that she could possibly be more beautiful, but . . . he didn't know what it was.

And then he did a double take because a stunning black woman with really short hair walked past him, and her profile made him think—

The woman stopped next to Monica, the two of them smiled at each other, and then he knew. This was her twin sister, Missy, who worked for CNN . . . who would, of course, have come to cover the president in her hometown.

And then they both turned to look at him. There was no use pretending he wasn't watching, so he approached them, and Monica rose to her feet.

"Hey, Missy, I want you to meet Special Agent Travis Beaumont of the Secret Service."

Missy wore a polite smile, then that smile deepened, and she gave her sister a quick, unreadable glance.

"Travis, my sister, Missy Shaw," Monica continued as if she hadn't noticed. "Or Melissa, if you want to go by her CNN name."

Missy wrinkled her nose. "I'm just Missy at home."

Travis held out a hand. "Missy, nice to meet you."

She shook hands, and he was surprised how alike the two women smiled, the way their brown eyes slanted. Missy looked a little thinner, with hollows in her cheeks, but he imagined the pressures of TV could get to anybody. But there was something about the way she held herself, the elegance of her clothes, the smooth, model-like way she had of moving, that seemed very different from her sister, who was sassy, sexy, and curvy like the girl next door.

"So you're Travis," Missy said, holding his hand a second too long as she stared at him. "You think I'd have noticed you in Washington."

"I'm usually behind the scenes," he said.

"So I hear you're commandeering my sister's flower shop."

Travis arched a brow as he glanced at Monica, who winced, and quickly said, "I didn't say that, Missy."

"Well, wait until the president arrives," her sister responded. "You might feel differently."

"We won't be interrupting her business," Travis said.

"Oh, that's right, you'll be *upstairs*," Missy answered.

Monica shot her sister another unreadable look. Travis could have sworn they spoke telepathically, as if they didn't need words.

"So Travis," Missy continued, "I don't suppose I could interview you?"

"I believe you framed the question like that," he said, "because you knew what my response would be. I cannot speak about the president's attending the private wedding of her son."

Missy sighed. "Yeah, I thought you might say that. Can't blame a girl for trying."

Even their voices seemed alike. But there was something in Monica's expression that was just . . . her, the mischievous light in her eyes, the way she saw the humor in everything and seemed to be secretly smiling.

And then she looked past him and waved at someone. "Hi, Royce! Come here and let me introduce my sister."

Royce was grinning before he even came to a stop. "There are two of you?"

Missy eyed his bald head, and the way his casual jacket didn't cover the fact that he had an impressive build.

"Royce Ames," he said, grinning down at her. "You look very familiar—and not because you're Monica's sister."

Monica leaned forward to get in their line of sight, but they were only looking at each other. "She's a reporter for CNN. You two live in the same town."

Royce shook his head with regret. "Reporters and Secret Service agents—we don't exactly get along. But what if I buy you a Cave Dust Bunny? You might think better of me then."

Missy blinked. "A Cave Dust Bunny? For that, I might tell my camera crew to take a break."

Monica looked around. "You're filming tonight?"

"Isn't that what you want, national attention for your cause?" Missy asked with feigned confusion.

"It is!" Monica grinned at her sister. "Thank you!"

"I was hoping representatives from the Renaissance Spa would come. I sent them word, asking for an interview tonight. Do you see anyone?"

"No, but I'm not surprised," Monica said. "They can't take the heat—not that that means they've changed their minds."

"Too bad," Missy said.

Monica turned to Royce. "Now don't distract her from her job."

"I'm easily distracted," Missy confided, and the two of them walked off arm in arm toward the food aisle.

For some reason, Travis felt immensely relieved that Royce had his own Shaw sister to focus on.

And *his* Shaw sister was giving him the sweetest smile.

"I have to get back to work," she said.

"No Cave Dust Bunnies for you?"

"On my next break. Although if Kyle was any example, they're pretty messy. I'm really a carnivore."

"Turkey leg, got it."

"Are you sure we should eat together?" she asked.

And then he remembered his professional duties. "I think we could sit side by side." He lowered his voice. "I might be able to keep my hands off you."

Her gaze lowered almost shyly, then met his again. "You make me feel so good," she whispered.

He wanted to cup her face in his hands, to kiss that upturned nose, to nibble her ear and smell the scent that was only Monica.

"Agent Beaumont?"

He recognized that voice and gave Monica a rueful

grin. "Duty calls." He turned toward the silver-haired lady bearing down on him. "Mayor Galimi, it's good to see you again."

He ended up explaining that once again, he would have to see what the president decided about her schedule. Soon he was alone, watching as the town turned out. He found it moving, how much the people around here cared about their causes. He didn't mind the mayor, or *Valentine Gazette* reporter Jessica Fitzjames wondering if the president had heard about the mammoth dig. Another person had sent him a note to see if the president wanted to be informed about natural-gas testing and drilling.

He liked the ambiance of Valentine. He never would have thought he could feel nostalgic for the small-town life he'd left behind. Though he had an important job to do, he felt more relaxed than he had in a long time—but that was a mistake, he reminded himself. He was in charge, he had to prove himself, and part of that was figuring out this protest and keeping everyone safe. So he wandered around the Mammoth Party, talking to the widows, who were manning various booths, and met Brenda Hutcheson for the first time.

When Monica finally had a break, they sat in the chairs between speeches to eat their turkey legs and corn. Lots of people sat around them, so they didn't stand out as a couple. Travis had seen several of his own people wandering around, enjoying themselves.

"I passed the flower shop several times this afternoon and never saw you," he said, watching as Monica chewed her turkey leg with gusto. When she wiped barbecue sauce from the corner of her mouth with a napkin, he wished it could have been his tongue.

Her dark eyes teased him. "And why were you looking for me?"

"Well, after a night like we had, I would normally send flowers, but that might not work this time."

She grinned. "Probably not. Extra work for me. I like anything made with sugar, of course—you could impress me with a Cave Dust Bunny. And before you ask again, I'll happily tell you where I was today—at the widows', getting ready for this."

"I believe it. You all went to a lot of trouble for the scientific community. It's an impressive event."

She smiled. "Thanks."

"But it's not your only event."

She took several bites along the length of her ear of corn, ignoring him.

Travis changed the subject. "So are your parents here?"

"One night with me, and you want to meet the parents?" she teased.

He watched her gaze search the room and her expression grow troubled. He saw her mom manning the dinosaur-kit sales booth, but he'd never met her dad.

"Monica, is everything all right?"

"Yes—no, I don't know. Oh, I'm fine, it's just my parents. They seem to have hit a rough spot in their marriage, and the three of us are worried about them. I haven't seen my dad at all tonight."

"That's too bad."

"I don't even see Dom—he's avoiding me and Missy." She lifted a hand. "Never mind, it's just an old quarrel. You don't need to hear all this."

"I like hearing about you."

She smiled at him, softly, sweetly, and he felt something stir inside him that wasn't just lust, and that had been happening more and more lately. He liked knowing everything about her.

"You better stop looking at me like that," she said, "or people will get suspicious. Where are your sunglasses? They always make you look remote."

"I don't feel very remote lately."

But they continued to stare at each other until someone called Monica's name, and she looked away.

Travis widened his eyes as someone dressed as a purple *Tyrannosaurus rex* approached. "I thought this party was about a mammoth," he said to Monica.

She laughed, even as the "mascot" pulled off his head to reveal a young man, with a red face and light brown hair matted down with sweat.

"I don't think this is a good idea, Monica," the man said, flinging his stubby purple arms wide with great drama. "This was the only dinosaur costume I could get, but kids are laughing at me."

"That's the point," Monica said patiently. "They're having a good time, Matt. Have you met Special Agent Travis Beaumont? Travis, this is Matt Sweet, Emily's cousin."

Travis automatically reached to shake hands, and ended up holding a rough purple paw. More than one onlooker chuckled—including kids. So he made a big show of keeping it solemn and serious, and was rewarded when the kids laughed, too.

Monica eyed him with a soft, sweet gaze, as if he'd done something heroic instead of just shaking a dinosaur's hand.

Whitney walked slowly toward them, her belly clearing the aisle in front of her. She was accompanied by a young man with deep dimples and black spiky hair.

"Hi, Travis," Whitney said, wearing a very knowing smile that made him wonder what she knew about him.

Whitney turned to Monica. "I wanted to introduce my personal assistant, Ryan Garcia. He flew up from San Francisco to . . . uh . . . help out."

"The lingerie business must be very busy during such a big wedding," Monica said straight-faced. "And you so close to delivering, too."

"Right!"

"I came for the wedding," Ryan admitted with enthusiastic honesty. "I know I'm not invited, but I'll have fun watching all the fuss." He glanced once, then twice at Matt Sweet, his smile slowly growing as he said with wide-eyed sincerity, "I couldn't believe Valentine Valley could be more interesting than San Francisco, but you were right, Whitney."

Matt held out a hand. "Hi, Ryan, I'm Matt Sweet, aka cuddly dinosaur."

The two guys smiled at each other, and Travis couldn't help wondering if he and Monica gave off such an obvious interested-in-each-other vibe as the two young men did.

Matt startled struggling to put the dinosaur head back on, and Ryan helped, then offered to guide him through the crowded aisles.

Monica watched them go, practically beaming, before leaning close to murmur, "It's sometimes hard in our macho ranching community for Matt to find a date."

"And Ryan's single," Whitney said.

Travis had almost forgotten Whitney was there since he'd been busy inhaling the scent of Monica's perfume.

"Ryan's not the only one who was curious about the president," Whitney continued. "Even my dad is at our Aspen condo although he swears he's here for the birth of his first grandchild. I'm not due for a few more weeks, so he's not fooling anybody. He was on the other side of the world when *I* was born." Then she stiffened. "Incoming. Gotta go."

Whitney was gone by the time he saw the three widows bearing down on them, Mrs. Ludlow in the lead, manning her walker as if she'd use it like a battering ram.

Travis stood up. "You ladies look upset."

"Did you see the Renaissance Spa people?" Mrs. Thalberg asked.

Monica stood on her tiptoes and looked around. "Must have missed them. They didn't cause a scene, did they?"

"I don't know how you could have missed the boos," Mrs. Palmer said, flinging her arms wide. "They had the nerve to say the dig will be officially closed next week. People aren't bein' allowed near the site anymore." She rounded on Travis. "What can the government do about this?"

"Mrs. Palmer, if it's private property, I'm pretty sure the government can't do anything," he said patiently. "But maybe this event will change minds, and more people will bring pressure on the spa owner. You ladies have done an excellent job here."

He was trying to mollify them, and though they gave him tight smiles of acknowledgment, they weren't happy. And he guessed they weren't finished with their own pressure on the spa owner. He wished he could fix things for Monica—for the widows—so they wouldn't have to do something drastic to get attention for a cause they deemed important.

"Monica, what—he's there, isn't he? Travis?"

Monica gave a throaty laugh. "I can neither confirm nor deny."

Brooke said something away from the phone. "Adam says it's time to hang up, that you have a private life, too. You don't have anything private from me, right, Monica? We always tell each other everything."

"I seem to recall you kept a certain Marine secret for a while."

Travis lifted his head and gave her an arched brow.

"Not you," Monica mouthed. Then, "Say good night, Brooke."

"Good night," she practically grumbled. "Details later!"

"Uh-huh." Monica pressed the OFF button and tossed her phone onto the bedside table.

Travis parted her thighs and pressed his mouth in between, and she cried out and forgot everything but him. He licked and sucked, seeming to take pleasure in bringing her so close to orgasm, then backing away. Before he was done, her arms and legs were moving restlessly, her head turning back and forth, soft cries she didn't even recognize coming from her mouth. An orgasm shuddered through her at last, and then he was on her, in her, a part of her, their mouths and bodies joined for a rollicking ride that she could swear moved the bed a foot by the time they were done.

They ended up dozing, wrapped together, and when at last he left, it was like a part of her left, too. She had to find some way to remember this was just for fun, to keep her distance, to not get too emotionally involved.

She feared it was already too late.

Tuesday morning, a day before the president's arrival, Travis held the first major agent briefing, including all the agents from field offices in the surrounding states. He introduced the site agents, went over the president's schedule in detail, began to coordinate where agents would be posted. The first big C130 had just landed at the Grand Junction Regional Airport, with all of their equipment and SUVs, as well as the Beast, the presidential limousine—two of them, so that no one would know in which one the president rode.

He'd asked for reports from stores if anything unusual was sold, and although his agents chuckled, one of them did announce that the local feed store had sold out of all their twine and cammo netting within a twenty-four-hour period—but there was no increase in gun sales.

Travis didn't laugh along with everyone else because he knew what ghillie suits were made of. How many suits did they need, and why? Those supplies weren't used at the Mammoth Party, so something else was still going down this week.

Sheriff Buchanan was also at the meeting, and when Travis questioned him, he got to his feet, harrumphing as he tugged on his waistband.

"Agent Beaumont, you wanted to know every strange occurrence, so I have to bring it up. Did you see today's *Valentine Gazette*?"

Laughter rippled across the room, and from the back, Royce called, "CAT will take care of it, don't you worry."

More laughter.

"I haven't read the paper yet, Sheriff," Travis said tiredly. "What did I miss?"

"There's a lot of unrest over the archaeology dig."

Travis was surprised at how uneasy the man seemed. "Spit it out, Sheriff. A lot of us were at the Mammoth Party last night, so we know how important it is."

"We've had to keep watch on the site, of course, worried about vandalism. But we received several calls, and it made the paper."

"Calls about what?" Travis demanded impatiently.

Buchanan sighed. "A Bigfoot sighting near the spa."

The place broke out in roars of laughter, but Buchanan wasn't laughing as he sat down stiffly, and neither was Travis. He knew a person in a ghillie suit could resemble Bigfoot from a distance. And though snipers wore ghillie suits, he just didn't believe that was the reason.

Did the widows think they could *scare* people away from the spa?

"**M**onica!" Mrs. Wilcox called. "You have a visitor!"

Monica was in the workroom, baskets and vases for the presidential suite spread out around her, the first greenery already embedded in foam. She frowned. "Can you take care of it, please?"

"It's lunchtime—you might appreciate this."

Gritting her teeth and forcing a smile, Monica walked through the swinging door and found Travis opening bags with the Rancheros logo on the counter. Immediately, all her stress faded away, and she had to stop herself from grinning like an idiot. He kept saying he'd soon be too busy to see her much, but he was still finding the time.

"I figured you might be too engrossed to eat," he said, wearing that faint smile beneath his sunglasses. "We can't let you get sick—we need your apartment for our observation post."

Mrs. Wilcox clapped her hands together. "We have been far too busy to order lunch yet. Agent Beaumont, you are a lifesaver. Monica, I'll take these customers," she said, as the door jingled when an elderly couple entered.

Travis came around the counter, and Monica gestured for him to sit on a stool. He'd brought a selection of tacos, burritos, and quesadillas, and her mouth watered. He tossed her a bottle of Coke and, after opening it, she took a swig.

"Did you see the paper today?" he asked, too casually.

Monica eyed him. "I read it with breakfast." She knew what he was going to mention, but she said innocently. "Do you follow baseball?"

"No. I was more interested in the local news. Weren't you? The unusual sighting?"

She filled her mouth with a quesadilla to stop her giggle, but she knew her eyes were shining at him.

He'd taken off his sunglasses, revealing blue eyes

that were more concerned than amused. "Bigfoot? Really?"

She shrugged as she chewed, and after swallowing, said, "Never heard of it around here before. Someone's obviously having a good time with the president's coming. You know, like the sheep?"

"We never did catch it," Travis said, frowning down at his taco.

"And now you have to chase Bigfoot. Honestly, I am just as clueless as you." And that was the truth. She'd gasped when she'd seen the paper, then laughed herself silly.

"I don't know if it's about the president so much as the spa. That was where the person was spotted."

"Person?" she asked, smiling.

"Person. And you can laugh, but you know this has already been picked up nationally because of the president's imminent arrival."

She sighed. "And we'll come off as a bunch of rednecks."

"Not what you wanted."

"I don't know anything about this, Travis, I swear to you. Hold on a sec."

She put down her food and went to help a teenager who seemed to be wandering aimlessly by the terrariums. Ten minutes later, she returned to try a taco.

"We are rednecks, you know," she said casually. "You can't believe how excited people got in Grand Junction when your military planes landed. We can't handle that size in Aspen. Can you tell me what they're for?"

"Motorcade vehicles and our equipment."

"Equipment?"

"Don't forget, we have to scan every visitor to every event. We use magnetometers, or mags for short, sort of like the rectangular doorways people walk through at airport security. We wand them, too."

"Can't take any chances," she agreed. And she imagined they had more-deadly equipment, too.

"Back to Bigfoot."

"Really?"

"Really. I wondered if you'd take me hiking near the spa. I'll have men keeping an eye on things, but I want to see it for myself."

She glanced toward her workroom. "I'm getting all the flower deliveries now, Travis."

"I can handle those whenever you need me to," Mrs. Wilcox said. "And if you two go in the afternoon, Karista will be here to help. And isn't your mom going to start working evenings?"

Monica nodded. "Dad and Dom are going to help with deliveries, too."

"It's a family affair," Travis said. "I won't take you away for more than a couple hours. Should I ask permission of your family?"

"No!" Monica said quickly.

He smiled.

"I'm surprised you even mentioned my family." She leaned toward him. "I do have a father and a brother, you know."

"I didn't think you needed someone defending your honor."

Mrs. Wilcox was watching them with interest, or Monica might just have kissed him right there.

She straightened up. "So did you solve Ashley's problem with the presidential staffer?"

"I tried. The woman actually had a meltdown right in front of me. Stamped her foot, thinking that would get her her way."

Monica gaped at him. "How old is this chick?"

"Not much more than midtwenties. I feel pretty old around her." He eyed Monica. "Guess she'll really have a meltdown when a protest interrupts her rigid schedule."

Monica dipped her quesadilla into a tub of sour cream and said nothing.

"You know, I've been patient but upfront with my concern for you. But I need to know what's going to happen, Monica. This ghillie-suit thing is crossing a line."

Her gaze rose up to his in surprise.

"Yeah, I know about them," he said soberly. "Did you know ghillie suits are used by military snipers?"

She stiffened. "You can't seriously believe anyone in this town is a sniper."

"I didn't say they were, but others might think it. I've been handling this little investigation myself so far because I'm the lead agent," he said, leaning toward her and lowering his voice. "I thought when you realized how important my duty is to me, you'd give me some explanations."

For a moment, an ugly suspicion made her feel cold, and she set down her taco as her appetite faded away.

Had he been using her to get details on the protest? She didn't want to believe it. The fact that she felt a sharp stab of hurt made her realize that she'd begun to fall for him, that this was more than a fling to her.

But maybe not to him. Maybe it was just a fun means to an end.

"Monica, this is about protecting the president of the United States," he insisted.

"Nobody wants to hurt the president."

Now Mrs. Wilcox was openly staring, and Monica strode into her workroom, knowing Travis would follow.

When he did, he stood with his arms folded across his chest as if in judgment of her—when she should be the one judging him and his motivations.

"I don't want you or your friends to get hurt," he said with a slow patience that rubbed her nerves raw. "I know you certainly don't want to hurt anyone."

"Thanks for being so concerned, but you'll just have to trust me that no one is going to get hurt," she said, her own patience strained. "This isn't just about the two of us. Too many people are involved, people who are important to me."

"You're important to me," he said softly. "I'm not important to you?"

The implication hurt—but maybe that was what he wanted. "Did you really just say that?" she shot back. "You've totally made it clear what we have is temporary fun. You're making me think you have ulterior motives for sleeping with me, Travis."

He flinched but said nothing, and her stomach plummeted with nausea.

And then icy tendrils of doubt wrapped her heart as she remembered the determination in his voice, the set of his jaw when he first told her he *would* figure out what the Double Ds were up to. And he hadn't been kidding. He'd done a background check on her, brought up the photo—had he thought to weaken her somehow with a hint of threat from her past? But still she'd told him nothing. He'd changed his tune, though, when she hadn't tried to hide her attraction to him. He'd kissed her, and she'd played right into his hands, thought he was so sweet to treat the widows as if they were important—maybe he wasn't being sweet at all. It was his first assignment as lead agent; she knew his job was important, and he wouldn't want to fail. She just hadn't wanted to see it.

"You know I wouldn't hurt you like that," he said calmly, even cautiously.

"Do I? We're done with this conversation. Nothing bad is going to happen, and three old women will have their voices heard."

But something bad had happened already, she thought, though it was just between the two of them.

They stared at each other until he spoke with disappointment, "Never mind about the hike. I can take things from here." He turned and went back into the showroom.

She now knew it was pointless to have any deeper feelings for him. They were using each other, she for fun, he for mixed reasons she didn't want to think about. It *was* just fun because if it were more, she'd have to feel worse than she already did.

That evening, just as Monica was about to leave for the boardinghouse, her phone rang, and she saw her dad's caller ID. They had a great relationship, but they didn't often chat on the phone.

"Hi, Dad," she said, juggling the shopping bags of jute she'd had to drive to Basalt to buy. "I'm heading out the door, but I have a sec."

"Hey, baby girl. I just have a quick question. Why is Dom upset with Missy, and no one will discuss it?"

Monica winced. "I'm—I'm not really sure, Dad. You know Dom—he can be so sensitive."

"Well, I don't like it. I don't like a lot of the tension going on these days."

Tension? Was he at last talking about himself and Janet? "Dad, I'm sure some things'll get better when the stress of the presidential visit is over."

"And then Missy will go back to DC, and every problem will be swept under the rug. I think we need a family dinner before she goes."

"It's a great idea, Dad, but I don't know if we can all find the time, between both Missy and me working for this presidential visit."

"And let's not forget this big protest you and your mother are involved in," he said dryly.

"You mean the Mammoth Party?"

"And Bigfoot?"

"That's not part of our protest," she insisted.

"Do you know who did that?"

"No, but I'm hoping to find out and put a stop to those kinds of stunts. It's not making Travis's job any easier."

"Travis, huh?"

"Never mind about Travis," she said hastily.

"Is this going to get out of hand, Monica? I don't want my girls hurt. Maybe you all need to dial it back a bit. Your mom's new at this and probably doesn't know what she's getting into."

"Really?" she said, wanting to stare at her phone in shock. "She's not exactly clueless, Dad, and you know what she'd say if you said that to her face. I don't know why you care so much about this protest. From what I hear, you like your freedom with your car racing, but you don't like Mom to have her freedom?"

"Where did you get that from?" he demanded with exasperation.

"You're the one who's upset with her activism. Maybe it's not me you should be talking to, but Mom."

He grumbled something she didn't quite catch.

"I've got to go, Dad. Talk to you later."

At the boardinghouse, the Dig Defenders' membership had expanded, as Brooke, Emily, Whitney, and Whitney's assistant Ryan returned to help them finish the sewing. They discussed the success of the Mammoth Party, which had led to Mayor Galimi promising to have another talk with the Renaissance Spa people.

Townspeople had donated more money to the cause. The widows had found several newspapers online who'd picked up the story because of President Torres's impending arrival. The evening had been an unqualified success.

But it hadn't stopped Travis's suspicions, Monica thought, feeling again the hurt of their argument that afternoon. Neither one of them had called the other afterward, and she'd told herself they were both just busy. She wondered if she could find a way to get back to the casual nature of their friendship without the deeper emotions that would only complicate things.

When they'd all eased their stiff fingers by digging into a cheese-and-fruit plate, Monica said, "We have to talk about Bigfoot. Who was it?"

Every young pair of eyes turned to the widows.

Mrs. Thalberg innocently popped a cube of cheese into her mouth. Mrs. Ludlow frowned.

"It was me!" Mrs. Palmer said brightly.

Brooke groaned, and Monica imagined how the old woman's grandson Adam was going to take it.

"I just couldn't resist! You know I love my costumes. I just wanted to see if those spa people were damagin' the dig in any way. I thought I was stayin' out of view, but I guess not."

And she didn't look all that sad about it.

"You know how this makes us look," Mrs. Ludlow coolly pointed out.

"And you think our Friday protest will look like the height of elegance?" Whitney asked.

"Mrs. Palmer, do you know what the Secret Service thinks of when they hear of ghillie suits?" Monica asked. "Snipers. Someone aiming rifles at the president."

Smiles died, and the Double Ds gave each other worried looks.

"Of course, Travis doesn't really think we're a bunch of snipers," Monica pointed out. "But he's been asking a lot of questions, and it's getting difficult to put him off."

"Oh dear, we didn't mean to get in the middle of your courtin'." Mrs. Palmer wrung her hands together.

"Courting"? Now *that* was an old-fashioned term applied to a very modern fling. Brooke was biting her lip hard to keep from laughing, and Monica wanted to elbow her.

"Let's just promise there'll be no more Bigfoot sightings," Emily said reasonably.

Mrs. Palmer made an X over her heart. "I promise."

Later, after making signs for the demonstration, they all left with boxes of calendars to distribute. Monica walked ahead with the girls, while Matt and Ryan stood talking on the porch.

"All right, spill," Brooke said to Monica once they'd put the boxes in their cars. "You talked a lot about Travis. Are things going well with him?"

"Well?" Theresa echoed, grinning. "Don't you mean are things *hot* with him?"

"They were," Monica said glumly, "but now he's upset I won't reveal all the protest details. I'm pretty sure I was a means to an end."

Emily touched her shoulder. "I've seen him with you. I don't believe that's true."

"It was great until today," Monica admitted, "when he wanted more answers than I would give. We ended the discussion on a bad note, and neither of us has called to apologize."

"He's busy, so are you," said the practical Brooke.

Monica remained silent.

Emily studied her. "Why, Monica, I do believe you feel more for this guy than you meant to."

"I'm starting to worry about that, too, since I've been feeling so down about our argument. He's . . . pretty special. But I can't keep thinking like that. He's leaving in a couple days. Maybe if I stay angry at him, these soft, gooey feelings will go away."

"Do you believe that?" Emily asked.

Monica sighed. "No. I—I really like him. Which is stupid because we can't have anything even if this protest weren't standing between us."

And she would have to continue to emphasize that to herself whenever she started feeling tender toward him. He was a man of strength and focus, but she'd thought he'd been yearning for something more in his life, just as she had. Too bad they couldn't be that for each other.

Chapter Nineteen

Monica had stayed awake far too late working, unable to sleep, wishing she'd called Travis when the hour was more reasonable. Angry words festered if they weren't talked through. She would put her own hurt feelings aside—emotions had no place in their relationship, and that was her problem, not his.

But their sexual relationship had been a cold-blooded attempt to use her . . .

And that thought had kept her awake, sick at heart.

She was still asleep when her doorbell began to ring at eight thirty. After pulling on yoga pants and an oversized t-shirt, she glanced at her wild hair and winced, trying to wipe smudged mascara from under her eyes. She went to answer in case it was an early flower delivery.

Instead, three sunglasses-wearing, nicely dressed Secret Service agents stood in her alley, carrying boxes and several cases with handles on them. For the first time, each agent had an earpiece with a curled wire disappearing under the collar of his suit jacket. Guess they

had to talk to each other more, once the president arrived. She imagined how sleep-deprived and exhausted
she must look—

And then she saw Travis, getting out of the car
last. She felt her body respond immediately, her heart
racing, her mouth going dry, like she had a junior-high
crush. He wore a suit and an official earpiece, as if
there was no longer any need to pretend he blended in.
It was like medieval armor between them, a reminder
that he didn't belong.

That he wasn't what he seemed.

She pressed a hand against the pain in her stomach
even as she knew it wasn't going away.

"Good morning, Miss Shaw," said the lead man
right in front of her.

She blinked and tried to focus on the threesome,
when everything in her yearned for the impassive man
behind them. How could she still feel this way when
she might have been only a means to an end to him?

The unfamiliar agent took off his sunglasses to
reveal Asian features beneath short dark hair. "I'm
Special Agent Nguyen. We need to set up the observation post for the president's arrival this afternoon." He
glanced at her clothing. "I was told Agent Beaumont
briefed you . . ." he began, then glanced over his shoulder at Travis.

"He did," Monica quickly said. "But I guess I didn't
get the memo about the time." Or maybe they'd been
too busy arguing for him to remember to tell her.

But he'd come with his men, when it would have

been easier to stay away, something she could reluctantly appreciate.

"I'm sorry for the miscommunication, Monica," Travis said, removing his sunglasses to look at her, his gaze serious, even earnest.

Which miscommunication was he talking about?

"It's okay," she said warily. "Guess you've all seen a woman who's just rolled out of bed."

Not that Travis had seen her the morning after, of course. Maybe that would have been too intimate, considering his questionable motives.

She swallowed and tried to shake away her morose emotions—there was nothing like having an argument with yourself, where you were creating all the guy's answers in your head. Pathetic.

She led the first three men up into her living room, where they ceased to pay attention to her as they began to set up their cameras and long-range equipment near the window. Travis moved past her at a careful distance, then stood with the other agents, only overseeing, as far as she could tell. He didn't even seem necessary, so she could only wonder why he'd come. But she couldn't keep standing there making pathetic puppy eyes at him. Whatever his reasons for attending, they couldn't talk about it openly.

She put coffee on, took a quick shower and dressed, then went next door to Sugar and Spice for a tray of pastries. She was laying them out on her dining table when the first three agents enthusiastically descended on them as if they hadn't eaten their pastry quota for the month. She stepped back and saw that Travis was still at the window, staring out at Main Street below. Before she knew it, she was standing beside him, her own focus on the hotel across the street instead of him. She didn't know what to say and was still baffled by how much he'd been able to hurt her.

"Sorry about the bad timing," he finally said.

"Do you mean the agents this morning, or something else?" she murmured coolly, finally risking a glance at him.

Those blue eyes captured her, held her. "The hurt in your eyes yesterday . . . I never wanted to do that to you."

She swallowed hard, embarrassed as her eyes filled with tears she didn't want to shed. "Just because you didn't intend an outcome doesn't mean you had the best intentions."

"Monica, I—"

"Hey, Monica!"

If only he could have finished that sentence. She whirled as two more agents arrived, dressed in black tactical uniforms with lots of pockets, and POLICE written across the back of their vests, and the small star of the Secret Service on the front left. She guessed their long cases weren't for telephoto lenses. She'd been so intent on the uniform, it took her a moment to recognize Royce Ames.

She smiled at him. "Hi, Royce. So the hard part of your job officially begins?"

"I'm hopin' it runs smooth as cream."

And then he looked past her at the other agents, and

perhaps his eyes widened a fraction on seeing Travis, but he asked no questions. She knew it was time to get out of the way.

After leaving her apartment key for the agents, Monica went to drop off boxes of calendars at her list of the various businesses who'd offered to sell them: the Royal Theater box office, the Open Book, Mountainside Deli, and the Vista Gallery of Art. In her flower shop, she put them on their own table at the front, opening the display copy to Josh's page, and arranging some of his work nearby. Okay, he'd been photographed snowboarding in December with a decorated Christmas tree nearby, but his handsome face would draw customers over at any time of the year, and Mrs. Wilcox or Karista could talk up his leatherwork.

Then Monica loaded her van with the flowers meant for the presidential suite. Just as she was getting in, Missy pulled up in their mom's car.

"Am I too late?" Missy asked. "Mom said you needed help delivering today."

"You're kidding, right? You're just trying to score an interview."

"I am not!" Missy said, faking outrage. "And besides, the president's not giving interviews this weekend—or so she says."

"So you thought you'd interview the Secret Service." She shook her head. "Thanks for the offer of help, but I've already pissed off Travis—I'm not going to add you to the mix."

"What happened with Travis?" Missy asked, her expression morphing into true concern.

"The protest and my insistence that I won't tattle on my friends. Surely you've run into this in your line of work."

"Yeah, but not tattling can get a journalist thrown into jail."

"It's not quite that bad. When I see him, I'll let you know what happens. Now you go join the press pool."

Her shoulders slumped. "We rotate, and it's not my turn—just as the president is arriving. Guess I'll go find some other news."

Monica drove around to the rear of the Hotel Colorado to the delivery entrance. All the added security had changed everything. She was stopped before entering the lot; luckily, she was on the approved list and waved through. There was a cart waiting for her, though first she had to walk through a "mag," then have her purse and all her flowers searched. To her surprise, the dog was pretty gentle with her arrangements.

When at last she was permitted into the lobby with her cart, several women stopped her to exclaim over her flower arrangements and ask her ideas for a luncheon they'd be hosting at the Sweetheart Inn. She slipped back into her regular persona, the successful florist with the unique, creative ideas. She was passing out business cards when she caught a glimpse of Travis on the other side of the lobby, talking with a group of agents, then speaking into the microphone up the sleeve of his suit coat.

When he saw her, though his expression didn't change, she felt the awareness, the pull of attraction, but thankfully not a wave of anger. She was too sad for that.

Deciding not to disturb him, she excused herself from the ladies and went to the elevator, where another agent stopped her. She'd just started to explain that her flowers had been ordered for the president's suite when Travis approached.

"I'll take this," he said to the other agent, who went back to manning his post.

Monica followed Travis away from the elevator, and though they were in the middle of a busy lobby, just being close to him made it feel very intimate. "Hi again," she said awkwardly.

He gave her that old faint smile. "Sorry for waking you this morning."

"Really, you didn't," she lied. "Not that I got around to running this morning."

"I looked for you at dawn."

She gave him a perfunctory smile. "Glad I was missed. Now about these flowers . . ."

"You can't go up. The rooms are being swept for bugs right now. You'll just have to trust that we'll pick the perfect place to display them."

He cocked his head as if listening to something in his earpiece.

"You have to work," she said. "Thanks for taking care of these for me."

"No problem. Will I see you later?"

"Aren't things going to be hectic for us both?" she reminded him, frowning.

He sighed, looking past her, his expression grim. "Yeah, you're right."

She swallowed the lump working its way back into her throat. "Okay. Well . . . bye."

He nodded and turned away, already speaking into his sleeve again.

She'd known they'd have little time together once the president arrived, but their relationship seemed to have ended so abruptly, what with their argument and now his job. It made her feel . . . sad and alone, in a way she'd never felt before. She'd broken up with guys, relationships she would have considered a lot more serious than this one, but hadn't experienced anywhere near the same feeling of loss. Maybe this abrupt ending was best, after all. She didn't want to imagine how she could feel worse.

Back at her shop, she worked hard all afternoon on the flowers for the rehearsal dinner, trying to concentrate on the satisfaction she felt when the flowers seemed to blossom anew under her skilled hands and inspired designs. And that's how she felt with flowers— inspired by their loveliness to display them even more beautifully. She wanted them to enhance the romance of the coming wedding, to make certain Ashley and Jeremy felt the specialness of their new start together.

Around four o'clock, Mrs. Wilcox excitedly called her name. Monica's mind left the gorgeous sights and scents of flowers and returned with a thud to her troubled reality.

"They're closing down Main Street!" the older woman cried, standing at the front windows of the showroom along with Karista and several customers. "My neighbor called me and said the president had landed in Aspen. Can you believe the president is actually here?"

Monica could believe it, especially since she couldn't relax in her own apartment because of tense, focused Secret Service agents. Somehow, it had seemed fun last week, imagining Travis in her apartment regularly. But that wasn't going to happen. She watched the show that was the prepresidential arrival, as agents blocked off the street. Working dogs were led from planter to mailbox to garbage container, searching for bombs. Crowds multiplied and were kept away from the Hotel Colorado by ropes. Cameramen gathered as close as they could, their microphone booms hitting each other as they set up.

"There's Missy!" Karista practically squealed.

At the customers' curious looks, Monica felt a little brag come on as she said, "My sister is a reporter for CNN."

But Missy wasn't getting any closer to the door than anyone else. Apparently, President Torres was pretty serious about not giving interviews during her son's wedding weekend.

When her customers went outside to join the gawkers, Mrs. Wilcox, Monica, and Karista exchanged glances.

"Come on, let's just go outside," Monica said, to everyone's relief.

It was like revelers waiting for the Thanksgiving Day Parade, as they emerged from restaurants and stores, only to have barricades keeping them from the streets. Emily joined Monica, while her sister Steph leaned in to say something to Karista, making both of them giggle.

Emily smiled sweetly at her sister, then glanced at Monica. "What do you think? Pretty exciting, huh?"

"Come on, you lived in San Francisco all your life. You must have seen lots of politicians and celebrities."

"To be honest, we mostly tried to ignore them. But this . . . this is different. The president's son is getting married to one of our own. Sounds silly, considering I just met the bride, but it feels personal, important." She eyed Monica. "You look like you're working too hard."

"And you have shadows under your eyes you didn't have before. No carpal tunnel, right?"

Emily flexed her hands. "I keep the instruments of my genius in good shape."

It felt kind of good to laugh. Fifteen minutes later, motorcycle cops blocked off side streets as the first black Suburbans glided into view in front of the hotel, several others following, surrounding two limousines. Secret Service agents walked into the street and along the crowds. Monica looked up at her closed apartment window, the glare of sunlight revealing nothing. But she knew that Royce and his countersniper agents were watching. There were other agents strategically placed along the street, and she saw several on the roof of the hotel.

And then on the far side of one of the limousines, agents opened the door and up popped the dark head of a diminutive woman who barely stood taller than the vehicles though she was the head of the free world. The crowds began to cheer, the US flags displayed up and down the street waved in the breeze. Agents surrounded President Torres and her husband, then whisked them inside.

Monica glimpsed Ashley Ludlow in the doorway of the hotel, and then she realized why. A young man emerged from the limo, taller, just as dark-haired as the president. He swept Ashley into his arms right on the hotel steps, and they hugged for a long moment.

"It's the groom!" Emily said, clapping her hands together.

The bridal couple disappeared inside, too, and the show was over. The Suburbans and limousines glided away, and soon cars drove down Main Street again. The crowds dispersed, and many headed right into her shop, so Monica went in and worked alongside Mrs. Wilcox and Karista. A lot of calendars were sold that afternoon, and Monica eventually retreated to her workroom with satisfaction.

She found herself wondering what Travis was doing. Would she be wondering that a lot over the next few months? Would she be second-guessing everything she'd done with him, or could she find some peace? It didn't seem possible at the moment . . .

Travis had been watching from the command-center windows as President Torres arrived. He'd seen Monica standing on the sidewalk across the street, and after that, it had been difficult to pull his thoughts back to his work.

It had been good to see her that morning—he hadn't realized how much until he'd seen her all sleep-tousled, then pushing her cart of flower arrangements, trying to charm his agent to let her upstairs. She'd looked beautiful, professional, and sexy as hell. But her gaze at him had been so hesitant and wounded, and he understood why.

He'd been upset he wasn't more important to her than her friends. Stupid of him. She'd spent a lifetime with them and only days with him. He'd known all that from the beginning, but somehow their relationship had changed so much that he blindly thought he was entitled to her trust, her belief. He was still surprised by how much he wanted more, how he wanted to be the one she entrusted with all her secrets, just as she'd entrusted her body.

The hurt in her eyes when she'd practically accused him of seducing her for information—it was still like a hammerblow to his skull. He'd been indignant at first that she could believe such a thing of him, leading to their argument. But now that he'd thought of nothing else ever since, he realized how his behavior had looked, how his demand for information had sounded. And he felt sick inside that he'd hurt her when he'd arrogantly assumed he was only doing his job—and that she might need his protection. But she wasn't part of his job, even if she and her friends might cause minor problems.

When the president and her entourage passed the command center on her way to her own suite, Travis stood in the doorway, nodding to the various members of the Presidential Protective Detail whom he recognized.

And then he saw his ex-wife, Mikayla Hunt, not two feet behind the president.

Their gazes collided, and he schooled himself to keep the surprise from his expression. She had short blond hair that managed to look no-nonsense and stylish at the same time; her green eyes swept the crowded hall with the cool intensity he'd always admired about her. She was tall, with the powerful shoulders of a swimmer. He hadn't known she'd made the "big show," and he suddenly felt his chest puff up with pride in her. They'd both wanted the same thing—to work their way up the ladder, prove they belonged on the most exclusive, prestigious detail in the Secret Service. And she'd achieved it.

He'd thought he might be envious of her promotion, but he wasn't. Part of his feelings was his happiness for her success, but he couldn't figure out the other part.

Where was the unease that always hovered just beneath the surface when he watched her do her job? He'd battled that daily until it seemed to take over his life. Now he didn't know what he felt, didn't know how to view his marriage through the lens of the past.

After the president and her entourage went past, he caught sight of Samantha Weichert, the junior staffer. Her short black hair was as styled as if she'd just gone to a salon, but her expression was pinched and pale as she practically glared at him. Did she think he was going to tell on her, like they were schoolkids?

Suddenly, a ripple of laughter moved through the

command center, and one of his agents called him to the window. He gave a sigh as he saw a sheep running down Main Street, chased by two local cops on foot. He could see another slogan painted on its wool, but couldn't read it and didn't need to know what it said.

His phone buzzed, and he found a text from Monica: *Did you see the Wool-a-Bomber?*

He chuckled aloud, relief flooding through him at the brief contact like the sun on a cold day, and more than one head swiveled to look at him in surprise. He never smiled on the job, usually took it so seriously because it *was* important.

But it wasn't the only important thing.

Did he still have a chance to make things up to Monica? Could she find a way to forgive him his stupidity, let him prove he'd never cheapen their lovemaking by using it to entrap her?

He stepped into the hallway, where agents stood at the door to the president's suite to his right. He headed left, back near the elevator, as he placed the call on his cell.

"Yes, Travis?"

Monica's voice, though strained and hesitant, rippled along his nerve endings, making him glad and horny all at the same time, regardless of the problems between them. "Hi, Monica."

"We're not behind the Wool-a-Bomber," she said coolly, firmly.

"I didn't think so." He remembered those haunted eyes so filled with the hurt he'd caused. How could he make her smile again, her face radiant with the happiness and optimism with which she usually faced the world?

There was an awkward pause until she spoke. "President Torres's arrival was impressive. It looks different in person than what you see on TV."

"We aim for intimidation." He winced at his bad joke; that sounded so awful that he hastily added, "I meant—"

"I know what you meant," she interrupted tiredly, but with a faint amusement that relieved him.

He hesitated before speaking again, not sure why he felt the need to tell her something from his past. "You know who else arrived with the president? My ex-wife, Mikayla. She's on the Presidential Protective Detail."

"That's impressive."

"I think so, too. She worked hard for it." And then he remembered his uneasiness with his wife's ambition, the tenseness every time she traveled on assignment. Why was he dwelling on this? Why was he trying to see the past a new way when it was something that should be behind him?

There was a long pause, then Monica said quietly, "Is it awkward for you, her being here?"

"Surprisingly, no. I haven't talked to her yet, though, but it's not like we ever fought much." And that was true. He hadn't been able to find the words to explain his disturbed feelings, didn't even want to admit he had them.

"I guess getting along with an ex is a good thing. What's she look like, so I can size her up?"

Her attempted joke sounded as awkward as their

conversation, but it gave him hope. "Green eyes, short blond hair, tall, athletic."

"Those eyes'll be behind sunglasses, of course."

"Of course."

"Gotta go, Travis. Flowers await."

When he ended the call, he found himself staring out the window. He didn't know if he wanted his life to go back to what it was. It might be a cliché, but Monica had made him feel alive again, excited for each day and the chance to see her—and now, the chance to make up for the hurt he'd caused.

For the first time, he wondered if a long-distance relationship could possibly work. Because he could no longer imagine his life without her.

Chapter Twenty

By eight o'clock that night, Monica was exhausted. She trudged up the stairs to her apartment, thinking only of hot chocolate and her bed, but when she emerged from the hallway into her living room, two Secret Service agents turned to stare at her.

"Oh. Sorry, guys. I actually forgot about you. Let me grab some stuff and get out of your hair."

Great, now she could go to her parents', who were silently feuding. As she packed a bag, her cell phone rang. Travis. She didn't know what to feel or do. But she couldn't ignore him, no matter how he'd hurt her.

"Hi," she said. "Don't you have a president to protect?"

"I'll leave that to my ex." He paused. "I wish I was there so I could kiss you and maybe find a way to convince you I'm an idiot."

Did he really mean that? Because she didn't know if she could trust his words. She was all tied up in knots over him—they'd met only two weeks ago, for God's sake! And he'd hurt her, made his job more important than anything they had together. She sank down on her bed and closed her eyes. This was a fling, no emotions involved. Just fun. Those were the things she'd told herself as they'd gotten closer. But her emotions *were* involved—*too* involved. She'd thought she saw things in him she'd never seen in another man, tenderness in the midst of strength, humor to ease the tension of his life-and-death profession. And now she didn't know if they were all a part of a façade he'd constructed to weaken her resistance, get her to spill the truth on people she'd known her whole life—reveal their secrets to a man who might as well be a stranger.

Was he really still a stranger?

"I don't think I need to be convinced you're an idiot," she said huskily, no teasing involved at all.

He sighed. "I deserve that, I know. And I don't want to talk over the phone about something so important. I hope we can clear things up face-to-face."

"You're awfully busy, Travis."

"I'm not too busy for you."

It was her turn to sigh. "We'll see."

"I'm actually calling on a work-related issue—and not about the protest, I promise. Have you seen the bride and groom?"

She blinked in surprise. "I haven't even *met* the groom yet, so no, I haven't seen them except from across the street."

"They seem to be missing."

"Well, they have just been reunited a couple days before their wedding. Maybe they just want some privacy."

"They didn't tell their agents that they were leaving."

"Oh. And I bet that's frowned on."

"You'd be betting correctly. It's hard to keep people safe when they sneak out."

"I know, but . . . Ashley's been having a hard time. You know that, and she's not your typical jittery bride with nothing to worry about. I could kick that Samantha chick for upsetting her like this."

"That 'chick' burned holes into me with her eyes today," Travis said.

"Great," she answered with faint sarcasm. "No wonder Ashley might have run. You know, it must be overwhelming knowing that the moment you say 'I do,' your life will change, armed guys will follow you around, and you can never do anything spontaneous again."

"It's not forever, just until the president's time in office is up. And the protectee can be spontaneous—we call an unplanned trip a pop-up. But we just like a little notice."

"That's easy for you to say. Can you just give Ashley and Jeremy some time? This is their wedding, not a political event."

"I can't. The risk is too great."

At least he sounded regretful.

"If you hear anything, can you let me know?" he asked.

"Sure. Good night."

Was that a sigh as he hung up?

She stared at her phone, frowning. Ashley's world was about to change, and in some ways, Monica could understand. Monica was certainly not getting married, but still felt like everything in her world had changed since she had met Travis. It was scary and humiliating and infuriating all at the same time.

When she got to her parents', she sat in her minivan, letting the quiet darkness envelop her, before calling Ashley's parents' house. Of course the Secret Service would have already done that, but she had to try. Nope, Ashley wasn't there. She wasn't at the boardinghouse either, and although Mrs. Thalberg sounded suspicious, Monica kept her inquiry light and innocent.

Then she tried Brooke, who'd known Ashley as well as Monica had back in high school. "Is this a bad time?"

"We're having wild sex, but I interrupted it for you."

"I'm flattered," Monica said, holding back a sigh.

"What's up?"

"Ashley Ludlow is missing."

"She's not missing—she's at our bunkhouse."

Monica let out her breath in a rush. "That's a relief. What's going on?"

"She just wanted some time alone with Jeremy. The hotels were booked solid, and the Secret Service follows him everywhere."

"For a reason."

"Says the girlfriend of an agent."

"I'm not his girlfriend," she said tightly.

"Oh, that doesn't sound good. What happened?"

"This isn't about me," Monica insisted.

"All right, all right, we'll talk about *you* another time. You know Ashley's been a wreck, so much so that she's even begun questioning whether they should marry."

"Oh, that's sad!"

"Turns out she hadn't been confiding in Jeremy, not wanting to worry him with the wedding stuff, and now he feels really guilty. So he wanted some time just for the two of them."

"Thoughtful of him. But I'm going to have to tell Travis, you know, to prevent a national incident."

"You mean the opposite of what you've *been* doing, keeping secrets?" Brooke teased.

Suddenly, Monica couldn't even speak, for fear she'd cry.

"Monica? I was kidding."

"I know. I—things are pretty bad between us," she admitted hoarsely. "But—but I can't talk about it yet. And . . . and he'll be gone in a couple days, so maybe it's for the best."

"Oh Monica . . . but will he be gone from your thoughts, too?"

"He should be. He's an idiot."

"Oh."

She started fumbling in her purse for a tissue. "This isn't like me," she suddenly said with intensity. "I don't cry over guys."

"We all have our weak moments, even you. You know if you want to talk . . ."

"I know. Thanks. As for Ashley, I'll try to convince Travis and his agents to stay away from the bunk-house."

As she disconnected, she saw her parents' front

porch light flicker on, but she didn't go in yet. She blew her nose, took several deep breaths, and called Travis.

He answered immediately. "That was quick. You have news?"

Even though she was in the middle of crying over him, his voice just seemed to resonate inside her. God, why did he affect her so much?

"Ashley's fine," she said impassively. "She and Jeremy just wanted some time alone after the stress of the last week." She heard him exhale.

"Where are they?"

"They're at the Silver Creek Ranch bunkhouse, but can you leave them alone? This isn't a political event but a wedding, Travis."

"Well, they've made it bigger than that. There's a rumor that a local reporter saw them leave without their Secret Service detail."

"Damn. We could warn them."

"They're not answering their phones."

"Then let me help, Travis. I recently met one of the local reporters—surprise, I don't know everyone in town. I'll give her a call and persuade her to let this go."

"That's great, thanks."

She closed her eyes and gritted her teeth, hating to ask a favor but knowing she'd promised the widows—and that he owed her. "Travis, I wouldn't ask this for myself but . . . the widows . . . they don't want to disrupt your schedule or anything. They want their little event to be smooth and quick. Is there a chance you can tell me a time when the president will be in her hotel suite on Friday? They won't try to intrude or anything, I promise. But it would be helpful to know."

"Monica," he began, then stopped.

She didn't say anything—what could she say? And she wouldn't beg.

"We don't distribute the details of the president's schedule," he said, his voice reluctant and maybe weary.

"I assumed as much, and I don't want you crossing a line for me. But I had to ask. Now I'll call the reporter I know and try to help."

"Thank you. I appreciate it. Good night, Monica."

Heaving a sigh, she opened her purse, and by the light of her phone, dug out Jessica's business card. She called her cell.

"Jessica Fitzjames," the woman said in a brisk voice.

"Hi Jessica, it's Monica Shaw."

"Oh, hi, Monica!"

Warmth had flowed into Jessica's voice, and Monica relaxed.

"What can I do for you?" the reporter asked.

"Well, I have a favor. I hear there's a rumor about Ashley Ludlow."

"A rumor? Well, I don't know about that, but I saw Ashley and her fiancé running out the back entrance of the hotel without their Secret Service detail."

Monica heaved a sigh that she'd gone to the right person. "She's just a jittery bride, upset by all the presidential craziness. If you print that, you'll just be making her life worse. She needed an evening alone with Jeremy."

"Then the wedding's still on?"

"Definitely," Monica assumed. "And let me make you a deal—if you hold off on putting Ashley's night out in print, I'll make sure she gives you an exclusive *after* the wedding. What do you think?"

"You have a deal."

After ending the call, Monica almost redialed Travis, then decided to text instead. She wrote that Jessica had agreed not to print the story. In his text, he thanked her and said he would reassure the president. And that was it.

She was surprised to find herself near tears again. Putting her head down on the steering wheel, she took deep breaths, trying to get herself under control before facing her family.

Though exhausted walking up the front porch stairs, inside she put on a smile, had some snacks, and played cards for an hour with Missy and their parents, trying to pretend everything was the way it used to be.

After Travis hung up with Monica, he entered the president's suite and reported what he'd heard about Ashley, Jeremy, and the reporter to the chief of staff, who headed in to brief the president. As Travis left the suite, he almost ran right into his ex-wife going off duty.

She smiled at him, and said softly, "Hello, Travis."

He smiled back. "Hi, Mikayla. It's good to see you."

"You, too."

She seemed to relax a bit after he first spoke, like she'd been waiting for a different reaction.

"Congrats on the assignment to PPD."

She blinked, not bothering to hide her surprise. "Thanks. That means a lot coming from you."

"You got a moment? It's too weird to talk in the hall like we're strangers. My room is at the end of the corridor, or we could go down to the bar in the Main Street Steakhouse for a drink."

"I could use a drink," she said tiredly.

He remembered that flying wasn't her favorite part of the job.

They decided to take a booth in the darkly paneled restaurant, and after they'd ordered drinks, she asked, "Are you enjoying being the lead agent here in Valentine Valley? You did flee your own small town, so this must bring it all back."

He shrugged. "I didn't flee it because I hated living there. And this is a nice place, with good people who've been easy to work with." *Especially one lovely florist,* he thought. "Even my job has been at a slower pace than normal, and I'm finding I like it."

"Even being in charge of the advance?" she asked in surprise.

"Amazing, huh?" Maybe he liked Valentine too much—or maybe he was just yearning for this slower pace because of Monica. His life in the Secret Service was never slow-paced. The moment he got used to one thing, the agency would make him move on to another after just a couple years. It could be tiring.

"What's your next assignment?" she asked.

"Advance work in LA although I guess I shouldn't assume too much. Maybe they'll see how this wedding goes before agreeing to make me lead agent again."

"Oh, come on, you're good at what you do, and you take it very seriously."

The waitress brought their drinks, and Travis studied Mikayla when she didn't meet his eyes. He knew they both could feel bitter that the marriage hadn't worked out. But he didn't want that between them.

"I'm not sure you'll think I'm on top of the job when a protest breaks out."

Those big green eyes looked up at him in surprise. "A protest against the president?"

"No, there's a local archaeology dig that's about to be closed prematurely to finish construction of an addition to a spa. People are angry, and they've decided a presidential visit is the perfect time to get national attention."

"Oh. You know about it, but you can't stop it?"

"I'm slowly gathering the details—maybe too slowly."

"I'm sure you'll figure out what to do." She bit her lip and took a quick sip of her drink.

"Are you laughing at me?" he asked skeptically.

"Not at all." But her voice quivered a little. "It's just that . . . protecting the president—protecting everyone—is so important to you that this must be making you nuts."

"Protecting people is the job."

"It's not just the job with you," she said softly, tiredly.

"But—"

"Never mind." She held up both hands. "It's in the past. But I do have a question. When I first saw you in the hall, frankly, I was worried about your reaction to my promotion. Does it bother you that I made the PPD?"

He touched her hand. "Not a bit. You deserve it, and I'm proud of you."

To his surprise, her hand actually trembled beneath his before she pulled it away.

"I'm glad," she said, her voice threaded with relief. "You've changed, Travis. There was a time you couldn't even express an emotion like pride to me. When we married, I logically understood you'd been affected by your sister's injury—anyone would be. But it took a long time for me to admit you'd simply . . . shut down, and that I couldn't change you."

He flinched as a sick feeling of shock and sadness clenched his gut. He'd told himself that stress and living apart had caused them to grow apart, and, of course, that was part of it. But . . . he thought back to their marriage, to his inability to protect his very capable wife from the dangers of the job—his inability to protect Kelly.

"Maybe you're right," he said slowly, soberly. "It was easier to focus on the job than all the things I couldn't control, the people I couldn't protect."

She looked at him regretfully as if she knew all this and was still hurt it took him so long to admit the truth. He hadn't seen it, hadn't understood it then.

"I didn't need your protection, Travis—it made me feel like you thought I couldn't do my job."

"It was never about that," he insisted.

"It took me a while to figure that out, but I finally get it."

He knew he'd been trying to protect Monica, even from herself and the consequences of her freely chosen actions. God, she must be really frustrated with him.

"I'm sorry." He stared into his drink, knowing he'd already failed once. Would recognizing his failures help him make better choices?

Mikayla touched his hand. "Really, forget about this. We're the past, and neither of us should dwell on regrets. Are things better now? I talked to some of the guys, and they said they actually saw your work mask crack with a smile."

"This place makes it pretty easy to smile."

Her eyes were full of curiosity, and he hoped she didn't ask about women—that would be too awkward with his ex-wife.

"How's your family doing?" she asked. "They must be proud of your new assignment."

So he started telling her about what his sisters were up to, leading to laughter as well as the knowledge that he and Mikayla could maybe be friends.

Thursday brought a lot of nerves, Monica thought, as she dressed at her parents' house before dawn and went off to work. Today, a big tractor trailer would be making the delivery to the Silver Creek Ranch, going in unobtrusively by the back roads to the south.

And there were flowers, of course, dozens of arrangements in urns and vases and huge displays. They'd be on different elevations of stands, and at the base of church columns, a display of the outdoors, of Mother Nature's incredible, natural decorations. She'd been working steadily and felt on top of things, but there was so much to do!

And then she got the call from Travis just after nine, telling her that President Torres had agreed to meet the mayor and speak to the residents of Valentine Valley at the community center late that morning. Agent Nguyen dropped off several press passes at the flower shop, so she and her friends could be up close for the ceremony. She was reluctantly touched that Travis had thought of her.

Before lunch, she, Emily, Brooke, Whitney, and Heather pushed through the crowds spilling out of the community center and showed their passes to the uniformed men at the door. They submitted to being searched, wanded, and magged—Monica bandied the term about like she was in the know—until at last they were in the large reception room, where red, white, and blue bunting was draped on the walls. A raised dais had been erected with stairs leading up to it. Standing intimidatingly at those stairs was Travis, wearing sunglasses, earpiece, and a tailored suit that showed off his impressive shoulders.

"He looks scary," Whitney said in Monica's ear.

Monica was guarding her front, so no one would bump into the pregnant woman.

"Bet you're turned on by that," Brooke said.

Monica rolled her eyes. But, God, he looked good,

coolly official, handsome in that square-jawed way that made her feel all melty in her stomach. *It's just desire,* she reminded herself. *Just desire.* But then she thought of his willingness to die for his president, and how much she admired him—even though he'd been a real jerk.

To distract herself while they awaited the president's arrival, she gathered the women about her.

"Guess who showed up at my flower shop this morning?"

"The First Husband!" Whitney practically squealed.

Monica shot her a mock frown.

"Well, of course I know; Josh told me all about it."

"But we want to hear a firsthand account," Emily urged in her usual diplomatic way.

"Two agents came in to check things out," Monica said, letting the excitement take her over once again. "That's how I knew something big was going to happen. I mean, I heard he wanted to visit, but I didn't know if he'd make the time."

"But he did!" Heather clapped her hands together. "You must have been thrilled."

"Well, I was practical—he was there to see Josh's work. And luckily, when I called, Josh was able to hop in his truck and arrive quickly." She turned to Whitney. "Did he tell you he was stopped in the alley by the Secret Service?"

Whitney covered her mouth as laughter escaped. "Oh, he left that detail out."

"He was gracious about the misunderstanding, and Dr. Torres actually apologized. The man seemed pretty starstruck."

"To think I knew my brother before he was famous," Brooke said, shaking her head.

"Josh gave the First Husband one of his beautiful framed mirrors," Monica continued, "and a shoulder bag for the president. Dr. Torres tried to pay him, but, of course, Josh wanted it to be a gift. I was pretty happy with everything, because after he left, customers entered in droves to ask what Dr. Torres had done, what he'd bought, etc. He even bought some roses for his wife, which was very nice of him," she added, smiling.

"Oh, look, it's Ashley!" Brooke said, as both Ashley and her fiancé appeared, hands clasped, smiles broad. As wild applause broke out, Brooke leaned in to whisper in Monica's ear. "She gave me a call to thank me and say she's doing better. I guess a lot of Jeremy attention did the trick." She smirked.

And then Secret Service agents emerged from a side door, preceding President Torres. A roar of excitement rose through the crowd. The president was dressed in navy blue pants and a patterned jacket, waving cheerfully. Though her dark hair was conservatively pulled up on her head, without the glasses she wore when giving a formal speech she looked younger. And of course happier—and why wouldn't she, when her only child was getting married?

Monica found herself scrutinizing the agents standing near the president, facing outward, watching the crowd. She spotted the tall blond immediately, the only woman among a group of men. Travis hadn't mentioned she was gorgeous, Monica thought, vaguely disgruntled.

She leaned back to the girls and tried to enunciate so they'd hear her over the crowd, telling them about Travis's ex-wife. Much more gawking ensued.

"Does it make you nervous?" Heather asked.

"No, because what right would I have to *be* nervous? He's leaving in a couple days, and I've barely seen him lately. We've mostly talked on the phone." And though he'd hurt her badly, and she still suspected his motives, he seemed to be trying to make up for it. But could he? And could she find a way to believe she meant something to him, so that she could look back on their time together without feeling bitter?

Brooke eyed her, but there wasn't any chance to talk because Mayor Galimi went to the podium for her welcome speech, then handed President Torres the symbolic key to the town. The president spoke about Valentine's graciousness and welcome, how it gave her son his bride Ashley, making him so happy. Though a couple reporters called out questions—including Missy, Monica noticed with a sympathetic wince—the president ignored them, saying that she hoped everyone understood they'd like some privacy for this momentous event for their family. And then she left the dais, Travis's ex right behind her.

"Good luck with any privacy in this town."

Monica heard the deep voice at her side and turned to find her brother there, as the crowd began to stream for the exits. "I think people understand about a wedding."

He snorted. "We'll see." He glanced at her friends, who were hanging back, chatting about the president, and spoke in a lower voice. "So did you tell Travis about the photo?"

"Dom, I told you it's Missy's call, so of course I've kept quiet."

He put up both hands. "I'm not trying to antagonize you. I've just been thinking how hard a relationship is when you're not honest."

"He and I don't have a relationship, not a long-lasting one." And had he ever been honest?

"I don't know. I've seen him with you. He seems possessive, serious."

She felt a flash of heat. "Really? No, never mind."

"And Monica, he needs to see that you're the kind of person who would do whatever it took for someone you loved."

She swallowed hard, feeling the sting of tears. "Dom . . ."

"I may not agree with them, but you've got strong beliefs, and you don't compromise on them. That's important to a guy. There, I've said my piece."

"I . . . thank you. That was nice."

He nodded. "Gotta go. I'm meeting a client soon."

And then he kissed her cheek, and she gaped, touching the spot.

"Was that really your brother or some kind of clone?" Brooke asked.

Monica didn't answer. Dom had forgiven her and said something nice! But . . . did he believe her to be in love with Travis? Did he think Travis was in love with her? She had a hard time believing guys could see those kinds of emotions in each other. And she didn't want it to be true because it would complicate everything.

Because if she loved him—no, no, she couldn't love him, because if she did, she'd have to believe in him, to accept that he hadn't wanted to use their intimacy for his personal gain. She'd have to experience all the pain of loss when he left.

But wasn't she already experiencing pain now?

Chapter Twenty-one

Brooke and Monica eventually returned to the flower shop. Emily had to bake, of course, and Heather was going to help. Whitney looked so tired that Monica insisted she go rest, since the parade was the next day. It ended up just being Brooke and Monica in the workroom, while Mrs. Wilcox and Karista dealt with customers through the lunch hour.

Brooke was an old pro at making bows, so Monica could focus on the expansive spray of roses, delphinium, and lilies meant for the church altar.

"I know you didn't want to talk in the crowd, but did our package arrive?" Monica asked quietly, eyeing the swinging door separating them from her employees.

"It did! You can't believe this incredible trailer with an air-circulating system for cooling, and small living quarters for the caretaker."

"Did anyone see the unloading?"

"Like I said, I made sure my parents were gone, and Josh was at the flower shop with you. I tried to hide it from Nate, but he got a phone call about the couple

riding lessons I'd canceled, and he came to the arena to
see what was going on. He'll keep quiet. Oh, and the
widows are coming over tonight. Will you be there?"

"Can you handle it yourself? I have to work. I
also might try to get more facts about the president's
schedule—probably not through Travis. He can't give
me details."

"Can you blame him?"

"No, but . . . I'm hurt he doesn't trust me to keep a
handle on things."

"That sounds like an impasse."

"Tell me about it."

"You really care about him."

Monica hesitated and gently put down the long delphinium. "I do. I don't want to, but I do. He's leaving,
Brooke. I've got to stop feeling this way."

"You can't *make* your feelings go away. I tried hard
enough with Adam, didn't I?"

Monica gave a faint smile.

"And you know," Brooke said in a softer voice, putting down the ribbon and looking into Monica's eyes.
"Maybe you should just tell him about the protest."

Monica frowned. "But—"

"If you feel so much for him, then you should trust
him. Maybe your instincts are trying to tell you that."

"But what if he tries to stop it?"

"What can he do? It's not illegal—my grandma even
got a permit from the town!"

"So she says. I never actually saw a piece of paper."

"She sweet-talked somebody," Brooke insisted.

Monica let that point go. If there was a permit, surely

Travis would have heard about it and come right to her. "Even if I wanted to talk to him, I have nowhere to do it—the Secret Service has my apartment, his hotel room is off-limits to us common citizens, and I certainly can't talk at my parents'. We've been reduced to talking in the alley or on cell phones."

Brooke dug in her purse and pulled out a ring of keys. "How about my apartment? Adam and I'll be at the bunkhouse."

Monica hesitated. Did she want to talk to him, to hear his explanations, to question whether they rang true? "Thanks," she murmured.

"Don't get too excited." Brooke took the key off the ring and threaded a piece of ribbon through it. "And don't turn it into a den of iniquity like Ashley did the bunkhouse."

"Like you and many generations hadn't already christened that bunkhouse before."

"Yeah, well . . . oh, okay, do what you must. But I'll need details."

Just after midday, Travis received a text from Monica.

I'm at Brooke's apartment above Sugar and Spice. I have too much pizza.

He smiled with relief.

"I'm beginnin' to recognize who your good humor is about these days," Royce said quietly from where he sat in front of a computer screen in the command center. Around them, men and women briskly circulated among computers, phones, and whiteboards.

Travis shrugged. "Can't help it. She's pretty amazing."

"So is her sister. We had dinner together last night."

"She was only trying to get an interview with the president," Travis said, keeping a straight face.

"And Monica is tryin' to get . . . *what* out of you?"

And that made Travis remember that she thought he'd lied to get the truth out of her.

"Gotta go." He grabbed his phone and keys and headed for the door.

"Never mind, she's already got everythin' she wants from you," Royce called, laughing, then glanced over his shoulder guiltily as more than one person turned to look.

Only everything I've been willing to give, Travis thought, and that hadn't been a lot where the women in his life had been concerned.

The doorway in the alley was right next to Monica's, and when Travis rang, she was there to meet him with a polite but wary smile. They stared at each other for a moment.

"Hi," she said.

Her voice was a little soft and breathless. He felt the need to put her against the wall again because he could never seem to be patient with her. But how they proceeded now would take every bit of his caution— because it mattered so much, and he was only just realizing that with every moment of their separation.

She led him upstairs, where he found an identical apartment layout to hers, but with a big couch underneath the main picture window and lots of books on every surface. There were several framed photos of a woman racing her chestnut horse around a barrel, leaning at an impossible angle.

"Brooke?" he asked.

Monica nodded. "She's got championship belts and everything." She sat down at the two-person little table against the wall near the galley kitchen and pointed to the pizza box. "Beer or Coke in the fridge. Brooke's treat."

She took a swig from her own beer bottle and silently toasted him as he shrugged out of his suit coat and went for a Coke before sitting down opposite her.

They ate their first slices in silence, just looking at each other—and he enjoyed the view. She wore a V-necked pink top that revealed just a little cleavage, enough to whet his appetite for more.

Monica set down her beer, and her expression changed into something that hovered between serious and sad.

"Monica?"

"You know, Travis, we started out as just fun and flirty, at least on my part. I wanted to get you to relax, to maybe see the guy underneath. I partly succeeded, but only partly."

"And that was my fault, I know."

"But things aren't just fun and flirty with us anymore. They've become serious and important, and I can't just ignore that."

"We're important?" he asked quietly, trying to see past the reserve that now filled her eyes when she looked at him.

"I think we are," she said ruefully. "I wanted your

trust—I wanted to believe you'd never use me to further your work agenda."

"I never wanted you to have that impression," he insisted. "It all came out wrong that night. I'm so sorry you were hurt. I've honestly been trying to protect you from the beginning."

"I know you're saying the right words now, but it all comes down to trust, doesn't it? I want to be able to trust you, and now I don't know if I can."

"Monica, I hope you can forgive me. I—"

"Just wait, please. Because if I want you to trust me, then I should trust you all the way. I can't justify keeping things from you even if maybe I should." She took a deep breath and let it out. "We're having a parade tomorrow along Main Street to protest the closing of the archaeology dig. There'll be people walking, holding signs that say stuff like, ANCIENT HISTORY IS AS IMPORTANT AS PRESIDENTIAL HISTORY."

"Impressive writing." He was hoping to be both serious and teasing at the same time. Though a corner of her mouth curved, she didn't really smile.

"Thanks. Knew you'd like it."

He studied her, thinking how . . . basic this little parade seemed, how unnecessary the secrecy. "Just a parade? Just signs?"

"Well . . . there will be a surprise during the parade."

"Aah. Does this have something to do with all those ghillie suits you wouldn't talk about before?"

She sighed. "Of course it does."

"I'm grateful you're trusting me with the truth, Monica, when I know I've hurt you. And I'm so sorry for that. I would never use you for my job, regardless of how it looked, or how my questions made it sound. I just let your secrecy screw with my head, and in some ways, it was like you weren't letting me help—letting me protect you. I know that's not my job, and maybe I go overboard with the worry—especially with worry that you'd try to live up to that photo and get hurt. Sometimes that's what all your secrecy seems to be about."

She winced. "I appreciate your apology, Travis, and I do accept it. I just don't know if it changes things. As for that photo, it isn't even me. I'm not the 'Heroine of the Revolution,' or whatever mythic figure that photo made people think of."

He smiled. "The moment I met Missy, I knew it was her, not you. I even rechecked the photo to confirm it. The hell with the facial-recognition software."

She gaped at him. "You knew? No one figured it out—not my family, not . . . anyone."

"I'm not just anyone."

They stared at each other for a long moment until she looked away.

"We were college students," she said quietly, "and it was true we didn't even realize someone took that photo until it started circulating on the Internet. They tracked us down, and Missy was in tears at the thought of what such notoriety could do to her future journalism career. So I said it was me. She was angry when she found out, but I insisted. What did I care, after all? I was going to own a flower shop, not pass background checks."

He took in Monica again, amazed anew at how selfless she was. "You do too much for everyone else," he said roughly.

"But they're my family, Travis, or friends as close as family. They're who I owe my loyalty to, the people I've spent my life with. Why else would I hold back the details of this protest? You're just going to leave, right?"

"I wish—" He broke off. He wasn't sure what he wished, and it would be bad to try to come up with the right words out loud.

"It's okay," she said sadly. "It's been nice, but this can't go anywhere, so maybe we should just end it now instead of dragging it out for a few more days."

"I don't want that, Monica. I know I'm not good at emotions. In the past, I've let them overwhelm me, so it was better not to feel them at all. But that's not healthy either."

"I don't want to feel anything, Travis," she said bleakly. "It'll just make it worse in the end. Go on, get back to work."

When he hesitated, she reached for his jacket and handed it to him.

"Please, Travis."

"Can we talk later?"

When she nodded, he crossed to the hallway. After closing the door behind him at the top of the stairs, he stood still a moment, feeling shell-shocked. What the hell had just happened? And then he thought he heard Monica crying, and the sound tore at his gut. He put a hand on the knob—and stopped himself. Was she right? Would emotions make everything worse when they had to say good-bye? He still hadn't brought up the idea of a long-distance relationship, and now that they were having trouble when they were still together, he didn't know what to think.

But Monica's grief clenched his chest painfully, and he wanted to be there for her, to make it better, to protect her from pain. But was that the right thing to do? Or would he fall into the same behavior again and drive another good woman away? After his marriage, he'd kept all his emotions inside and focused on the job. When was the last time he'd even had fun before Monica and Valentine Valley? She'd changed him, made him want to see his mistakes and become a better man.

He was walking down the alley toward the hotel, a light misty rain starting to fall, when he realized that she hadn't even told him what the ghillie suits were for. And he knew she'd meant to.

Suddenly, it didn't matter. Before he could think about the consequences, he texted her: *She'll be in her suite between ten and twelve.* His mouth was suddenly dry as he realized what he'd done. He'd told a protest group the president's schedule.

But he *trusted* Monica. And he wanted to earn back her trust.

Had he fallen in love with her? If so, he didn't have the faintest idea what to do about any of it.

Monica stared at her cell phone in disbelief. Travis had given her President Torres's schedule. Even after that argument—hadn't she broken their relationship off by the end? Did this mean something? No, she wasn't about to question it.

Without thinking too deeply, she sent an e-mail to the Double Ds with the details, and soon got a reply that they'd all meet at the indoor arena at 9:00 A.M. It looked like all the pieces for their protest were lining up—hopefully nothing would go wrong.

But late that afternoon, she got a call from her mom telling her to come home for dinner. When Monica tried to protest that she had to work, Janet simply insisted that everyone had to eat, and she was to attend. Monica cut her grumbling short, reminding herself that maybe her parents needed help remembering how wonderful they were as a family. Now that things were better between her and Dom, that could only help.

She ended up working a half hour later than she'd meant to, and the sun had already dropped behind the mountains as she drove the few blocks home. When she arrived, she hurried up the walk, glancing at all the cars lining the street. Since the president's arrival, everyone in Valentine Valley had to park in their driveways because the side streets were full of tourists parallel parking.

Inside the house, it seemed strangely quiet, but as she moved into the kitchen, she could hear the sound of her sister's voice on the back deck. She slid wide the sliding glass doors and made her entrance.

"I'm sorry, I know I'm late but—" Her voice faded as she frowned. The men were nowhere in sight.

Her mom stood at the grill, where hot dogs and

hamburgers were sizzling, and Missy was laying out macaroni salad and a veggie tray on the picnic table. Shadows darkened the back lawn, although white columbines marked the landscaped gardens.

"Hi, baby girl," Janet called, smiling at her over her shoulder.

She seemed relaxed and happy, and Monica couldn't resist answering with a tired grin. "Hey, Mom, I thought I'd find you guys already eating."

"No, the men had stuff to do in the garage," Missy said, shaking her head as she unloaded condiments from a tray.

"That old Mustang." Janet's voice sounded good-natured rather than resentful.

Monica widened her eyes at Missy, who only shrugged.

They heard deep voices coming through the kitchen window.

"Wash your hands before you come out," Janet called. "Dinner's ready!"

Monica was standing near the grill, holding a platter for her mom to pile the grilled meat, when the back door slid open again. She glanced over her shoulder, smiling—and saw Travis coming out between Dom and their dad, his short auburn hair more chestnut than red in the twilight.

She knew her mouth dropped open, and she saw Missy do a double take at her expression. Janet just hummed and acted like she hadn't exploded a bomb over her daughter's head.

"Travis was right," her dad said, clapping him on the

back. "The rattle under the hood was because I left the wing nut on top of the filter cover. Who knew Secret Service agents had time to work on cars?"

"Not so much lately," Travis answered, grabbing the beer he'd obviously left on a side table and taking a swig. "Which is why I'm okay on an old Mustang, rather than a newer car."

And then he smiled at Monica, a broad, happy, almost intimate smile, as if everyone here knew what they'd recently begun to mean to each other and they were just fine with it.

Not her, of course—her stomach was tight with nerves and sudden tension. Why had he accepted her mom's invitation?

Oh, she knew why, she realized, even as he came toward her across the deck, all handsome in a buttoned-down checked shirt and jeans. He wanted to make things up to her, to prove he wasn't the jerk he'd come across as.

But it was pretty jerky of him not to warn her he'd been invited. But then again, her sneaky mom might have told him Monica knew. And then to her surprise, he kissed her cheek, and she barely withheld a gasp of astonishment.

"Can I get you something to drink, Monica?" he asked, as if he was so comfortable with her family he could speak for them.

How long had he been here waiting for her?

"Uh, I . . ." And then the words simply died.

Dom smirked good-naturedly, and Missy was obviously trying hard not to laugh at her.

"I've already poured her an iced tea," Missy said. "Come on and sit down, Travis."

"I—I need to change," Monica said, heading for the door. "I'll be right back. Just start without me."

"You look fine," Ben called. "Let's eat."

"Well, I should at least wash my hands," she said with exasperation, then fled inside.

Missy followed her, and they both ducked into the kitchen and peered out the window to the deck.

"What the hell is happening?" Monica demanded in a furious whisper.

"I thought Mom was just being polite, inviting the guy you've hung out with, but the look on your face . . . so you didn't know a thing?"

Monica shook her head, then washed her hands absently at the sink, listening to the laughter float through the backyard.

"He's a really nice guy," Missy said lamely. "And he knows about cars."

"I didn't know that," Monica grumbled. "So he and Dad were okay when they met?"

"Dom introduced them like Travis was some kind of national hero."

"Well, he sort of is," Monica admitted, sneaking another glance out the window. "He helped save the last president in Afghanistan—not that he'll talk about it."

"Oh," Missy said with interest. "Even I didn't hear about that."

Travis was sitting at the glass-top patio table, gesturing with his hands as he regaled her parents and Dom with a story. He looked so relaxed, so at ease, so . . . at home. The tiny flame of hope she'd been nurturing suddenly blazed a little higher. He said he didn't want to end their relationship, and now here he was, schmoozing with her family. Could she actually believe him?

"We should get out there," Missy urged halfheartedly.

"One more question. What did Mom or Dom tell Dad about Travis and me?"

"They both said you and Travis had hit it off, and he didn't deny it. Dad seemed fine with it, national hero and all."

Monica took a deep breath. "Okay. Okay, I can do this."

"And you thought you couldn't because . . ."

Monica spoke low and urgent and too fast. "Because maybe I'm falling in love with him, and there's no maybe about the fact that he behaved badly although he claims a good excuse, and he apologized, and—"

"Whoa, wait a minute." Missy put up both hands. "So I don't have to ask him to leave to defend your honor?"

Monica chuckled, forcing her shoulders to relax. "I guess not."

"Girls!" Ben called. "We're starving!"

Missy put her arm around Monica's shoulder and led her to the door. "Then let's just see how it goes, okay? Color me intrigued."

Monica gave Travis a perfunctory smile as she sat down in the chair beside him. While she'd been gone, her dad had lit torches around the deck, and the flickering light caused shadows on their animated faces. It was surreal and strange all at once.

"So tomorrow's the big day," Ben said, as he loaded his burger with tomatoes and lettuce.

Monica stiffened and exchanged a frown with Janet.

"You know, the Double Ds' event?" he continued, looking at Missy's stunned expression. "Come on, Travis already knows something's happening."

"Sure," Travis said, "but the Double Ds? Isn't that . . ." He trailed off awkwardly.

"A woman's bra size?" Dom said dryly as he scooped macaroni salad on his plate. "You bet. But then the widows seem to have a thing for bras."

"It stands for Dig Defenders," Monica said archly. "And no, I didn't come up with it."

"Like I said, the widows." Dom leaned toward Travis and spoke conspiratorially. "Do you know what a bra tree is?"

Travis swallowed the carrot he'd been chomping. "Those crazy trees beneath a chair lift, where people drop stuff on them?"   .

"Not just stuff—bras," Dom said patiently. "The widows got it into their heads to use a bra tree last year to demonstrate on behalf of Whitney's Leather and Lace—"

"Against the porn charges," Travis interrupted.

Janet grinned. "You're up on your Valentine Valley history already."

"Anyway," Dom continued, "they tossed their bras into the tree right in front of town hall." He glanced at Monica. "And they weren't the only ones . . ."

"Whitney needed my support," Monica said firmly.

Travis's smile grew wide, and she felt her face heat. Why couldn't he be all solemn and stoic right *now*?

And why did she have to really like this hidden side of him, the side only she'd been able to see—or so she thought. Apparently, he'd included her family in the inner circle, and she felt . . . touched.

"Just like the widows need our support now," Janet added.

"How about if we eat rather than talk about this?" Monica asked brightly.

She thought for sure Travis would want to continue the conversation, but he bit into his hamburger and chewed with relish.

"Delicious, Mrs. Shaw," he said after he'd swallowed.

"It's just a hamburger," Missy teased. "I don't know about you, but when I'm on the road, I eat too many of them."

"But not home-cooked," Travis pointed out. He studied his hamburger as if he were about to fill out a judging form. "And isn't there cheese cooked *inside* this burger? That makes it."

Janet beamed.

"You know, Monica once had this boyfriend," Dom began.

"Hey!" Monica knew exactly where he was going. "We don't need to go there."

"I don't mind," Travis said earnestly. "We need to support family history, after all. What about Monica's boyfriend?"

She kicked sideways under the table, but missed his

foot. "You cannot be curious about the men I used to date."

"Sure I am."

Her dad looked between them with happy interest, as if they were putting on a show. Monica hadn't seen him look so relaxed in . . . well, in a long time, she realized. Then she looked at her mom, and wondered if this little drama was distracting them both, making them realize how important family was—

Not that Travis was family, she hastily assured herself. But she was all flushed again, and looking at him out of the corner of her eye, and he was looking at her . . .

"Your boyfriend?" Travis urged with way too much interest.

Dom grinned. "He was a chef who specialized in— get this—hamburgers."

"*Gourmet* burgers," Monica said, nose in the air. "And he was a nice guy—friendly, outgoing, artistic."

"Seems like you're describing yourself," Travis said smoothly. "Didn't dating someone just like you get a little boring?"

Dom laughed aloud. "He *was* boring."

"Hey!" Monica shot back.

"Surely there were other guys over the years," Travis said, leaning back as he sipped his beer.

"You make it sound like millennia have passed during my adulthood. There haven't been all that many guys. And why are you all that interested?"

His smile was light and endearing. "Because I'm interested in you."

Dom snorted, her parents smiled at each other, and Travis captured her with those blue eyes. God, he was up front and obvious. She wanted to be offended, especially since she still wasn't sure she forgave him.

"If you're interested in my sister," Dom said, "then let me tell you about the string of men she's left in her wake."

"Dominic!" Monica said sharply.

"It's okay," Travis said. "I don't need to hear it. I imagine all those idiots are kicking themselves about now anyway."

Dom winced, then smiled at Monica as he told Travis, "You're ruining the fun, you know."

"No, I just understand how they feel."

"Another burger, Travis?" Janet asked gently, as if he'd just complimented Monica with romance instead of a buried apology.

Travis held out his plate. As they all ate, the conversation lightly skimmed the presidential wedding, but no one asked too many questions, as if it was silently understood that Travis was off duty. He had opinions about things as varied as politics and sports when asked, but he didn't dominate a conversation. Monica felt like he let her family shine, like he was simply, honestly, enjoying himself. It took all of her control to keep from looking at him with her heart in her eyes.

Later, when her family proposed a Trivial Pursuit challenge, he joined right in on her mother's team, full of military and geography knowledge. It was hard for her to even concentrate, the way he openly laughed and seemed so at ease and normal.

Like he was hers.

By the end of the evening, she was starting to wonder how disappointed her family would be if things *didn't* work out with Travis.

When it was time for him to leave, they stood in the front hall alone while her family remained in the kitchen.

Travis gestured toward the back of the house with his head. "You're very lucky. I really like them all."

"Thanks. But you have to be used to families—you have more siblings than I do. And in-laws, too. I think that's why you were good with mine."

"You thought I was good?" he said, eyes twinkling.

"Well, I'm not about to lie," she said huskily. "You must get along with your family really well."

"I do. I don't see them enough, lately only at Christmas and once in the summer, but it's like no time has passed. Your family . . . they made me feel comfortable, not like an outsider. It's rare I feel that way, except back home."

And then he stared at her for so long, she became mildly uncomfortable.

"What's wrong?" she demanded.

"I'm just thinking of you with other guys. Dom seemed to imply there was a huge list."

"Hardly. Only two lasted more than six months."

"You must want me to shut up about it. After all, I have an ex-wife."

"Was she your only serious relationship?"

He nodded. "When I was in the Marines, I was too conscious of the risks of my job."

"And you were protecting any potential woman from getting hurt by whatever happened to you," she said softly.

"Maybe." He reached and tugged a curl above her ear. "There are some who would say I worry too much. So what happened with those two guys?"

They weren't you. But she didn't say those words aloud, only gave an embarrassed shrug, and said, "I think I was waiting for it to feel right."

He cupped her face in his hands. "I think it feels right."

And then he kissed her, right in her parents' front hallway, not with openmouthed passion but gentle understanding.

Oh God.

He finally stepped away and put his hand on the doorknob. "Looking forward to the parade tomorrow."

Her eyes widened. "Maybe I should warn you about—"

"No," he interrupted. "Let me be surprised. I'm sure whatever your group came up with will live up to a name like the Double Ds."

Then he walked outside, giving her a final wave before turning away.

Monica closed the door and leaned back against it, feeling a little weak.

Missy was standing there, holding out a dish towel. "Just because you're in love, doesn't mean you get out of the dishes."

"I'm not in love," Monica said—too quickly. But she took the towel.

Chapter Twenty-two

Friday morning in the command center, Travis checked his watch one more time. It was five of ten. He glanced out at Main Street and finally he saw some action—two policemen were blocking Main Street off right in front of town hall. Traffic slowed and finally stopped altogether; if he leaned really close to the glass, he thought he could see another set of wooden barriers being set up a couple blocks down. Just to be safe, he'd already alerted Royce and his countersnipers about the event.

"Excuse me, I need to see the president."

By now, that voice felt like nails on a chalkboard to Travis. He turned around and saw Samantha Weichert, his favorite junior staffer, in the hallway outside the command center.

"Can I help you, Ms. Weichert?" Travis asked impassively as he approached the hallway.

Mikayla stood in front of the doors to the president's suite, and though her face was impassive, he could tell she didn't think much of the junior staffer.

"I doubt it," Samantha said coldly.

He knew she was remembering how she'd broken down in a childish tantrum right in front of him and was now glad to have information she thought he didn't. "Why don't you try me?"

She gave an exasperated sigh. "If you must know, I have a contact at town hall, and was just told about a parade permit being granted for today—*today,* of all days. This will distract the president, and she needs to get through that file from the UN ambassador."

And people thought *he* took his job seriously.

"It's a parade, Ms. Weichert. If the president is concentrating, she won't see it. If she needs a mental break, she'll watch. This is a private weekend for her, remember. I have orders from the chief of staff that she's not to be disturbed."

"We'll see about that."

She marched toward the door, Travis eyed his ex-wife, and she stepped forward.

"I'm sorry, Ms. Weichert," she said, "you won't be seeing the president right now."

"But—"

"Hey, come look at this," one of the agents called from her table near the window. "You're not going to believe what's coming down the street."

"It's a parade," Samantha said with exasperation.

"Not just any parade," said the agent, and began to laugh.

Travis crowded the window along with a half dozen other people. First came a 1920s roadster, tooting its horn. He could swear it was being driven by Mrs. Ludlow, her walker sticking out of the backseat, a long white scarf draped around her neck and fluttering. Then came about a dozen people carrying signs and a broad banner promoting the museum involved in the dig.

"What do the signs say?" someone asked.

"It's a protest against the closing of the archaeological dig at the Renaissance Spa," Travis began—and then his mouth dropped open.

Lumbering behind the protesters was a woolly mammoth, curled tusks and all.

Mikayla was peering over his shoulder. "Is that . . ." And then her voice died away.

Travis started to laugh—he couldn't help it. His stomach hurt by the time he was done, and although many others were smiling, most were staring at him in amazement, including Mikayla.

"Sorry," he said, wiping his eyes. "I knew something about this, but not . . . that." He chuckled some more. "Ghillie suits. They sewed ghillie suits and put them on an elephant. Where the hell did they get an elephant?"

"Who's 'they'?" Mikayla asked.

"Monica Shaw and her cohorts. She owns the flower shop across the street, and there are these three widows—"

"Oh my God," one of the older agents called, "there's an elderly woman dressed as Pebbles Flintstone."

Travis snorted another laugh. "Either Mrs. Thalberg or Mrs. Palmer. I'm betting Mrs. Palmer."

Mikayla was smiling at him even through her curiosity. "You've gotten to know these people pretty well."

"Oh please, there's only one of them *he* cares about," Samantha said disdainfully. "And it's not one of those old ladies. I've seen him at the flower shop way too much—and he didn't need to set up the observation post there."

Travis shrugged toward Mikayla, who only shook her head, smiling.

Just then, Ashley Ludlow leaned into the command center. "The president wanted me to make sure you were all looking out the window—she's having a great time in Valentine. I knew she'd love it."

Samantha left the command center in a huff.

Travis went back to the window, smiling as he watched little kids fall into line behind the elephant, who was being led by a man with a long stick he used with light touches for guidance. Considering that Travis had spent the last two weeks trying to discover and stop this protest, he couldn't believe how relieved he was to simply watch and enjoy. He'd known from the beginning that Monica hadn't meant to thwart him personally—it was about her town and what she felt passionately about. She never focused on herself at all. It was about helping the widows when not many other people cared what the elderly did.

Ashley stepped back in. "Hey, Travis, the president wants more details about the parade and the protest— and I figured you might have them. My grandma's been pretty quiet about it around me." She blushed when she met his gaze, and he knew she was remembering when she'd let slip about the protest last week.

He smiled at her reassuringly. "Of course. Lots of detective work on my part to figure it all out."

Her relieved smile was brilliant.

In the best suite of the hotel, old-fashioned charm mixed with modern conveniences. Wooden columns separated the living and dining rooms, and plush leather furniture inspired relaxation. A wet bar had been added, now being well used by Jeremy Torres, who poured coffee in mugs and brought them to his parents.

President Torres, who looked larger than life on TV, always surprised him with how tiny she really was, especially next to her lanky husband. The president was relaxing in a pair of khakis and a buttoned-down blouse, her reading glasses on, a file now forgotten on the coffee table. Her husband, a professor of Latin American Studies at George Washington University, had gray hair and mustache, and looked relaxed in a sport coat and open-necked shirt. The two of them were smiling as they paged through the "Men of Valentine Valley" calendar.

Ashley tugged on Travis's arm. "President Torres, this is Travis Beaumont, the lead agent for your advance team. He discovered information about the protest before today."

"The whole thing is pretty harmless, Madam President," Travis said, nodding.

"And I have to be honest," Ashley added, giving a cute blush. "The woman driving the old car? She's my grandmother."

Jeremy grinned and saluted with a Coke. "I already like everything I'm hearing about my new family."

"Don't discuss the parade with my mom," Ashley said in a fake whisper. "She's probably mortified."

"She's the mother of the bride," the president said, smiling. "Of course she wants everything perfect this weekend."

Travis explained all about the mammoth dig and the protest, and even the Valentine Valley Preservation Fund, which was selling the calendar.

"But the elephant—I mean mammoth," Dr. Torres said, shaking his head. "Now that was inspired."

Travis grinned, and out of the corner of his eye, he saw Mikayla staring at him as if he were a ghost. Maybe he really had changed.

For a few minutes, he answered questions, watching the way the president and her husband discussed the local guys on display in the calendar, the elderly widows running the town, and it dawned on Travis that even the head of the free world took time for her husband, for fun. She knew how to separate the private and public parts of her life—something Travis had never mastered. If even the president could focus on the job without fixating on the dangers to her family, what the hell was *his* problem? She trusted the Secret Service to protect her family, then she put her fears aside without shutting down all her emotions.

He wasn't going to make that mistake again, not ever. He was thirty-five years old—and he had the chance to leave behind the loneliness, the isolation, he'd only caused himself.

He didn't want to lose Monica—he really had fallen in love with her. Somehow, he had to find a way to keep her in his life.

Monica spent a lot of time walking backward, watching the spectacle that was their growing parade. Not only kids were following, but adults, too. People had cheered their signs, howled with boisterous delight at their "mammoth," even if the papier-mâché curly tusks were kind of drooping on one side where they hung from the elephant's harness.

She'd walked beside her mom, and when she saw Missy waving and pointing with her thumb at the camera beside her, Monica and Janet had slung their arms around each other and waved for CNN and their global audience.

She thought she'd seen Travis, too, and had definitely noticed people in the window of the presidential suite. Success felt good.

To her surprise, her dad had appeared in the crowd, laughing, and her mom had gestured to him. He'd joined the parade and spent the last blocks chatting with Janet. Monica tried not to look at them too much, tried not to feel too hopeful that maybe they were at last finding a way to communicate rather than spend their evenings and weekends apart. Tears actually stung her eyes, and she realized she'd been denying how truly worried she'd been about her parents.

As they left the center of Valentine Valley, she could see Mali the elephant's special trailer waiting for her. Monica was kind of glad it was all over. All three of the widows were crowded in the roadster now, and they were looking tired—not that they'd admit such a thing.

As she helped untie and remove the mammoth cos-

tume, she felt such a feeling of satisfaction even though
the protest had been a wall between her and Travis. She
wished she could have seen his face when he saw the
"mammoth." In the end, he hadn't stopped her—he'd
even helped her.

Just walking in the parade, she'd let herself begin
to feel hopeful about their relationship again—even as
she scoffed at herself. They lived across the country
from each other. But . . . they'd both broken down and
risked everything by telling each other the truth. He'd
apologized, insisting that he'd never used sex to get answers. And she was starting to believe him, to let the
hurt go. Surely, that meant something good.

Not that she knew what it could lead to—but she
wasn't going to think about that right now.

"We did it!" Mrs. Palmer practically crowed, an arm
around each of her best friends.

It was hard to take the woman seriously with the fake
bone once again in her hair and the green dress with
tiny black triangles all over it, like Pebbles Flintstone
used to wear. Not that Monica remembered the show
all that well, but her mom had roared with laughter on
seeing Mrs. Palmer. Monica couldn't help grinning at
the threesome, whose eyes sparkled even though they
looked tired.

"You ladies did an amazing job," Monica said.

Brenda held an armful of signs she'd collected. "I
admit, I didn't think we'd pull it off."

"Did you see Mayor Galimi's shocked expression?"
Matt asked. He elbowed his new friend. "I pointed her
out to Ryan, and we both thought she looked like she

couldn't decide if she should throw herself in front of the parade or just laugh."

"She chose to laugh," Theresa said smugly. "She's pretty cool. Guess no one told her about the parade."

"I wonder how that happened?" Mrs. Thalberg said innocently.

Monica shook her head. "Your pockets must be lined in gold for all the bribes this must have taken."

"Now, Monica," Mrs. Ludlow said in her teacher voice, "don't underestimate the appeal of our beliefs. People wanted to help."

"Even the Secret Service," Mrs. Thalberg added, eyeing Monica with interest.

Monica felt her face getting a little hot. "Well . . ."

"That nice Agent Beaumont did come through in the end," Mrs. Palmer said. "Surely it took somethin' other than pockets lined with gold to persuade that man to leave us alone."

All three widows looked at her with interest, and she was very happy when Mali's hula hoop went rolling past.

"I'll get it!" Monica cried, and quickly hurried after it.

As Mali was led toward her trailer by her handler and the long guide he carried, Brooke said wistfully, "I'm going to miss the old girl. My dad got the shock of his life this morning when he came to find me and ran smack-dab into Mali."

Emily covered her mouth as a giggle escaped. "Oh no! Was he upset?"

"Nope. His mouth did drop open for so long I thought birds would roost, then Mali rolled her ball at him. How can you resist that? And besides, he's pretty resigned to Grandma's 'projects.' "

"I raised him right," Mrs. Thalberg said emphatically.

After Mali entered her trailer, the elephant handler waved good-bye and climbed into the cab with the driver. And then it was over, and suddenly, a feeling of determination swept over Monica. There was nothing left to focus on but the wedding and making sure Monica's Flowers and Gifts put on the best display of small-town charm and décor. Emily obviously felt the same way because she and Steph barely said good-bye before jogging back up Main Street toward the bakery, their signs trailing in their hands.

At Monica's Flowers and Gifts, Brooke and Whitney were waiting to help put displays together under her direction. When it was time to take them to St. John's, Dom and her dad showed up, and her mom arrived after the medical clinic closed for the weekend.

Monica bossed her friends and family around, and almost felt normal again—except for Travis. She wished he were there, too.

Chapter Twenty-three

That night, Monica retreated to her old bedroom in her parents' house by nine. She'd tried to stay awake, playing Trivial Pursuit with her parents and siblings like the old days, but she just couldn't keep her eyes open. And she had even more flowers to finish and deliver in the morning.

She was smiling all the way up the stairs, listening to the happy laughter drifting up behind her. God, it sounded good.

When she arrived in her old room, she heard her phone ringing from the depths of her purse, and by the time she found it and saw that it was Travis, she thought for sure she'd missed him.

"Hello?" she said breathlessly.

"Hey, Monica, are you okay?"

His deep voice made her close her eyes and shiver. "Yeah, sorry, we were playing Trivial Pursuit, and I didn't hear the phone, and—"

"You were playing without me?"

But he was chuckling as he spoke, and it sounded

just wonderful. She sank onto the bed and closed her eyes, pretending she could see him.

"Your parade was pretty impressive."

She grinned, so glad that the weight of secrets had been lifted between them. "Thanks. I did mean to tell you about the elephant, I swear, but we got off topic yesterday afternoon, then my parents' dinner wasn't exactly private, and—"

"I know. I'm sorry."

"Me, too."

There was a long pause, and she felt on the brink of something major, but she didn't know what—and didn't want to talk about any of it on the phone.

"I wish I could see you," she finally said.

"I'll make time. I always have time for you." His voice dipped lower, huskier.

The tone caught her by surprise, made her throat catch, but he went on before she could even begin figuring out what was going on.

"I was called in by the president as the parade was passing by," he said.

"She really saw it?"

"She did. She thought it was cool."

Monica closed her eyes on a sigh. "Oh, that's good. It made CNN, too. I got a text from the widows a while ago that they were getting all kinds of interview requests. And the owner of the Renaissance Spa wants to talk. It worked, Travis, it really worked."

"You know, the widows even got to talk to the president about it themselves."

"They did? Oh, that's right, they were at the rehearsal dinner! How did it go? Wait, wait—I don't want to have this discussion over the phone. Can we meet?"

"The restaurants and bars are packed, or so Royce tells me. And I don't really want to share you with everyone you know."

She smiled even as the warmth of happiness spread through her. She prayed she wasn't making a mistake encouraging this. "Why don't you come over here?"

"Your dad having car trouble again?"

"No, I'd rather keep you to myself this time. Don't come to the house, sneak in back. I'll be waiting for you on the swing."

"A playground? Kinky."

She laughed. "Don't make me wait!"

After hanging up, she went to brush her teeth and check her makeup. Which was silly, considering it was pitch-dark outside. She didn't know why she was so excited—lately, every time she and Travis were together, they argued. But she kept hoping that *this* time . . .

This time what? He'd be leaving Sunday. And the thought was like a punch to the gut. She'd been telling herself to keep emotion out of their relationship, but obviously *that* wasn't working. Then what? What did she want or expect from him?

Or from herself? Was she supposed to make a grand gesture to be with him?

The thought was frightening and exhilarating all at once—when she didn't even know if Travis wanted to be with her beyond this final weekend. Although during their argument, he'd said she meant more to him . . .

Looking at herself in the bathroom mirror, she put on delicious-tasting lipstick, too.

She crept down the stairs, hearing everyone laughing in the family room. Opening the front door a crack, she slid through and eased it shut behind her before hurrying down the porch stairs and around the stone path that led to the backyard. The sky was like black velvet flecked with stars, and she knew he didn't see stars like this in Washington, D.C. She followed the path through the lawn to the big two-person swing, the kind you often saw on porches. But her parents, just like her, preferred to look at the stars when they sat together.

Not that this old swing had seen much of that lately.

Monica put that out of her mind and sat down on the cushioned bench, giving a little push with her feet and leaning back to look up. Not much time passed before she heard Travis's deep voice.

"Now that swing has possibilities."

She laughed and slowed to a stop, patting the seat beside her. He sank down, and it creaked with his weight. She looked at him, and he looked at her under the moonlight. He was wearing a light jacket over a dark polo shirt, with jeans.

"You don't wear jeans much," she said, "but when you do, you make this small-town girl just swoon."

"Glad to hear it. I dress with purpose."

He reached for her hand, then pushed off gently with his feet. They swung silently for several minutes.

"God, it's beautiful here," he said, looking up at the night sky. The jagged silhouette of black mountains was the only thing that interrupted the perfection of stars that glittered like sequins.

"I know. I love living here." Internally she winced—that sounded like a specific comment on their relationship though she hadn't meant it that way.

But Travis only nodded solemnly. "I feel like we're back in high school, and you snuck out of your parents' house to see me."

She laughed softly. "I did, didn't I?"

"So tell me about the elephant. How the hell did the widows manage *that*?"

"Oh, they are mysterious about their contacts, but I can tell you that Mali is retiring and is on her way from California to an elephant preserve in Tennessee, where she'll roam free over hundreds of acres for the rest of her life. They persuaded the new owner to allow us to borrow her for a few days on her way across country. The owner thought it was wonderful she'd be marching in front of the president and was glad Mali had a good break from being confined in her trailer. And she's used to costumes since she occasionally was used at Indian weddings. We were very careful to make the ghillie suit light and airy so she'd be comfortable."

"Where did you keep her? I can't believe I didn't hear about it," he added with teasing reproach.

She smiled. "At Brooke's indoor riding arena, where Mali had a good time spraying people with water. And the food! Two hundred pounds of grain and hay and fruit, along with fifty gallons of water every day. Brooke just kept a hose running in the trough all day long."

Travis shook his head. "Well, you certainly got your point across."

"Thanks. And the media are responding. The widows will be busy for days if not weeks with all the interview requests they're getting. But now tell me how the rehearsal went!"

"I didn't stand post at the rehearsal itself although Mikayla told me it went well."

"It's still . . . okay working with her?"

"It's fine. We always worked well together. It was the marriage part that we failed at."

He spoke so matter-of-factly that something tight she hadn't known she felt eased inside her. And it was good that he wasn't the kind of man to dwell obsessively on the past.

"But I was at the rehearsal dinner, and watched Ashley introduce the widows to President Torres. Let me tell you, I didn't think the president was going to get a word in edgewise for a while there."

Monica laughed. "Oh, I wish I'd been there. Hope Ashley didn't mind."

"No, she was pretty much focused on Jeremy the whole evening. Kind of sappy."

She gave his hand a tug. "Hey, they're about to be married. I'd be disappointed if they weren't sappy about it!" She sighed with satisfaction. "I'm so glad they're doing well—and that our protest didn't cause problems for them. I really worried about that."

"And her grandmother didn't?"

"Mrs. Ludlow always seems to know what she's doing—or she gives that impression anyway. Maybe

it comes from living a long life—no point worrying
about stuff unless it happens. You know, Travis"—
she turned to face him, her knee against his thigh—
"maybe it's too little, too late, but it really was hard for
me to keep the protest from you. Not at the beginning,
of course. I didn't know you, and I would never disap-
point the widows if I could help it. But after we got to
know each other . . ."

He squeezed her hand. "I understand because I
know just how you feel."

"I think I didn't want to see that the protest could
have serious consequences to you because to me, it was
all about the widows and protecting something so fragile and easily lost when no one else seemed to care. I
know there are other digs, but there are none like *ours*.
I felt . . . serious about it, and I only feel serious about
certain things."

"You're very serious about your business."

"But those are flowers, and I love them, and I love
using them to make people happy. I think . . . I think I've
spent my whole life trying to make people happy, even
when I was a kid. I grew up knowing every day that my
grandpa was so sick he could die, and I wanted him to
have the best memories. How could I be sad or serious
about anything when he needed me to be happy?"

He cupped her cheek with one hand. "That's a big
burden for a young girl."

"It didn't feel like a burden." She briefly leaned her
head into his hand.

"So that's why you help the widows, why you took
the rap for your sister."

She shrugged, then leaned against his side. He put his arm around her, and she sighed, feeling content just to absorb the warmth of his big body and listen to the evening birds chirp. It was so peaceful, she didn't even realize she'd dozed until Travis shook her gently.

"Monica?" he murmured against her hair, "you have a big day tomorrow. Maybe you should go inside."

Smiling, stretching, she looked up at him, then pulled his head down for a kiss, so gentle, so tender, without all the crazy lust that usually exploded between them. When he lifted his head, she stared up at him solemnly, but the night shadows hid his eyes from her, and she couldn't read anything.

She let him walk her around to the front of the house to say good night. Hugging herself against the chill, she watched him until he got in his car and drove away.

She tried the front door—and it was locked.

"Dammit."

And her mom had stopped leaving a hidden key since they were all grown-up now. Half grumbling, half laughing at herself, she went around back and tried that door, but it, too, was locked. She stared up at her window, knowing there was no way she was going to climb the tree like she'd done when she was a kid. So using the age-old method, she grabbed a handful of pebbles and started tossing them at Missy's window.

After a few minutes, her sister threw the window open and looked down.

"Monica, is that you?" she hissed.

"I'm locked out! Can you let me in?"

A moment later, Missy unlocked the back door and

stepped outside to say, "What the heck are you doing out here? You went to bed!"

"Well . . . Travis called, and I wanted to see him, and he came over, and we've been sitting on the swing . . ."

Missy smirked, opened her mouth, but Monica held up a hand.

"I know, I know, it was just like high school all over again. Including the kisses. But mostly we talked about how the rehearsal dinner went. It went well, and the widows got to talk to the president about the dig."

"And Travis?"

Monica shrugged. "I don't know. He's leaving Sunday, right?" Suddenly, the quiet rightness of the evening mixed up in her brain with the thought of his being gone, and once again, she burst into tears.

"Oh, Monica!" Missy slung her arms around her.

"I never cry!" Monica moaned with impatience. "Why does he do this to me? I just—I just—I don't want him to leave."

"But he'll be in D.C. You can come visit."

Monica straightened up and took the crumpled tissue Missy pulled out of her pocket. "It won't be the same. And on the advance team, he's all over the country— all over the world—and it's not like I could visit those places and see him. I feel like two people—half the time I'm so happy to be with him, and half the time I'm so sad."

"Sounds like love."

Monica winced. "I don't want to be in love."

"I don't think you have a choice. Come on, let's get something to drink, and you can cry on my shoulder.

Or I'll cheer you up and tell you how Royce and I plan to get together in two weeks when he's back in D.C."

"Oh, sure, rub it in." But Monica smiled, glad for her sister.

"Isn't it cool we're both dating Secret Service agents," Missy gushed. "And we're twins!"

By the time Monica went to bed, she was telling herself to be optimistic, to see what happened. If it was meant to be, it was meant to be.

That was what Grandpa used to say, and she let good memories console her.

Chapter Twenty-four

The afternoon wedding of Ashley Ludlow and Jeremy Torres was as beautiful as any ceremony for two people in love. Though Monica was magged by the Secret Service going into church, and her purse was searched, she didn't mind. She was at last able to feel exhausted and peaceful because her work was done. Earlier that morning, she'd delivered all the flowers for both St. John's and the Sweetheart Inn, getting within the perimeter of the events though blocks of Valentine Valley were closed off and manned by motorcycle cops for the presidential motorcade. She'd had a lot of help from friends and family and hadn't let a little thing like bomb-sniffing dogs in her arrangements bother her. The First Family's being safe was all that mattered. She was able to take lots of pictures of her work before the Secret Service decided it was time for her to leave, just as the dogs were going from pew to pew. The security wasn't any less delivering flowers at the inn, and when she caught sight of Theresa in the banquet room, they sent each other a quick, frazzled wave but never had a chance to talk.

But all the work was now done, and Monica could simply be a guest, relaxing beside her family. It was wonderful to watch Ashley preceded up the aisle by her nieces, Zana and Miri, and her sister, Kim, as her matron of honor.

For the first time, she caught sight of Travis, standing motionless near a side door close to the altar. He wasn't wearing his sunglasses inside the church, so she could see his eyes constantly scanning the crowd, his face impassive.

She thought of the first time she'd seen him, wearing that same expression—and then thought of the man who'd held her in his arms underneath a starlit sky and kissed her tenderly. Whatever happened, she couldn't regret anything, not their affair, not the way she'd stood up for her own beliefs, not the loss she might soon feel.

She found her eyes welling up with tears as Ashley's voice broke on the vows, and seeing the heartfelt way Jeremy looked down at her. Monica felt a little melancholy, wishing she could have that kind of love and devotion.

If she and Travis could only be friends, then so be it. But their friendship would have begun in love, for he was the only man she'd ever fallen in love with, truly in love, beyond infatuation or lust.

He put himself between the presidential family and harm, showed more courage and dedication than most people could even hope they might feel. He'd served his country in one kind of war, now he served it in defense, and cared so much. There was so much to admire about such a man. And yet he was a tender lover, funny at rare and surprising moments, and all the things that made being with him a joy.

"The wedding's up on the altar," Missy leaned in to say, giving her an elbow.

Monica's gaze left Travis and focused on the couple doing their "you may now kiss the bride" moment to enthusiastic applause. "Sorry," she whispered out of the side of her mouth.

"Don't be. Can't blame you for looking. Think positive. If it was meant to be—"

"It was meant to be," Monica finished, smiling into her sister's lovely brown eyes. "As the widows would say, from your lips to God's ear."

"What?" Dom asked, leaning around Missy from the other side.

"Shh!" both women whispered.

That evening, at the wedding reception, Travis manned his post near the bluegrass band. He'd been well trained to watch crowds, his senses peaking every time there was a surge of activity near the president. Mikayla and the rest of the detail were in place, but that didn't keep Travis's gaze from flicking to people's eyes, then their hands. His earpiece was a constant stream of calm chatter as agents reported the position of the president as she moved around.

He was looking for people who displayed unusual symptoms—hands in their pockets like they were cold, nervous behavior, overly or underly enthusiastic responses near President Torres. Along a motorcade route, he often had to ask people to take their hands out of their pockets, and if they didn't do it immediately, they were taken away and frisked. He hoped that didn't happen at Ashley and Jeremy's reception. But so far, everything was running smoothly.

And then he saw Monica dancing with her sister. She wore a floor-length pale yellow halter dress that left her back enticingly bare a long way down. The material occasionally glittered when the light caught it just right.

For just a moment, he remembered sitting on the swing last night, thinking he could be with her forever, even if she just slept in his arms. He loved her—he'd almost said the words, but it hadn't seemed the right time. She was so sleepy, maybe she wouldn't have remembered, he thought, smothering a smile.

He wanted to be the one to dance with her, wanted the right to be a part of her family instead of the one always on the outside looking in. His impatience was startling, so he fell back on his training and resumed his focus on work.

Monica did her best to have fun even though she longed to bring Travis into the heart of her friends and family. He stood alone and practically motionless through the dinner and the early part of the dancing. She knew it was his job, and she was proud of him, but she wanted him as her date, selfish as that was.

During the dinner, she'd focused on her happiness

over her parents' reunion. They told her about the camper they'd bought so they could attend his vintage-car races together on the weekends and explore the countryside, talking over each other in their excitement. They held hands like teenagers in love, and at one point, Missy clutched Monica's hand under the table, and Monica knew they were both trying hard not to cry tears of happiness and relief.

During the dancing, Monica never had the same partner twice. When she dragged Josh onto the dance floor at Whitney's urging, it was hard to keep his attention because he kept looking back at his wife.

"She's okay," Monica called above the music. "You're making her a wreck with your fussing."

The tall cowboy frowned at her. "Something's wrong. She seems tired and overly quiet."

"She is about to have a baby in a few weeks," Monica pointed out dryly.

He glanced back again at Whitney, whose head was bent, her hand on her stomach. "I don't know. Sorry, I can't dance any more."

Monica followed him back to his table and watched as he dropped to one knee beside his wife.

"Whitney?"

Her smile was tense even as she glanced at Monica. "Hi. You didn't dance very long."

"I can't keep him away from you," Monica said, shaking her head. "It's kind of pathetic."

Whitney nodded almost absently, and if Monica hadn't been paying attention, she'd have missed the slight wince in her expression.

"All right, that's it," Josh said firmly. "What's going on?"

Whitney sighed. "I was hoping these were just Braxton-Hicks contractions, you know, false labor."

He took both her hands, and said slowly, "I know about false labor. This isn't false, is it?"

Biting her lip, she shook her head. "Babies take hours, Josh. Let's not make a big deal of this."

Monica knelt beside her, felt a flash of unease at the pain that briefly etched its way across her friend's face. "Maybe you guys should go to the hospital. How long has this been going on?"

Whitney winced, then gave her husband a hesitant glance, even as her breathing deepened and quickened. "A few hours," she admitted faintly. "But I thought it was false labor, remember?"

They were attracting the notice of Josh's parents, Doug and Sandy, who now stood up from their seats on the far side of the table.

"Josh?" Sandy said with concern, leaning forward on her cane.

He was still a lot calmer than most expectant dads, his voice reassuring for his wife, but Monica saw his wide eyes as he looked at his parents.

"I think Monica might be right," he said.

"I don't want to miss the rest of the reception!" Whitney cried, then let out a groan, doubling over, her dark, layered hair falling forward to shield her tightly closed eyes.

Monica looked down at the spreading puddle on the

polished wood floor. "Uh . . . I think your water broke, Whitney. This kid has other plans."

Whitney swore, and Monica had to press her lips together to keep from laughing.

"Time to stand up and head for the car," Josh said. His wife's hands were clenched tightly together, and he had to pry them apart to lift her to her feet.

She swayed, then leaned against him heavily.

"Oh, damn, I think I have to push!"

"You've barely been in labor," Josh said, his voice finally showing a crack of unease in his usual calm.

"Babies don't care about schedules," Mrs. Thalberg told her grandson. "Not sure this one's going to wait."

"Someone call an ambulance," Josh said, even as he swung his wife up into his arms.

Ripples of disturbance spread out around them, people turning their heads to gawk or leaning together to whisper.

"What's going on?" Travis asked as he approached.

"Baby's coming," Monica told him.

He said something into his sleeve, then spoke to Josh. "Ambulance is called. A second one. The first just left on a run because someone might have broken an arm. Don't worry, I hear first babies take a while," he added lightly.

Josh stared at his wife, not noticing the teasing.

Monica did. Her man was not only cool under pressure, he could even attempt to ease fears.

"Let's find someplace private," Travis said. "There's a lounge nearby."

"I'm sure you know the whole layout," Monica teased.

"I do."

He led them through the nearest door, away from the reception, although it seemed like dozens of people followed, but Monica knew them all, concerned friends and relatives of Josh and Whitney. Theresa Sweet rushed forward and followed them into a lounge near the ladies' room.

"How do you feel now?" Josh asked as he laid Whitney down on a couch.

Between gritted teeth, she said, "Like this baby wants to come right now."

"Try not to push," Travis said, taking off his jacket and rolling up his sleeves.

Monica stared at him. "What are you doing?"

"Getting ready to deliver the baby if the ambulance doesn't arrive on time," he said matter-of-factly. To Josh, he said, "I take refresher courses in emergency medicine all the time."

Josh nodded absently, his focus on Whitney.

Not everybody could fit into the lounge, and Monica noticed Emily keeping people out. Mrs. Thalberg, Doug, Sandy, Nate, and Brooke got through, of course.

"I think you'd better remove her lower undergarments," Mrs. Thalberg said with practical efficiency. "And let's get some soap, hot water, and towels."

"I'll be right back with the supplies," Theresa called, rushing out of the lounge.

Travis caught Monica's eye. "Go find one of my colleagues and ask for someone from the president's medical staff."

By the time she got back after relaying her message, there was a doctor in the lounge as well as family. Monica and Emily stood outside the door to answer questions, but all the while Monica kept glancing back inside, trying not to feel too nervous. Women had babies all the time, right?

Just as paramedics came through a door at the end of the hall, wheeling a stretcher, a newborn baby started crying.

Monica and Emily gripped each other's hands and just grinned. Then they looked back inside to see Travis take the wrapped baby from the doctor who'd delivered it and lay it on Whitney's chest, the umbilical cord still trailing down between her thighs.

Monica watched Travis in amazement and wonder, feeling so proud and full of love for him. He'd been calm and commanding and reassuring, having no problem stepping aside for the experts.

And then the paramedics pushed past them and cleared the lounge of everyone but the parents and grandparents. Travis emerged, nodded to Monica and Emily, and headed for the men's room, his hands in a towel.

Emily looked at Monica. "I think you need to keep that man," she said reverently.

Brooke seemed a little shaky as she held on to Adam's hand. "I agree."

"I'm going to do my best," Monica answered, just as serious.

The paramedics pushed their stretcher back through the door, with a beaming, perspiring Whitney holding the baby. "Oh, wait!" she called.

They all looked down at the tiny little face, delicate eyelids closed, serene as she rested so peacefully in her mom's arms.

Smiling, Whitney said, "Little Olivia, this is Aunt Brooke, Aunt Monica, and Aunt Emily. They've promised to do lots of babysitting."

"Oh, we will," Emily said with quiet determination.

Whitney waved tiredly as her stretcher was pushed away.

Emily glanced up at her husband, and a brilliant smile grew on her face. "Maybe we need to start looking more seriously into adoption."

Nate grinned at her. "I knew you wouldn't be able to resist a baby once this one arrived."

After Whitney and Josh left in the ambulance, and the grandparents went looking for their cars, Monica waited in the corridor for Travis. He emerged from the men's room, unrolling his shirtsleeves and buttoning them at the wrist. But he smiled when he saw her. She didn't care that he was on duty, she simply went to him.

He enfolded her in a big hug and spoke against the top of her head. "This has been an exciting wedding reception."

She laughed and looked up, her arms around him. "That's what we do in Valentine."

He looked into her eyes, and his smile gradually faded. "Last night, I had some things I wanted to say, but you were too tired—and I wanted to see your face, anyway."

She let out her breath on a heavy sigh. "Good-byes are so difficult." She averted her gaze, hoping he wouldn't see the tears she was trying to keep hidden.

"We don't have to say good-bye."

She looked up at him, hope beginning to rise in her chest. "You wouldn't mind giving a long-distance relationship a try? I was afraid to even bring up the subject. But my sister is in D.C., and I'd always have a place to stay, and—"

"I was thinking the same thing early in the week, but now, it's not going to be enough." He cupped her face in his hands. "I love you, Monica."

She inhaled swiftly, the rush of joy overwhelming. "Oh, Travis, I love you, too. We can make this work, I know we can."

"You haven't asked me, so I don't know if you've been thinking about it, but would you mind if I moved here to be with you?"

Her mouth fell open. "You'd—you'd move to Valentine Valley?"

"It's not like I don't know small towns—I was raised in one."

"What about the Secret Service?"

"I've struggled with that all week. It's difficult to take the stress for more than ten or so years. Hotel room to hotel room, city to city, sometimes getting little sleep, or not even knowing where I am when I wake up. I realized I could no longer give it the focus it needed when I sent you part of the president's schedule."

She winced. "Oh, Travis, I didn't mean to make you betray your principles."

"No, no," he hurriedly said, kissing her forehead. "It's

not you. I just don't have the drive necessary anymore. I don't seem to be able to be healthy about it, to find time for myself so that I'm sharp and focused. I was so wrapped up in my job, I thought it ended my marriage, when it was really me. I couldn't protect my wife from her duties; I couldn't save my sister. I just retreated from it all emotionally, became the job instead of a whole person. Then I met you, and it was like I had the chance to be a part of true love, a chance to show you that you're my world. I can't do that in the Secret Service, from across the country. This incredible feeling came over me when I watched that baby being born. I want babies, Monica, and I was wondering if you wanted babies, too."

She laughed, even as the first tear slipped from the corner of her eye. "Oh, yes, I want babies—your babies. I love you so much!"

She flung her arms around his neck and kissed him, and felt herself briefly weightless as he lifted her off the ground.

When they surfaced for air, she grinned up at him. "Speaking about babies makes this a very serious conversation, Travis Beaumont. Are you talking about marriage?"

"I am. Not right away, of course. Maybe I should have chosen a better place for this discussion than someone else's wedding reception," he said, sending a guilty glance back toward the main doors to the banquet room. "And we've only known each other a couple weeks—maybe we shouldn't even talk about anything too serious until I move to town and date you properly."

"Wow, proper dates where we have fun adventures

instead of talking about observation posts and activism." She waved a hand before her flushed face. "How will I bear such normalcy?" Then she stared into his eyes. "I don't think that'll matter to me, Travis. I know everything about you that I need to know. I would marry you today. You're smart and funny, two things I really admire and want in my husband. And did you see how calm and reassuring you are when a baby's being born? Wow!"

"Don't forget, I sometimes don't see what's right in front of my face, and I can totally miss the subtleties of life—but you'd still love me anyway?"

"I will—I do. And you're sexy as hell, let's not forget that. And you make me feel like the most important woman in the world to you."

He slid his hands up and down her back. "I don't ever want you to forget that. You're first in my life, from now on, Monica Shaw—although I promise you can make your own decisions, and I won't let my worries interfere."

"You'll talk about them instead of bottling them inside?"

"I promise."

"But . . . what about your job? What will you do here?"

"There's a lot I could do although that might surprise you. I'd probably start out doing security consulting—seems like Aspen might need some of that. Maybe I'd even set up an executive protection firm of my own. But I'd oversee, not do all the heavy traveling myself. I'm done traveling unless it's with you."

"Wow," she breathed, staring up into his beloved face. "My grandpa always told me what was meant to be, was meant to be. And I tried to believe him, but it wasn't until now that I truly understood that love can change anything. I think my grandpa's up there pulling strings." Her voice shook, and her smile was watery. "I hope it's not selfish, Travis, but I want to put us and our future first—I'll work so hard to make sure we're both happy."

He laughed. "I don't think it'll be hard work loving you."

She bit her lip. "I almost gave you up, didn't even know if I should fight for you because I thought I could never compete with your job, with the exciting life— the important duties—you already had. But dammit, this love we feel *is* important. We deserve to be happy." She kissed him gently, then stepped back. "But today you have to make sure someone else's wedding day is perfect. I can be patient."

He caught her hard against him. "It'll be difficult to wait for our life to begin, Monica. But knowing you're here waiting for me? I'll do my best." He kissed her. "Remember I love you, and you're going to hear that every day of our life."

As she watched him shrug into his suit coat and walk back into the reception, she knew it would be the last time he'd walk away from her, the last time she had to hide what they were feeling. She was no longer the Last Single Girl in Valentine.

Suddenly, her life and her future spread out before her—and it was full of love.